The Treasure of Maria Mamoun

WITHDRAWN

Michelle Chalfoun

Farrar Straus Giroux
New York

Farrar Straus Giroux Books for Young Readers
175 Fifth Avenue, New York 10010

Printed in the United States of America
Designed by Andrew Arnold
First edition, 2016
1   3   5   7   9   10   8   6   4   2

mackids.com

Library of Congress Cataloging-in-Publication Data

Names: Chalfoun, Michelle, author.
Title: The treasure of Maria Mamoun / Michelle Chalfoun.
Description: First edition. | New York : Farrar Straus Giroux, 2016. |
    Summary: "An island adventure about a girl from the Bronx on a journey of
    mystery and discovery"—Provided by publisher.
Identifiers: LCCN 2015026267 | ISBN 9780374303402 (hardback) | ISBN
    9780374303440 (ebook)
Subjects: | CYAC: Adventure and adventurers—Fiction. | Buried
    treasure—Fiction. | Lebanese Americans—Fiction. | Martha's Vineyard
    (Mass.)—Fiction. | BISAC: JUVENILE FICTION / Mysteries & Detective
    Stories. | JUVENILE FICTION / Action & Adventure / Pirates. | JUVENILE
    FICTION / Social Issues / New Experience. | JUVENILE FICTION / Social
    Issues / Self-Esteem & Self-Reliance. | JUVENILE FICTION / Lifestyles /
    Country Life.
Classification: LCC PZ7.1.C475 Tr 2016 | DDC [Fic]—dc23
LC record available at http://lccn.loc.gov/2015026267

Our books may be purchased in bulk for promotional, educational, or
business use. Please contact your local bookseller or the Macmillan Corporate
and Premium Sales Department at (800) 221-7945 ext. 5442 or by e-mail at
MacmillanSpecialMarkets@macmillan.com.

For Ashly and Carlos, with thanks to Yaya
(because we wouldn't have the Vineyard without you)
and in memory of Papa "Jiddi" Salim

Author's Note

All the people in this book are fictitious. Any resemblance to real persons, living or dead, is purely coincidental. And while many of the places in this book are real, some are not. I leave it to readers to find out truth from fiction, should you so choose.

Also, a note about the sprinkling of Arabic words in the story. The correct spelling of many Arabic words in English is up for some debate. For example, *Maalish*, which means something like "Whatever" or "Don't worry about it," can be found on the Internet as *maalish*, *malish*, or *ma3lish*. (The *3* represents a sound we don't have in English.) Even my Lebanese relatives weren't sure. So, as far as which spelling is correct, remember that it doesn't really matter.

Maria Theresa Ramirez Mamoun

THIS IS THE STORY OF THE SUMMER THAT changed everything for a girl named Maria. It starts with something bad. Nothing magical; something quite ordinary, in fact. Ordinary, but bad enough to give her belly a sickening, swooping feeling whenever she remembered it. And bad enough to make her mother change everything about their lives.

Maria's full name was Maria Theresa Ramirez Mamoun. *Mamoun* rhymes with *baboon*, as Maria's classmates frequently pointed out. And though she did not look like a baboon, Maria Theresa Ramirez Mamoun was certainly not a beautiful princess. Nor was she powerfully strong, or extraordinarily brilliant. In fact, according to the old lady at the grocery store, Maria was weak, thin, and sickly, like an overcooked vegetable.

"You look like a canned string bean with glasses," Tante Farida would say. "A girl should have some color in her cheeks. You need to run around outside. You need fresh air and sunshine."

It wasn't Maria's fault she needed fresh air and sunshine. She had lived her entire twelve years in the Bronx, under the elevated train tracks between the Prospect and Intervale Avenue stops, where the tall, gray structure shaded Westchester Avenue most of the day. She left for school before the sun rose and walked in the shadow of gray tracks, past gray apartments until she reached her school. Yes, someone had tried to cheer things up by painting the façade of Bronx RiseUP! Charter School red, but the back side, where the students generally entered and exited, was gray cinder block with steel wire mesh over the windows.

When Maria returned home, the sun had disappeared behind the buildings on the other side of the street. And the noise! By midafternoon, the 2 or 5 train rattled and screeched continually overhead, competing with the rattles and bangs of construction as the last brownstones were torn down to make room for more high-rise housing projects. And with few trees and no yards, it seemed there were not enough plants to freshen the air dirtied by the endless parade of cars, trucks, and buses.

But there was one spot of green—in the empty lot on the other side of Rev. James A. Polite Avenue. Maria sometimes crossed the wide street (even though it was on the wrong side for her walk) just to watch the chickadees flitting among the weeds and white lacy flowers. She looked them up in the school library: Queen Anne's lace. She wondered at the names of the other plants. She monitored the growth of the vine slowly creeping up the wall of the hubcap shop beside the lot. She sometimes imagined the lot-vine taking over the whole street—and the other plants escaping the chain-link fence and covering the rest of the block in a wash of green and lacy white flowers. And butterflies and birds would come, and everyone would just stop and stare and love it and then let flowers and vines cover the whole neighborhood. She silently cheered for the grass that forced its way between cracks in the sidewalk beyond the empty lot.

Other than her daily walks, Maria had little time outside. She spent most of the day in cinder-block classrooms, waiting for the minutes to tick slowly by. After school, she spent the empty evening locked in her apartment watching TV, waiting for her mother to return from work. Maria was not supposed to go anywhere but school and the apartment because nowhere else was safe, and she had no adults to take her anywhere nice. Her mother, Celeste Mamoun, was a nurse. She worked two jobs: one in a hospital in Manhattan and another in a nursing home in Queens, and so between her long hours and long commutes she was gone twelve hours a day, six days a week.

Once, Maria asked Celeste why she had to work two jobs.

"Because there's only one of me," Celeste said. "And you need two paychecks to make it in this town."

On Sundays, Maria and Celeste went shopping. Though there were plenty of stores right there on Prospect Avenue, they took their two shopping carts and walked the two blocks east and three blocks south to Al Janed, which according to its sign was an AMERICA, SPANISH, AND MIDDLE EASTERN GROCERY.

Maria loved everything about that store. She loved the photos of the fried meals that decorated the windows: chicken legs, plantains, enchiladas, falafel, french fries, and so much more than she could ever try. She loved the way a string of brass bells chimed when they opened the door. She loved the weird curly writing on the canned foods. But most of all she loved the smells—smoky red paprika, piles of fragrant persimmons, braids of papery garlic, vats of stinky cheeses swimming in milky water, tubs of olives, and packages of cardamom and allspice.

The old lady who owned the store, Tante Farida, would always come from behind the counter and clasp her mother's hands, murmur *"Kifak, chérie,"* and kiss Celeste's cheeks—first the right, then the left, then the right again. Then Tante would slip Maria a *maamoul* cookie or a piece of *baklawa*.

"To fatten the string bean," she would say, pinching Maria's cheek.

"Merci," Maria replied. Her mother taught her to thank Tante in French, because that is how nice Lebanese girls do it "back home." Though Lebanon had never been Maria's home and Maria didn't speak French.

Her mother would then speak to Tante in a mix of French and Arabic. To Maria, Arabic was a mysterious language of whispers and sighs. Her mother never spoke Arabic to anyone but Tante—in their neighborhood most people spoke Spanish, English, or Creole—and so Maria had never learned more than a few words.

As they left, Tante Farida would fill Maria's pockets with sesame crunches and pistachio nougats, refusing Celeste's money. "You're family," Tante would say.

"Are we really related to her?" Maria had once asked. She didn't see a resemblance between her beautiful mother and the old woman.

"No. We call her aunt out of respect," Celeste said.

"Then why does she give us all the free stuff?"

"She's just lonely." Celeste sighed. "It happens to old people."

"Oh," Maria said.

Celeste stopped walking. She cupped Maria's crest-fallen face. "I'm sorry, *chérie*. Sometimes I don't say things right when I'm tired. I meant she likes us like family, so she treats us like family. Even though she's not in our family. Do you understand?"

"I guess," Maria said. There were so many things she wanted to ask her mother, but didn't, because Celeste was always so tired. Like why didn't they have a bigger family? And what happens to lonely old people?

They carted home the value-packs of chicken thighs and the big bags of basmati rice, lemons, lentils (red for *keftah*, brown for *mujadarah*), and chickpeas. Then they spent the afternoon cooking the meals Maria would heat up for herself in the microwave all week long. This was their routine, and it was rarely broken.

Once, the summer Maria had turned ten, Celeste had taken her on the 2 train to Penn Station, then on a train to Long Island, and then on a bus to Jones Beach. They spread an old blanket on the sand and ate a picnic lunch. Maria made friends with a girl sitting on the beach blanket next to theirs. They spent the afternoon building castles from the warm gritty sand and dodging in and out of the chilly waves.

It was the best day Maria could remember. Whenever she felt bored or anxious she closed her eyes and remembered that day at the beach.

She told herself she didn't mind being alone. She was quiet and shy, and she wasn't sure she would want to hang out with the other kids in the neighborhood even if they invited her. They seemed too loud and rough. She'd just as soon avoid them, even if that meant she had no friends. Still, Maria didn't complain. She understood, really she did. And Maria knew she was luckier than most. She had a clean apartment, a room of her own, and a mother who loved her fiercely. Celeste did whatever she could to keep Maria safe and happy, and Maria did whatever she could to be grateful.

Even though, sometimes, she wished things were different.

And then one day they were.

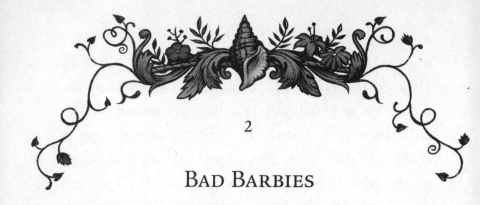

2

BAD BARBIES

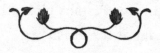

MANY OF THE ROUGH KIDS FROM SCHOOL lived in Maria's building. There was a pack of particularly loud, laughing girls who hung out together and who were also in sixth grade. Something Maria had done way back when she was younger, something she didn't remember or understand, had put her outside of this group. Growing up, she was not invited to their parties, and now they never knocked on her door to invite her to hang out.

Though they weren't actual members of a gang, Maria called them the Bad Barbies in her mind, because they were glamorous and mean like the girl gang that had terrorized the Bronx a few years back. In the building, she often heard their mothers cursing them out and calling them in. At school, they cowed teachers and students alike. Though everyone had to wear a uniform at school, the Bad Barbies managed to make theirs look unique. Shy Girl poofed her bangs and drew black eyeliner across her top lids, Skinny rolled her plaid skirt so it showed her thick upper thighs, and Sharpie glued sparkling jewels to her stiletto-shaped nails. Maria wasn't sure if it was the daggerlike manicure or the black felt-tip wielded to tag nearly every surface in school that had earned her that name, but Sharpie was definitely the leader.

They mostly ignored Maria when they ran into her with Celeste in the hallway or on the stairs, but when Maria was alone outside their apartment building she was fair game. And at school the Barbies found tormenting Maria to be a source of endless fun.

The Barbies were in most of Maria's classes. Science, Social Studies, and Specials—Art, Phys Ed, and General Music. In Art, Maria found her painting wet side down on the floor, though she knew she'd hung it up to dry on the clothespin line. Her abstract sculpture, stored safe on a high shelf, was smashed before it was graded. In Phys Ed, she was tripped, hit with balls, and clipped with lacrosse sticks so often she spent more time getting ice from the school nurse than playing, and the Phys Ed teacher marked her down for slacking. In the locker room after PE, Maria often found the clothes she'd left in her dry locker in a damp clump in the shower. In Music, there was not much the Barbies could do to her, and they generally chose to braid each other's hair or apply lip gloss instead of singing. Sometimes they looked up and giggled in Maria's direction, and she got the feeling they were laughing about her.

But the worst came when their Science teacher announced they'd be doing photographic family trees to study genetics. It was a horrible assignment even if you had a "normal" family; but it truly sucked when you didn't even have a picture of your dad. Maria had no family to speak of at all—at least none she'd ever known. All that was left of her family was in her name.

Maria Theresa Ramirez Mamoun. "Maria" for the Virgin and her maternal grandmother, whom she'd never met. *And never* will *meet*, Celeste would always say, but she wouldn't say why. "Theresa" for the Blessed Saint, though Maria hadn't set foot in a church since her christening at Our Lady of Lebanon down in fancy-pants Brooklyn Heights. "Mamoun" because that was her mother Celeste's last name. And the "Ramirez" wedged in between like a second middle name, because that was the name of her father, whom she'd also never meet, according to her mother.

Her father had gone back to Puerto Rico before she was born, and Maria didn't think about him much. Many of her classmates had no fathers, and some had no mothers either. Quite a few children were being raised by aunties and grandmas. Some lived in foster care. Even most of the Barbies didn't live with their dads. In fact, she'd have been hard-pressed to name a kid in her class who had access to both parents and two sets of grandparents.

Nevertheless, the Barbies found a way to tease Maria at the lockers after class.

"This should be a easy A for you. All you got to do is go down to the animal shelter and get some pictures of the mutts there," Sharpie said.

Shy Girl slammed Maria's locker shut and leaned on it so their noses were inches apart. She sniffed at Maria as if she were smelling something bad. "Yeah, but how she gonna know which dog is her daddy?"

"Who's your daddy! Who's your daddy!" Skinny chanted.

"She don't know."

"That's 'cause her daddy took one look at her ugly face and ran all the way back to PR with his tail between his legs."

Maria did as she always did; she put her head down,

ignored their comments, and waited to gather her books after they'd gone laughing down the hall.

It was because of the Bad Barbies that Maria made sure to leave for school early in the morning and come home carefully in the afternoon. In the morning, she left the apartment building before the Barbies pulled themselves together and exited in their squawking flock. And after school, she walked behind the Barbies so she could keep them in her sights. She wanted to be sure all the Barbies were inside their apartments before she entered the building. If she saw them hanging out on the steps, Maria detoured to Prospect Avenue and hung out in Linda 99¢ Plus, where she'd spend a long time browsing the soap selection or feigning interest in socks. If they still hadn't left and the man behind the counter was giving her dirty looks, she circled back to La Vida Librería and pretended she could read the *Literatura Cristiana*. She understood enough Spanish to know it was *Abierto de Lunes a Sabado* (open Monday to Saturday) *hasta* 4:30 p.m. So she was covered for two hours at least.

This was, of course, against her mother's rule about going anywhere except school and home, but Maria could see no other way of avoiding the Barbies and she didn't want to bother her mother with something like this. Celeste Mamoun was already overworked and overtired. She would leave even earlier than Maria in the morning and she would return home even later, sometimes even after Maria had put herself to bed. Maria figured the last thing Celeste needed was more stress trying to find affordable after-school care for her daughter who, at twelve years old and nearly done with sixth grade, should be old enough to take care of herself.

The uneasiness Maria felt was well-founded, if possibly misplaced. Though kids did get hurt at school and in the neighborhood, she didn't know for sure that it was the Barbies who did the damage. Still, girls got hurt. Especially lonely girls.

Once, in fifth grade, a teacher Maria didn't even know pulled her off the yard during recess to escort one such injured girl. The victim was tiny; recently from El Salvador and still friendless, and either she was too upset or didn't speak English, but she didn't say a word to Maria as they walked the long halls to the school nurse. The girl held a wad of bloody paper towels to her face, and when the nurse gently pulled them away with her gloved hands, Maria saw the scratches that started up in the girl's hairline, ran through her eyebrow, and tracked down her cheek to her jaw.

But on most days Maria got to school and back home

just fine. On most days the steps were clear and she could go right to her apartment and eat a snack and do her homework and watch TV in peace. If there ever were an emergency, she could call 911. So Maria was just fine, really.

Until she wasn't.

3

THE REPUBLIC OF UGLY

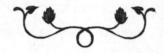

IT RAINED THE DAY THEIR FAMILY TREES WERE due. And it was one of those terrible spring rains, where the wind drives the raindrops so hard they feel like hailstones. Maria rolled up the poster board and tied it with a shoelace. Then she slipped it into two kitchen garbage bags and taped them securely with white bandage tape from her mother's home first aid kit.

She had done a good job on the project, despite the challenges of having no photos to work with. She'd drawn an actual tree with wide spreading branches and applied green paper leaves for the different ancestors. Since she didn't have photos, she drew flags to represent relatives from different countries: a cedar tree for the Lebanese contingent, and the red, white, and blue of Puerto Rico for her father. People born in the U.S.

got an American flag. Celeste had provided names and dates as best she could. If she forgot this or that one's name or birthdate, Celeste flicked her wrist and said, "*Maalish*, it doesn't matter: Mr. Kapusta has no way to check anyhow. What? He is going to call Beirut?"

Under each family member Maria detailed whatever genetic traits her mother recalled: blue eyes and peaked hairline, diabetes and heart disease. It had taken her the better part of a week to complete, and she was pretty sure she would get an A. Probably half the class did theirs on notebook paper over breakfast. Mr. Kapusta was a tiny, rabbity man, whose old-fashioned vests made him look even more like the Easter Bunny. Maria imagined him grateful and relieved that at least one student had completed the project correctly.

She'd gotten a late start, what with wrapping up her project because of the unexpected rain. As Maria stepped from the apartment, her umbrella turned inside out, rain slicked her hair so that it fell over her face, and raindrops obscured her glasses so that she could not see more than blurs of gray.

On such a rainy day she didn't expect to run into the Bad Barbies. They were the last thing on her mind. She was concentrating on getting herself and her project to school as quickly and as dry as possible. But the

Barbies, even if they were around, would be running through the rain, eager to get to school quickly, too, wouldn't they? And so Maria ran, with head down and glasses fogged, for the shelter of vinyl awnings that covered the shops under the elevated train.

Unfortunately she couldn't see that, as if they were waiting just for her, the Barbies had gathered beneath the rotting overhang of the Olympic Theater. She ran across the street and bumped right into them. She stopped, took a deep breath, and held it.

Shy Girl said, "Watch yourself!" She brushed at her jacket as if the impact with Maria had left some sort of stain.

"What's that? You taking trash to school?" Sharpie jutted her sharp chin at the kitchen bag package.

"What, you don't answer us?" Skinny's fat head swam on her neck like a serpent. "Why you so rude?"

Maria's hands tightened around her family tree. "It's my science project. They're due today."

Sharpie took a step toward her.

"How about I turn this in for you? I forgot mines. I could just say this is mines. You okay with that?"

Shy Girl was even bolder. She simply snatched the slippery bags from Maria's hands.

"Let's see this." Shy Girl tore through the plastic.

Immediately raindrops darkened the paper. She unrolled it full length and handed one end to Sharpie.

"Hoo-oo! What's that Christmas tree?"

"Your grandaddy a Christmas tree?"

"Answer the question. Don't you be rude."

"It's a flag," Maria said.

"Oh, yeah!" Skinny pointed. "It's a flag from the Republic of Ugly."

Sharpie rolled Maria's project up. "I guess I can't use this then. My family ain't terrorists."

For a moment Maria thought Sharpie was going to hand her the project. But the Barbie snatched it back from Maria's reaching hand.

"Why you always got to be the goody-goody, doing your homework on time, handing it in like you the best? You always trying to make the rest of us look bad."

"I'm not trying to make you look bad," Maria said. "Can I please have it back?"

"Can I please have it back? Can I please have it back?" The girls passed the project over Maria's head.

Maria was tired of it. She wanted to get out of the rain. She wanted her project. She lunged for the poster and missed. And her open hand came down hard on Skinny's beefy shoulder.

"Oh no you didn't!" Skinny grabbed Maria by the hair, sending her barrette flying.

Now they all joined in, pushing her back and forth, tripping her so she stumbled and catching her just before she fell, only to push her again. The sidewalk became a blur of hair and hands and ugly voices. Their sharp nails flashed, and Maria covered her face with her arms . . .

Suddenly Tante Farida hurried over in a great blustering fury, waving her umbrella and calling Maria's name. She swung through the Barbies, her tiny feet amazingly swift, and grabbed Maria by the arm and steered her with surprising force across the street and into the Colony Fried Chicken. Then she locked the door behind her, much to the fry cook's surprise.

"What you doing locking my door? I'ma call the police, you don't go right now," he yelled.

"You'll keep the door locked and hand me that phone if you know what's good for you, Mr. Sesay," Tante Farida said. She peered through the glass door. The Barbies huddled under the shelter of the Olympic Theater and stared across the street at the Colony Fried Chicken, talking to one another.

Mr. Sesay handed Tante his cell phone.

The Barbies crossed the street and came up to the door. Shy Girl tried the handle. Then she cupped her hands to the glass and peeked through. Tante Farida glared back at her and gestured to the phone.

"I'm calling 911!" she yelled, though in fact she was calling Celeste Mamoun.

"We was just messing with her! Jeez, lady!" Sharpie threw Maria's project to the curb, where it was promptly run over by the Riverside bus.

* * *

Later that night, Maria took a long hot bath. Celeste sat on the tile floor, looking worriedly at her. It had been years since she'd sat with Maria while she bathed, but Maria didn't mind tonight. It made her feel safer.

"But what did they do to you, *chérie*?" Celeste asked for what must have been the tenth time. "Did they hurt you?"

"No, Mama. They just pushed me around."

"Well, I'm going to make sure they get more than in-school suspension. What good is that? They can still get you walking home. It's like that gang stuff is happening all over again . . ." Celeste pressed her fingers to her lips. "I'm so sorry, *habibti*."

Habibti is Arabic for "my darling," and Celeste only

called Maria this when she was very worried. It worried Maria to see her mother so worried, and she struggled to stay calm herself.

"Really, it's no big deal," Maria said. "They're not a real gang. They're just wannabes."

"But what about in a few years? When they go from wannabes to actually being? What if something really happens?" Celeste said. "I could get you a phone, but who would you call? And I'm so far away I can't help."

Maria nodded. It had taken her mother hours to get home. She had to hand her patients off to another nurse, then take two trains back. The whole time Maria waited, shaking, in Tante's apartment. The old lady had given her a dry T-shirt and sweater that smelled of her husband's hair oil, even though he'd been dead for over five years.

"I wish we had someone else nearby," Maria said. "Someone around all the time. Like real family."

"I'm sorry. I'm all you've got," Celeste said.

"But what if something really does happen?" Maria had tried not to ask that, but her mother had asked it first.

Celeste hugged Maria though she was sopping wet. Maria couldn't help it: she suddenly started to cry. She cried great big racking sobs. She sobbed until her stomach hurt and the bathwater cooled. Her mom hugged her and waited. When she quieted, Celeste said, "*Qu'est-ce que c'est?* Tell me the truth."

"Even when everything is okay," Maria said, "I hate it here. I hate this building, those girls, and my school." She hadn't realized it till she said it, but once she had, she knew it to be true. "And I never see you! You're never here! I'm always alone!"

"I know." Celeste's voice sounded tight. "I'm sorry."

"It's just . . ." Maria didn't want to upset her mother any more than she already had. "Do you remember that day we went to the beach? I loved that. Why can't we do that kind of thing more?"

Celeste stopped stroking Maria's wet hair. "It's not always so easy to find the time."

Maria worried she'd gone too far.

"I'm okay now, Mama. I was just upset. And it won't happen again. I'm usually more careful. I just messed up."

Celeste stared at her for a long time, as if she were thinking about something important.

"You didn't mess up," Celeste finally said. "I messed up. You shouldn't have to be careful."

"It's not your fault."

"But it is." Celeste looked grim and determined. "I'm the adult."

"But what can you do about it?" Maria said.

"I don't know, *chérie*," Celeste said. "But I'll think of something."

Celeste didn't make Maria return to school the next day. And anyway, Maria didn't want to go back to school and face the Bad Barbies. She was pretty sure they'd be looking for revenge.

So Maria sat at the kitchen table, doing the school-work she was missing. Principal Toussainte had at least that much mercy—after Maria's mother called him to explain, he agreed to let Maria finish out the year at home.

Mostly, Maria spent her days listening. She listened for the Barbies coming back from school, roaming around the building, their hooting laughter, their mothers' hollers and slammed doors and stomped feet. She was scared all the time, though she pretended to be okay for her mother's sake.

But Celeste knew she wasn't okay. She knew, because she was watching her daughter closely. The day after the attack she quit both her jobs. So now she didn't go to work and she didn't leave Maria alone in the apartment except to go shopping for necessities.

Celeste spent her days on their ancient computer and on the phone, and her nights sorting and packing and making more phone calls. On the sixth day, Maria woke to an empty apartment. Everything was gone: to the curb as trash, to the building superintendent for donation, or stuffed into four large duffel bags.

"*Fais vite, chérie!* Our taxi is coming!" Celeste hovered in the bathroom door. "Wash your teeth quickly!"

"*Brush* your teeth, Mama."

"You should brush your hair, too, but we don't have time." Celeste snatched the toothbrush, still wet, from Maria's hand and shoved it in her purse. "Help with the bags."

Celeste locked up the apartment and slipped the keys under the floor mat. The Bad Barbies were nowhere to be seen. Maria followed Celeste down the building stairs, and out the double doors one last time.

Tante Farida was waiting for them on the sidewalk. The old lady looked particularly tiny and her eyes were red and wet. She grabbed Celeste and gave her three quick kisses, right, left, right. Then she handed Maria a plastic bag filled with pistachio nougats and sesame treats.

"To fatten my string bean." She patted Maria's cheek. She handed another bag to Celeste. "Grape leaves, *zeitoun*, *kibbe*, and breads for lunch."

Their taxi pulled up. The cabbie threw their bags in

the trunk. More kisses, more hugs, more Arabic whispers, more kisses again. The cabbie honked and they climbed in.

Tante waved until they turned the corner.

"But, Mama, where are we going?" Maria asked.

"To the beach," Celeste told her. "To get some sun."

4

FISHY BUTTER AND FUNNY ACCENTS

THEY WOULD BE LIVING ON AN ISLAND OFF THE coast of New England called Martha's Vineyard.

"Who's Martha?" Maria asked.

"I don't know," Celeste said. "Maybe we'll find out when we get there."

Celeste explained that she was going to be taking care of an old man who owned an estate.

"What's an estate?" Maria asked.

"It's a big place with lots of land and buildings—"

"Like a town?"

"No, more like . . ." Celeste paused. "You know those TV shows about rich people in England in the olden days? Not knights-in-shining-armor old days, more like horses and carriages and butlers and maids?"

Maria tried to picture it. She imagined women in

tight corsets and voluminous gowns drinking tea with their gloves on and their pinkies up, chattering in British accents. She couldn't see what that had to do with an island off the coast of New England. Unless New England was like Old England. She wondered if it was.

"He's some kind of billionaire," Celeste said. "He's also very, very ill. That's why he needs a nurse twenty-four–seven. I just hope he's not dying anytime soon. It would be my luck to have him die just as soon as we get there. Then I'd be out of another job."

Maria felt a sick tickle in her stomach. Her mom sounded worried and it was all Maria's fault. If she had been paying attention, she wouldn't have run into the Bad Barbies. If she hadn't run into the Barbies, her mother wouldn't have quit her jobs. And now they'd uprooted themselves because she'd been overly dramatic and said she hated everything.

Maria stared out the bus window. They had been traveling all day, it seemed: first the long taxi ride from their apartment to Port Authority, and then hours and hours on an interstate highway with nothing to look at but trees, trees, and more trees. It wasn't that she didn't like trees—she did. Especially at first. But after a while it became monotonous. Maria had never seen so many trees. Every so often the trees parted and she could see the backyards of houses near the highway. These suburban homes looked like the sort she saw on after-school TV shows, with patios and barbecues and swimming pools.

She remembered her own small but cozy bedroom. The flowered bedspread—her mom had put that in the donation bag because it was too big to pack—the yellow dresser with green knobs, also donated. Tears pricked her eyes. Why did she suddenly care about those worn-out things? She shook her head and closed her eyes. She would not care. She would not miss it, any of it.

"Hey, sleepyhead," Celeste said. "We're nearly there."

Maria sat up. "How long was I asleep for?"

"Not long. Look—" Celeste pointed out the window.

The bus was pulling into a large parking lot filled with cars and people. At the far end of the lot stood a huge white building, and behind it was the ocean. Suddenly the front wall of the huge white building opened up, and an orderly line of cars began inching toward the open wall. People with suitcases and duffel bags walked up ramps and disappeared into a side door. Maria had never seen anything like this before. Not even on TV.

"That's our ferry," Celeste said.

"Oh!" Maria readjusted her brain. The white building was *not* a building after all. It was a ferryboat. And they would take it to the billionaire's island.

The next few minutes were a blur of activity. Celeste hustled Maria out of the bus and told her to stay put while she monitored the transfer of the duffel bags from the bus to a little trailer loaded with passengers' luggage. Then she hustled her up the aluminum ramp and onto the gigantic boat. A man in a white nautical uniform took two paper tickets from Celeste and handed back two stubs.

"We'll keep these for a souvenir," Celeste said, pocketing them. "Do you want to ride outside or inside? We can see the sunset from the top deck. And we can get something to eat from the cafeteria."

"I want to sit outside. In front. I'll get seats while you get food," Maria said.

She picked the two best seats at the front of the boat. The glowing sun hovered near the horizon, turning the sky a neon pink and the waves a molten gold. A loud horn blew, the engine rumbled, and then the ferry glided away from the dock so smoothly Maria could scarcely feel it. The ferry picked up speed, and the salty wind whipped Maria's hair across her face and chilled her.

She liked the way the air smelled—damp and clean—like that day at the beach. A gull sailed along on the wind, hovering just off the rail.

The little town with the ferry terminal quickly receded, and soon they were on open water. Maria looked around for her mother and was surprised to see they were alone on deck, except for a few travelers with dogs.

"How come everyone's inside?" Maria asked Celeste. "I can't believe they'd want to miss this." She tipped her chin toward the pink clouds.

"They're probably all Island natives. This is routine for them. It's still too early in the season for tourists." Celeste handed Maria a cardboard tray with four cardboard cups. "Hot chocolate and clam chowder."

"Have I ever had clam chowder before?" Maria spooned up the thick white liquid and watched it drop back into the cup.

"No. But I think we'll be eating a lot of it now," Celeste said.

Maria sniffed her spoon. "It smells like fishy butter."

"You should try it," Celeste said. "It reminds me of a soup I ate in Paris, with cream and *moules*, how do you say it? Mussels."

"No offense, Mama, but that sounds kind of gross."

Maria put the strange soup to one side and turned back to the view.

But now that the sun had set, there wasn't much view anymore. The ocean turned deep purple with silver shimmers. The shore had disappeared entirely, swallowed up by shadows. She'd never been anywhere so dark. The only lights came from their boat and the occasional buoy. And the stars. She'd never seen so many stars in real life. The city's lights had always blocked the stars. She marveled at how they filled the black sky.

"It's pretty," Maria said.

"It is," Celeste agreed.

"But kind of scary," Maria said.

"How so?"

"Well, it's so empty." Maria looked out over the black water. "And it feels like if you fell in, no one would notice."

"Well then, don't fall in!" Celeste said. "But good thing you know how to swim."

"I guess. But I still say that pool was crazy crowded," Maria said. Two summers ago, her mother had made her take swimming lessons at the Crotona pool. Every Monday she'd joined a gaggle of loud, rough children in the overcrowded city pool because her mother had insisted she learn the basics.

"Well, now that we'll be living near a beach, you can swim in the not-crowded ocean," Celeste said. "You should thank me for saving you from drowning, in advance."

"Thanks for saving me from drowning in advance," Maria said. She cupped her hands around her hot chocolate and settled back to enjoy the ride.

Nearly an hour later, a bell sounded and a man's voice anounced, "Vineyahd Haven, Vineyahd Haven."

"Here we are." Celeste patted Maria's knee.

"I thought we were going to Martha's Vineyard," Maria said.

"It's a big island. There are more than a few towns. Vineyard Haven has a ferry terminal."

"Oh. Vine*yard* Haven. I thought he said Vine*yahd*."

The man told all *passenjahs* with *cahs* to go down to the *cah* deck, and all walk-off *passenjahs* to exit from the *stahbud* bow. Maria smiled and repeated the words in the strange accent to herself. She wondered if everyone here spoke like that.

The ferry was pulling into the brightly lit dock, bumping gently up against massive logs hung with old tires. A woman in a bright orange reflective vest caught a giant rope and looped it over something that looked like a metal hook lying on its side, and then she caught another. Meanwhile, two men climbed a series of ramps and began stretching a walkway toward the docking ferry. Beyond the ramp spread another ferry terminal, like the one they had left. But this one had no cars lined up, waiting to board. They had taken the last ferry. There would be no return trip that night. A handful of people in the parking lot below waited to pick up family members. A man stood at the base of the ramp with a cardboard sign that said MAMOON.

"There's someone waiting for us," Maria said. "He spelled our name wrong."

"I arranged for a taxi." Celeste tossed their trash. "Come, we have to get the bags off the luggage cart."

"Okay." Maria took one last look. Just beyond the ferry terminal, she could make out the shadows of a small town, but there were few lights to see it by. Just a white dot here and there—possibly streetlights or porch lights. No colored lights, though. No traffic lights, no flashing WALK/DON'T WALK signs. No neon signs advertising PIZZA or PUPUSAS. So strange, that a town could just turn off its lights and go to bed.

"It's so dark," Maria said.

"Wait till we get out of town. See that?" Celeste pointed to an even darker expanse beyond the terminal. "That's where we're going."

5

Into the Woods

CELESTE WAS RIGHT. BY THE TIME THEY reached the estate, there were no lights at all, just the headlights of their taxi. If Maria looked out the front window, she saw an empty road with a forest on either side. Every so often a dirt road broke through the trees. After about half an hour, the cabbie turned off the main road and onto one of these smaller, dirt roads. Suddenly the woods closed in around them. It felt to Maria as if they were traveling down a narrow hallway, except on either side, instead of walls there loomed enormous trees.

"Mr. Ironwall owns all this, right down to the ocean," their cabdriver explained. "You can't see the beach from here, but it's out there. One of the nicest on the Island and private, too. No public access. Your place is up ahead."

Through the gloom, Maria could just make out two statues of ancient Chinese soldiers flanking either side of an open gate. After they passed through the gate, the trees disappeared and the sky opened up. Vast fields glowed silver under the rising moon.

"It's a castle!" Maria said.

"It's not a castle. It's more of a mansion," Celeste said. "And anyhow, we won't live in the main house. There's a guesthouse."

After a few more minutes, the taxi pulled off the main driveway onto a little side path and stopped in front of a small cottage.

"We're here," the cabbie said.

In the taxi's headlights, the little house looked like a gingerbread cottage from a fairy tale. A glittering white footpath led to the red door. Evergreen shrubs squatted like gumdrops on either side. White trim frosted the dark windows and dripped from under the overhanging eaves. The lemon-yellow window boxes were empty of all but dirt, but Maria could easily imagine them filled with colorful flowers. She wondered what would grow.

The cabbie shone his headlights while Celeste hunted for the key under the licorice-colored mat. Maria stood beside her, waiting. The cool night air had that same salty tang she'd smelled on the ferry. She could breathe it forever.

Finally Celeste shoved against the door with her shoulder, and they stumbled into a cold, dark room. She wrestled their duffel bags inside. Already the cab was pulling away. Celeste turned her cell phone on and shone a pale blue glow around the walls.

"I can't find the switch to open the light," Celeste said.

"*Turn on* the light, Mama," Maria said.

"*Maalish.* Whatever. Maybe I will find some candles."

Maria had never been anywhere so quiet. In the city, there had always been noise. Kids like the Barbies roaming around the building, shouting and laughing no matter what hour. The elevated subway trains ran all night, rumbling and screeching past their living room windows. And she was often woken by the loud thumping bass from the stereo of a passing car, or a honking horn, or a siren.

Celeste lit the stump of candle she'd found in a drawer. The small flame revealed a main room with a kitchen area to the left and a living room of sorts to the right. In the middle of the main room squatted a weird black metal cube, like an old-fashioned bank safe, the kind Maria had seen in old cartoons. A pipe stretched out of the top, took a sharp turn, and exited out the wall over the fireplace.

"It's a woodstove," Celeste told her. "I don't want to burn this place down our first night, so let us leave it be. But I would guess that's our only heat, so we're just going to be cold tonight."

It was surprisingly chilly. Maria hadn't realized how far north they'd traveled. Back in the city it was already hot enough to sleep with the windows open.

"You want to snuggle in with me?" Celeste bustled about as she spoke, unfolding the sofa into a bed and spreading a fresh-smelling quilt on the creaky mattress. The pillowcases smelled fresh, too, as if someone had just laundered them.

"The housekeeper said there was a loft upstairs that could be your room," Celeste told her, "but I think it's too dark, late, and cold to deal with that now, no?"

Maria would have loved to see the loft. But her mother sounded tired and Maria didn't want to make things difficult for her, so she nodded.

"I think this will be okay," Celeste murmured, as if she wasn't sure that it would be okay at all.

6

CAPTAIN MURDERER

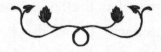

THE NEXT MORNING, MARIA WOKE TO HER mother clattering around the kitchen. The cottage felt deliciously warm.

"Did you find the radiator?" Maria asked.

"No. No radiator. But there was a note explaining the woodstove. I must have been too tired last night to notice." Celeste grinned proudly at Maria. "Who would've thought a city girl like me could make a fire?"

Golden sunlight streamed through the windows, and the aroma of cinnamon and buttery sugar filled the air. Maria burrowed under the colorful quilt and squinched up her toes with glee. She felt supremely happy. She couldn't remember the last time her mom had made a hot breakfast.

"The housekeeper left us a pan of cinnamon rolls in

the fridge," Celeste said. "They're baking now. And the coffee was all set to brew. The smell woke me up!"

"So there is electricity."

"Yes." Celeste placed a mug of hot chocolate on the table beside Maria. "Hattie even bought groceries!"

"Who's Hattie?"

"Mr. Ironwall's housekeeper." Celeste held up the housekeeper's note. "She says there's only as much hot water as the woodstove heats up—apparently the pipes run through it somehow. Which might be a problem in August when we won't want to light it because it will be too hot . . . but I guess we won't want hot showers then anyhow."

Maria sat up with the quilt wrapped around her and looked about. Now, in the bright morning light, she could see their new home properly.

The space was small—just one room really. Only the furniture defined the difference between the kitchen, living room, and dining room. Celeste could cook while Maria sat on the sofa, and no wall separated them. But instead of feeling crowded and jumbled, the design felt friendly and cozy. And, Maria thought, it was a fascinating room.

The wood floor shone from years of polish. Crocheted blankets and embroidered pillows brightened every chair. The walls were painted sky blue and odd ornaments hung all about: shells, fish skeletons, glass globes, and other bits and pieces of weird stuff.

Strangely enough, there seemed to be no TV. At least none that Maria could see. Just a fireplace where a TV should be. The mantel over the fireplace held more bric-a-brac: a stuffed parrot under a bell-shaped glass, a primitive drum of bark and skin, and a gourd carved with tiny pictures. A big, ugly painting of a ship in a storm loomed over the collection. Two mismatched, overstuffed chairs snuggled up to the fireplace. They looked perfect for curling up in on a rainy day. Each chair had a little table beside it for a snack and hot chocolate. Bookshelves lined two of the walls. Yellowing paperbacks, stacks of games, decks of cards, puzzles, and various other vacation pastimes crowded their boards.

The curtainless windows opened up to gray fields and misty woods. Pieces of smoothly polished glass, shells, and other intriguing items littered the windowsills. Yet despite the clutter, nothing was dusty. Someone, most likely this Hattie person, had carefully taken down, cleaned, and replaced each item.

"It's very nice here, Mama," Maria said.

"Yes, *chérie*." Celeste smiled. "Cozy."

In the back corner farthest from the kitchen, a black iron-lace stair spiraled up to the loft.

"Can I go see the loft now?" Maria pointed to the spiral stair.

"Yes—just be careful and don't touch anything. I haven't had a chance to look at it myself."

Maria crept up the twisting stairs and through a hole in the ceiling. The loft was an attic, empty but for a few trunks and suitcases of varying age, an antique croquet set missing the red mallet and most of the wickets, and a wrought-iron daybed with a blue-striped mattress. On either side of the attic were circular windows of the sort found on boats—with one directly above the bed so that if you lay upon it, as Maria did now, you could see loads of sky. She knelt on top of the bed and peered out the window. More swaths of silvery-gray grass led to a huge white house. It was as big as a castle, with columns in front and row upon row of windows. The driveway from their cottage to the mansion ended in a circle with an ornate marble fountain in the center. Maria couldn't tell whether it had water. Behind the mansion lay the ocean. It was the color of steel and whipped with white waves.

She squinted and pushed her forehead against the cool glass. Farther off, a dock jutted into the sea, and a boat bobbed alongside. It had two poles rising from it—the kind sails hung off of, but Maria couldn't see any sails. It looked like a sailboat just the same. Maybe the sails got put away when they weren't being used. Maybe that was the white clothlike thing below the naked poles. Maria didn't know. She'd never been on a sailboat. In fact, she was pretty sure she didn't even know anyone who had ever been on a sailboat. She wondered if she and her mom would get to use it. She craned her neck to see it better. The pressure of her head against the glass pushed the window open a crack and the cries of gulls filled the room.

She pulled the glass shut and looked around. The sloping roof formed the walls on either side and the exposed wood beams were carved with letters and numbers. Maria traced the carvings in the nearest beam with her fingers: *JM 1689, 1230, FH 1718, SI 1812*. She wondered who put them there, and why. She figured they were some kind of old-school graffiti: the letters were initials and the numbers were years. *JM* was here in 1689, *SI* in 1812. But *1230* made no sense. She knew there weren't any houses like this in America back in 1230. The Pilgrims hadn't even come over yet.

The insulation between the beams looked as though it was made of clay and coarse hair. Maria touched it. It seemed like it came from some kind of animal—a horse's mane or tail, perhaps? And what was this? Hay? And newspapers? It seemed whoever lived here had stuffed any old thing in between the eaves to keep out the cold drafts.

Her fingers found something hard. She worked her hand a bit deeper. Whatever it was didn't want to budge. She pinched it and wiggled it, until finally it slid out in a cloud of dust that showered her bed. She sneezed. The thing fell on the floor with a thump.

"Okay up there?" Celeste called.

"Fine!" Maria looked at the strange item.

It was a tube about a foot long, open on both ends, with two leather straps wrapped around and secured with square knots. She turned it over in her hands. Something was written on it, pressed into the leather and rubbed with fading ink:

Property of Captain Jean Murde er, 1689.

One letter was too squiggly to read. Captain Jean Murderer? What a horrible name. Maria wondered if it was made up.

"What are you doing?" her mother called from downstairs.

"Nothing." Maria dropped the tube on the bed. "Looking out the window. There's a beach!"

"But of course there's a beach—the cabbie said so last night!" Her mother popped her head through the hole.

"Can I sleep here?" Maria slipped the tube under the pillow. For some reason, she wanted to keep it hidden. At least until she knew what it was.

"Well, if the floorboards are safe and there's nothing dangerous for you to get into. I'll have to check it first—but now it's time for breakfast. And after that we go to the Great House to meet Mr. Ironwall."

"The great house?" Maria followed her mother downstairs.

"With a capital *G* and capital *H*. Apparently that's what they call it, according to this note." Celeste put the cinnamon rolls on the kitchen table and looked at her dusty daughter. "Of course, you'll have to clean up first."

"Of course," Maria replied. But she was thinking of the strange leather tube, and Captain Murderer, and wondering when she could get back and explore the attic for more ancient treasures.

7

THE GREAT HOUSE

THE WHITE FAÇADE OF THE GREAT HOUSE ROSE before them. The dark mirrors of its many windows flashed in the early morning sun. They were bumping down the long drive in a golf cart, the wheels crunching on the white surface, which Maria realized was made of smashed-up clamshells. Maria and her mother sat in the back seat, as the driver, a stocky man with graying brown hair, talked continually like a nervous tour guide.

"Mr. Ironwall hasn't had guests in the cottage for years. I hope you were comfortable enough. Sorry about the cold. If Hattie had told me when you were coming, I could have lit the stove." Their driver turned and smiled apologetically. He had a homely, friendly face. His eyes were a strange color. Green? Hazel? Maria couldn't tell. The changeable color of the ocean, she thought. His skin was tan, as if he spent most of his days outside, and he had the rough hands of a carpenter. Maybe that's what he was—a carpenter or a gardener.

"We were fine," Celeste said. "Hattie did a lovely job with the cleaning and shopping . . ."

The air was brisk, and the blue sky Maria had seen out her attic window was rapidly giving way to clouds. They drew close to the house and the driver parked the golf cart behind the dry fountain.

"It was really something in its day," the man now said. He lifted Celeste's bag from the back. "When the fountain was working and there was a team of gardeners. I mow the lawn and trim the hedges, but there's no one to do the flowers or topiary anymore."

"Is there a servants' entrance?" Celeste asked.

"Through the kitchen, around the side."

But he led them directly through the massive front doors. Maria scarcely had time to take in the marble entryway, sweeping staircase, and crystal chandelier before they were whisked through a series of halls where all the furniture was covered in white sheets. They went down a smaller corridor and ended up in front of a double set of white doors.

"Well, this is it." The man knocked and then walked

away, leaving them standing alone. They waited for what seemed like an extraordinarily long time.

Just as Maria was about to ask her mother if maybe there were some mistake, the right-hand door swung open and a large, gruff woman with red cheeks, white hair, and blue scrubs grabbed Maria's mother by the arm.

"Ah you Celeste Mamoun?" the night nurse wheezed. She turned her *r*'s into *h*'s just like the ferry announcer. "I've been waiting for you. I got to make the ferry. You have to crush the meds and mix them with applesauce. He's on smooth foods since the stroke— You do speak English, right?"

"Of course," Celeste said.

The nurse's face turned a deeper red. She stepped briskly back into the bedroom. Celeste rolled her eyes at Maria, then she followed the nurse.

Maria stayed in the hall. She peeked through the open door and saw a gigantic bed, in the middle of which a huge gray dog lolled regally, one outstretched paw held between the two skeletal hands of an ancient man.

Mr. Ironwall.

The old man's pale, sunken face was nearly lost in the mound of pillows. Beside the bed stood the sorts of machines and apparatus Maria had seen before in the many hospital rooms where her mother had worked: a portable toilet and Hoyer Lift and suction and oxygen and a stainless-steel table with syringes and pink plastic basins. The room had a strange, stale smell. The old man looked up and caught her eye, and then she was roughly shoved out of the doorway by the gruff night nurse.

"Mr. Ironwall don't want to see no kids right now," she said to Maria's mother. "We got to do his bed bath and I want to show you the med orders . . ."

Celeste just had time to mouth "See you later" to Maria before the door shut.

Maria stood alone in the empty hall wondering what to do. She and her mother hadn't had a chance to discuss it. She wasn't particularly worried about being left alone, as many other children might have been, because she'd already spent so much of her life alone. And somehow she knew she'd landed in a safe place—or safe enough, at least compared to her old neighborhood.

But what should she *do* all day? She hadn't really given any thought to how she was supposed to spend her days while her mother worked.

Celeste was going to be busy all day most days, so Maria supposed she'd be entertaining herself. Perhaps that's what she should do. Go back to the cottage and examine that strange tube. Maybe explore the beach and find that boat.

She wandered back through the mansion in what she hoped was the way they came, but she couldn't be sure because the hallways in this wing all looked the same. Every so often she tried a doorknob, but all of the doors were locked.

Just as she was beginning to get tired and starting to despair, she found a knob that turned in her hand. At first the door stuck as if it had not opened in a long time. But when she shoved it with her shoulder, she stumbled into a large, dark room. Though no one had said as much, and there were no signs forbidding entry, she was pretty sure she was not supposed to go in. But there was no one around to tell her the rules, and what did they expect of a twelve-year-old girl left alone in a billionaire's mansion? Who wouldn't be curious? And so Maria pulled the door quietly behind her, careful to keep it slightly open—she wasn't foolish enough to lock herself in—and began to explore.

Dark curtains covered the windows, and only a little light penetrated the dusty gloom. Maria stood still for a moment, blinking and waiting for her eyes to adjust. Rows and rows of wine-colored velvet chairs—enough to seat at least fifty people—faced a stage with a plushy wine-colored curtain. It looked like a small theater. Maybe it was. Maybe he was rich enough to have his own private theater!

Old-fashioned posters covered the walls: *The Last Privateer*, an Ironwall production, *Joie de Vivre*, directed by Peter Ironwall, *To Have and To Hope*, produced by Peter Ironwall.

She wondered if Peter Ironwall was the Mr. Ironwall upstairs in the bedroom.

"Is anyone in here?" a female voice said.

Maria startled and turned.

A woman was peeking around the door. Upon seeing Maria, she stepped all the way in.

"You don't want to get lost in this big house," the woman said. "You may get locked in a room and we'll find you three years later, mummified."

"I'm sorry," Maria said. "I left the door open a crack . . ."

"That's how I found you. If I hadn't, who knows what might have happened with you snooping about."

"I wasn't snooping," Maria said. "I just couldn't find the door to outside."

"Well, that's not surprising. Typical of Frank to leave you high and dry."

The woman looked neither old nor young. Her ruddy skin stretched tightly over her broad, unwrinkled forehead. Her eyes were big and bright, the color of the ocean (just like the gardener's, Maria thought), but her hair was a thin silver braid and she had the long yellow teeth of an old lady. Her clothes were wild and gypsy-like with embroidery and beads. Maria guessed she was about her mother's age but had lived a much harder life, or else simply didn't believe in hair dye and dentists.

Suddenly the woman stuck out her hand. "Oh, I'm sorry. I'm Hattie, the housekeeper."

"Maria." She stuck out her own small hand. "You made the cinnamon buns. My mom and I loved them, thank you."

Hattie took Maria's hand and turned it over, as if she were inspecting it. "You look like you could use more. You're a skinny one. And pale, too. I'd bet you don't get outside much."

"Tante Farida, this old lady my mom and I know, always says I look like a canned string bean," Maria said. "She runs a grocery store. In the Bronx."

"Well, this isn't the Bronx," Hattie said. She began tidying up the place, stacking books and papers. "You'll be outside a lot now. My boy, he's about your age, is out all the time. Every second he's not in school. And half the time when he should be in school—that's why his grades are so poor. Fishing, biking, skateboarding—we can't keep him home. It's like he was raised by wolves." She turned and squinted at Maria. "Why aren't you in school?"

"My mom said it would be too awkward for me to enroll here for the last few weeks, and I could just go next year if—" She stopped talking. She wasn't sure if it was appropriate to say *if my mom keeps this job*. She didn't want to make it seem that there might be some reason she shouldn't.

"Well, you'll need something to do or you'll get bored. Ironwall House isn't a great place for children."

"I think it's wonderful! It's like something out of a fairy tale—a mansion, the ocean—"

"What I mean is, Mr. Ironwall won't want you hanging around the mansion because he's sick and noise isn't good for his heart."

"I'm very quiet," Maria said.

"And you'll find the ocean isn't much fun for a while yet," Hattie continued as if she hadn't heard Maria. "It's too cold for swimming till nearly mid-July."

"What did Mr. Ironwall do?" Maria asked. "I mean, is this all his movie stuff? Is that how he became so rich? Like, was he a famous actor?"

"Not an actor, but he did something in film." Hattie dusted a golden statuette and clucked her tongue. "He was a producer and a director. I think he even wrote some of the screenplays. But he didn't need to work, really. He was always rich. Family money."

"What's 'family money'?" Maria asked.

"His ancestors were all rich sea captains. Whalers, navy men, maybe even a pirate or two. And they married money . . . daughters of other captains . . ." Hattie paused each time she removed and dusted another statuette.

Maria wondered if any of the rich ancestors were the mysterious Captain Murderer.

"Anyhow, our Mr. Ironwall is the last heir to all that fortune. So that's how come he can keep this place even though he hasn't worked in years." Hattie grabbed a folding chair to reach the top shelves. "I don't know when the last time was I dusted in here. These pictures need to be packaged up properly—the paper's getting all dry and cracked . . ."

"Yes, there are a lot of old things." Maria looked at all the movie memorabilia. Between the posters hung many black-and-white photos. They showed lots of glamorous, laughing people. Maria hoped to recognize famous actors, but none of the names or faces meant anything to her. On the far wall was a large photo of two men standing proudly beside a sailboat. The cramped handwriting in the corner said *The Last Privateer—1963.*

Maria wondered if it was the sailboat she'd seen from her window. It had two poles sticking up. She peered more closely at the photo. In it, one man held a bottle tied with a ribbon. The other man, equally young and handsome, stood beside him. The crowd around them had their hands up as if they were caught applauding.

"Who's that?" she asked, pointing to the man with the bottle.

Hattie stopped dusting and peered closely at the photo. "Oh, that's Mr. Ironwall when he was young. Christening his yacht. The other fellow is an actor. Used to be very famous. I forget his name now. My parents would know. He lived here for years, but that was before my time."

"Mr. Ironwall looks so young and happy," Maria said. She could hardly believe the strong, handsome man in the photo was now the old man in the bed. "Does he still have this boat? I mean, is it the one down at the dock?" She looked closely at the picture. "It's got those two stick-things coming out of it like this one."

"Those sticks are called masts. It might be." Hattie

dusted the photo, then all the photos beside it. "I never get down there myself. Always working inside."

"Does Mr. Ironwall still go sailing?" Maria asked.

Hattie scoffed. "Oh, Mr. I hasn't been out of the house in years. He got the diabetes, and then had a stroke . . ." She wiped her hands and surveyed the room. "Come on, I'll get Frank to drive you back."

Maria realized Frank must be the gardener with the golf cart.

"Oh, you don't have to do that," she said. "It's not far, and like you said, I need the fresh air. Anyhow, I'm sure I can get back to the cottage once I find my way out of this house."

"Well, I'll show you that much."

Hattie walked briskly in front of Maria, explaining the wings and hallways as they went. Maria wasn't sure she'd remember any of it. Suddenly they were back in the grand entryway but heading in a different direction, away from Mr. Ironwall's room.

"We'll go through the kitchen so you'll know where to find me," Hattie said. They went through a ballroom, a dining room (all tables and chairs covered in more white sheets), and then a set of swinging doors. They landed in a restaurant-size kitchen. The broad stainless-steel counters, giant walk-in refrigerator, and enormous stove were spotless, as if food hadn't touched them in years. The only part that looked used was a worn wooden table with an open newspaper, a coffee mug, and a pitcher of daffodils upon it.

Hattie held open the door to the outside for Maria. "You come by tomorrow for lunch and I won't take no for an answer. And we have to find you something to do all day. You can't be wandering around alone. Or who knows what sort of trouble you'll get into." She turned and shut the door behind her, as if this were a perfectly normal way to say goodbye.

TWICE TWICE TWO

MARIA HURRIED BACK TO THE COTTAGE. AS SOON as she got there, she raced up the spiral stairs to the attic, flopped on the bed, and pulled the leather tube from under her pillow. She ran her fingers over the name.

Captain Murderer. He sounded like a pirate.

With the straps untied, the tube unrolled into a flat leather rectangle. Inside was a sheet of paper. But it wasn't really very paperish. It was more like very thin, soft fabric. If she looked closely, Maria could see the weave of fibers. The edges were yellow and crispy, and in a few places it was nearly worn through. The paper seemed very old. Maria smoothed it carefully on the quilt.

It was a map of an island, roughly triangular in shape, with the apex at the northern tip. The lacy shoreline had been inked by a careful hand. A few landmarks had been drawn: a series of cliffs, some small lakes—but a great deal of the island was blank as if it had not been explored, and there were no names or marks to help identify the place. Sea monsters and mermaids swam in the ocean and an elaborate drawing of a compass decorated the top right corner. The whole thing looked ancient. At the bottom was a note written in a fancy hand:

> Twice twice two,
> Then twice that more.
> Take one from the first,
> The Queen treads upon the door.

Maria stared at the parchment for a long time. She turned it over, but there was nothing on the back except for some unidentifiable tea-colored stains. She looked at the front again. There, off the northeastern corner of the island, floated three small circles, which she'd previously overlooked as just inky smudges. They looked like tiny rocks, compared to the big, triangular island. Across the circles, as if they'd been a mistake, was a large, flowery squiggle.

Maria reread the cryptic note. *Twice twice two, then*

twice that more. Some kind of math problem. Boring. And who was the Queen? And what was the door? And what was that squiggle? A mistake? Someone crossing something out? Was it an X? On TV, X's on maps usually marked the spot for buried pirate treasure. And Captain Murderer certainly *sounded* like a pirate's name.

Maybe it was a treasure map with an X to mark the spot. Maria rolled onto her back and considered the possibility. She stared through the circular window at the gray-blue sky.

A pirate map. A pirate treasure map. A real pirate treasure map.

What else could it be?

And why not? This place was already so strange, this estate, this cottage. Everything was like something out of the TV movies she loved. Maybe this map was her chance for an adventure. If she could use the map to get her hands on a real pirate treasure, she would be set for life. Her mom wouldn't have to work all the time, they could settle down, buy a house of their own somewhere safe and quiet and nice, like here maybe—no more apartments, no more subways and cement and Bad Barbies . . .

But where did pirates usually bury their treasure? The Caribbean—she knew that much from TV—but she had no way of knowing which Caribbean island was triangular, with three small rocks off its northern tip. Was there a famous Queen in the Caribbean? Anyhow, how could she even get to the Caribbean?

Maria stared at the carved beam above her bed. *JM, 1689.* That could be Jean Murderer. In fact, it had to be. Captain Jean Murderer, the guy who owned the map. He'd hid it in the eave and marked it with his initials. She carefully rerolled the map and tied it shut. Maybe there were other clues buried in the eaves. It wouldn't hurt to look.

Maria started at one end of the attic. She figured she could work her way along the eaves, up and back, and then tackle the trunk. She slipped her hands behind the first wooden beam, closest to the window. It looked promising: someone had carved an elaborate sailboat on it.

After a few minutes of picking through the scratchy horsehair insulation, Maria had found nothing more interesting than a sheet of yellowed newspaper with an ad for five-cent Cokes and a story about war bonds. She wasn't even sure which war, or what a bond was. She stuffed the paper back into place and moved on to the next beam. This one had only a crude heart with *PI + CA* on it.

After many hours, she had found a tin of rusty bobby pins, a child's book of nursery rhymes, three necklaces of colored glass beads, a mousetrap with a mummified mouse (this she'd flung across the room with a squeal), lots of candy wrappers from lots of candy bars she'd never heard of, and a flower made out of what looked like human hair. She stared at the pile of nonsense, then swept it into the trunk—which had turned out to be full of disappointing mildewed clothes, old magazines, and weird wooden tools. Maria flopped onto the bed and sneezed at the billow of dust.

By now it was nearly dark. The sky through her porthole window glowed orange and the ocean was tinged with gold.

Downstairs, the front door opened. Maria jumped from the bed.

"Hi, *chérie*—I'm home!" Her mother slammed the front door. "Where are you? Are you up there in the dark?" Celeste called from the bottom of the stairway. Maria stuffed the map and its leather wrap under her pillow.

"I'm in the attic," Maria called back. "I wanted to check it out. Can I sleep up here tonight?"

"Yes, but come down for dinner now—Hattie sent food again."

Maria came down the spiral stairs and found Celeste

laying paper and logs in the firebox of the woodstove and chattering away.

"Frank—that's the guy with the golf cart, apparently he's Hattie's brother—says she can't stop cooking too much though there's hardly any staff and Mr. Ironwall can't even eat." Celeste set a match to the pile and it caught immediately. She smiled proudly at Maria.

"And how in the world did you get so dusty again? We have got to clean that attic . . ."

But Celeste didn't stop talking long enough for Maria to answer. She spun in circles getting dinner ready and talking about her day. While Maria washed up in the kitchen sink and then set the table, Celeste chatted on about poor, sick Mr. Ironwall, and the tough night nurse. Joanne was her name.

"She's not really mean, but just kind of ignorant. She keeps asking me questions about city life and you can tell she gets all her information from TV shows." Celeste clicked her tongue. "You know how they always give the characters enormous apartments even though they're only waitresses? And they all wear fashion de-signer clothes? She thinks New York is really like that."

Maria sat at the table and rested her head on her arm. She only half listened to her mother; she was still thinking about Captain Murderer's treasure map.

"You look tired, *ma chère*." Celeste put steaming bowls of clam chowder and a platter heaped with strange white disks on the table.

"Clam chowder again?" Maria asked. "Can't we have chicken, or something normal?"

"I haven't had a chance to shop or cook," Celeste said. "And this is normal for here. Try the crab cakes, at least."

Maria tried a tiny bite. It was strangely good. She tried the soup. It was buttery and clammy, but okay. She took another spoonful. It warmed her throat and cleared her head.

"It's not bad," Maria said. "But not as good as your food."

"I promise we'll go shopping soon." Celeste sat opposite her. "Now tell me, did you have a good day? What did you do?"

Maria thought back. Her visit to the movie room seemed as if it had happened days ago. She was sure Celeste would not like her sneaking about Mr. Ironwall's mansion. What else could she say? She hadn't done any cleaning. She'd really just snooped around the attic and gotten awfully dirty. Celeste looked at her, waiting for an answer.

"Well, I met Hattie," Maria finally said.

"Oh, yes?" Celeste squeezed lemon on her crab cake. "That poor lady."

"Why is she a poor lady?"

"Her husband was killed a few years ago. He was doing reconstruction in Afghanistan. Roadside bomb. It's really sad—Frank was telling me on the way home. She has a boy about your age, maybe a little older. Apparently he's quite difficult. That's why Frank moved back to the Island. To help her out a little. They all live in some crazy family compound up-island—I think Frank works such long hours to get away, though he didn't say, so I'm only guessing . . ."

Maria remembered that Hattie had mentioned her son. The boy raised by wolves. A kid troublesome enough that his uncle Frank was needed to help control him. She hoped she wouldn't have to meet him.

"You're very quiet," Celeste said. "Are you feeling all right?"

"I'm fine." Maria paused and looked into her soup. Somehow she'd finished the whole bowl without noticing. "May I be excused?"

"Don't go far." Celeste began clearing the plates to the sink. "There's dessert."

Maria wandered into the living room.

"Did you unpack at all?" Celeste asked from the kitchen.

"A little," Maria said. "Mostly just rested."

The items on the mantel looked piratey, now that she really looked at them. She wondered if any of the knick-knacks had belonged to Captain Murderer. Maybe that had been his pet parrot, perched on his shoulder while he stomped around on deck. Didn't pirates wear parrots? The bird in the bell jar *was* an actual stuffed parrot that had once been alive. Its rainbow plumage had faded with time, but its glass eyes still fixed her with a quirky, accusative stare.

She turned the bird to face the ugly painting over the fireplace. It was an old painting—the oils had darkened and cracked so that the storm-tossed boat was a smudge of grays and the sea was nearly black. It had two sticks— two masts—like the sailboat the young Mr. Ironwall had been christening in the photo. But it couldn't be the same boat. This painting was ancient. But then again, Mr. Ironwall was ancient. The artist's signature was unreadable. She stood on tiptoe trying to decipher the words engraved on the brass plate tacked to the or- nate wood frame. The script was fancily curled and dif- ficult to read under all the dirt, but it seemed to say:

She looked over her shoulder to see if her mother was watching, but Celeste stood at the sink washing their empty dishes. Maria peered at the brass plate again. There was more underneath the tarnish and stains. She licked her finger and wiped. Her fingertip turned black, so she spit on her cuff and really scrubbed. More script emerged.

*Le Dernier Corsair, Schooner of
Captain Jean Murdefer, Privateer, 1689.*

Maria felt a strange chill. *Murdefer.* Like *Murderer.*

Maria raced up the spiral stairs and took the tube from under the pillow. There it was, the same name: *Captain Murdefer*—she could see that now—what she had thought was an extra-squiggly *r* was actually an *f*. So Captain Murde*r*er was actually Captain Murde*fer*, and he owned a two-masted sailboat just like Mr. Ironwall . . .

Celeste called up. "There's rhubarb pie."

"What's rhubarb?" Maria yelled back.

"Apparently something Hattie grows in her garden and turns into pie. You have to come down and tell me if it's edible."

"Okay!" Maria put the tube under her pillow and went down the spiral stairs.

"Why did you disappear?" Celeste met her at the bottom with a wedge of pie.

"I just had to check something." Maria took her dessert to one of the squashy chairs. "What does *privateer* mean? Is it like a pirate?"

"I don't know. Why?"

"It's just on that picture there." Maria pointed her fork at the mantel.

Celeste got up to look at the painting. She clicked her tongue. "Did you rotate this parrot?"

"It was freaking me out."

"*La, la, la, la, la!*" Celeste scolded. "I do not want you touching poor Mr. Ironwall's things. If we didn't bring it with us, *touche-pas!* We are guests here. There are a lot of old things around here that could break—*c'est compris?*"

"Understood."

Maria certainly wouldn't tell her mother about the map, now. If her mom got that upset over her rotating a parrot, she certainly would have strong feelings about Maria taking the map from the eaves. Celeste would probably make her return it to its original hiding place, or give it to Mr. Ironwall, and then she would never find the treasure.

Her mother was still scolding. "... and I don't want you snooping around that poor man's house! Frank told me Hattie found you—"

"I wasn't snooping! I was lost. That's how I met Hattie—she helped me out."

"And what did she say when she found you?" Celeste eyed her suspiciously.

Maria did her best to look innocent. "That I should have lunch with her tomorrow. And that I need something to do."

9

SOMETHING TO DO

THE NEXT MORNING, FRANK ARRIVED AT THE cottage with a white paper bag in one hand and a big dog on a leash in the other. Maria recognized him as the dog from Mr. Ironwall's bed.

"My sister said your daughter needs something to do," Frank told Celeste. Celeste glanced at Maria, who gave her mother an innocent I-told-you sort of shrug.

"His name's Brutus because he's a big brute, but he's a good boy." Frank rubbed the dog under its chin. "Aren't you a good boy, Brutus? Say hi to our guests."

Brutus snuffled Maria's hand and then bowed his head to rub it against her palm. He felt velvety and lovely. He leaned in for more petting, nearly knocking her down.

"Would you like coffee?" Celeste said to Frank. "I just made some."

"Please," Frank said. He handed the leash to Maria. "Mr. Ironwall says you can walk the dog to earn your keep. He'll give you seventy dollars a week—"

"Seventy dollars a week!" Celeste said. "But that's too much. We can't take his money like that."

"It's just ten dollars a day," Frank said. "And if she walks him for an hour it's not much more than minimum wage."

"What does a twelve-year-old do with seventy dollars a week?"

"I can save for college," Maria said. College savings was one of the reasons her mother worked so many hours, so Maria knew that it was inarguably important.

"I still think it's too much," Celeste grumbled.

"Well, that's his offer, so take it or leave it," Frank said. "He's not used to being contradicted." He turned to Maria. "But it has to be a long walk. Take the Brute to the beach, run him around, make him tired. Then he'll stop whining so much." Frank tousled the dog's ears. "You're a big spoiled baby, aren't you, Brutus Maximus?"

Celeste handed Frank a steaming mug. "I'm still not sure it's such a good idea—Maria doesn't know her way

72

around yet and she's just getting over that incident . . ." Celeste looked meaningfully at Frank, and Maria realized her mother had told him about the Barbies.

"From what you've told me, Maria is a sensible girl, Mrs. Mamoun." Frank gave Maria a quick smile. He could be nice-looking if he were a little less scruffy, Maria decided.

"I'm *not* a *Mrs.*," Celeste said. "Just Celeste."

Frank's neck turned red. "Well, anyhow, if you don't want her to, I can take Brutus back . . ."

"Please, Mama?" Maria said. "I can't stay inside all day. And it would be great to earn some money." And, she thought, it would give her an excuse to explore the grounds, the beach, and that abandoned sailboat.

"Brutus will keep her safe," Frank said. "And no one comes onto the property. Not even the postman."

Maria looked at her mother with what she hoped was a pleading yet responsible expression.

"Okay." Celeste smiled tightly. "But you don't leave the property."

"Great! Thanks!" She started to head out the door with the Brute.

"You're going now?" Celeste asked.

"Yeah, why not?"

"Don't you want breakfast?"

"Sure." The dog sat at Maria's feet, looking up expectantly. "To go."

"I'll see you later when you drop the dog off. Come straight to Mr. Ironwall's room when you're done. But be quiet—in case Mr. Ironwall's sleeping." Celeste handed Maria a doughnut.

Maria and Brutus walked toward the beach that she'd seen through her attic window. She found a gap in the hedge behind the Great House. It led to a sandy footpath flanked by thorny bushes hung all over with tight pink rosebuds. The beach roses gave way to a grassy dune with an old wood-slat boardwalk barely visible under the drifting sand, and then suddenly over a rise, there was the ocean. It was not yesterday's flat steely gray, or last night's gold-tinged blue, but a shifting kaleidoscope of colors. About a half mile off, the sailboat bobbed at the dock. She started toward it. The wind whipped her hair across her face and Maria wished she'd worn a jacket. She ran as fast as she could, dragging the reluctant Brutus.

The dock was a long wooden walkway that came straight off the beach and extended into the water on wooden stilts. About a hundred yards out, a metal ramp led down to a floating metal platform with the boat bobbing alongside. Now that she was close, Maria saw the boat was much larger than she'd realized. Longer than a bus. The masts seemed as tall as a two-story building.

She skittered down the ramp, but Brutus stood at the top, pulling against the long leash, eyeing her nervously.

"Come on! Come!" Maria yanked the leash. She slapped her thighs. Brutus backed up and sat down. Maria shook the doughnut bag at Brutus. He tipped his head, as if he were considering the offer. She pulled the doughnut out and offered it on her flat palm. "You want a doughnut? You want it?"

Suddenly Brutus bolted down the ramp, his hind-quarters gyrating from his manically wagging tail. He launched himself off the ramp and onto the dock, and snatched the entire doughnut off Maria's hand in one slobbery lick.

"Fine," Maria said. "You can have it. I'm checking out the boat."

Up close, it looked ancient. The hull was made of some kind of wood painted pine green, and scrolled all over with fading gold decorations. The rail posts curved like fancy table legs, and a mermaid figurehead swam from the front. A long stick stuck out over the mermaid's head, and a weird black net was strung underneath, the rope rotted through in parts. The top of the boat was covered with a tent made of waterproof canvas. The two naked masts jutted out of the top of the tent, but the canvas was lashed tightly to the rails. Still, it looked like it might be the same sailboat from the photo in the movie room. The one a young Mr. Ironwall had christened. Or maybe the boat from the painting over the mantelpiece. She walked toward the back and there, painted in chipping gold, was the name: *The Last Privateer.*

Privateer. That word again. She wondered what it meant and why she kept finding it all over the estate: on the poster in the movie room, on the painting over the fireplace, and now on the boat. She realized this boat was too new to have anything to do with Captain Murdefer—no way a wood sailboat could survive hundreds of years. And anyhow, his boat had some weird foreign name. Still, she couldn't help feeling there was some kind of connection.

Maria really wished she could climb aboard, but there was no way to get past the tent. She walked slowly along the side, touching the rope that lashed the canvas to the rails, looking for a gap. She wasn't brave enough to untie it. That seemed too much like trespassing. But if it happened to be already loose . . .

Brutus whimpered and pushed his cold, wet nose into her free hand. He didn't seem to like the weather. It was rough and bitter here by the sea. A cold spray blew off the wild waves and chilled them both. She should take Brutus home. And, she thought disappointedly, a closer inspection of the sailboat would have to wait for a warmer day.

10

MR. IRONWALL

CELESTE MET MARIA AT MR. IRONWALL'S BED-
room door.

"Joanne's in there with him now," Celeste said. "I just
wanted to make sure you were ready."

"Ready for what?" Maria asked.

"Oh, *chérie*, you're a complete and utter mess." Celeste
combed her fingers through Maria's windswept hair.
"And that dog is all sandy."

"I took him to the beach, like Frank said."

"But couldn't you have kept him clean?" her mother
said. "He has to go up on the bed."

Maria knelt down and tried to shake sand out of Brutus's shaggy coat. She lifted a muddy paw and brushed
it on her jeans.

"Maria!" Celeste whisper-hissed. "You're getting mud on your jeans!"

"I'm sorry!"

"Lower your voice," Celeste said. "Oh, I wish you weren't wearing that shirt."

"What's wrong with my shirt?" She glanced down.

"Mr. Ironwall wants to meet you." Celeste rubbed at some imagined stain.

"Okay," Maria said.

"Look at his face when you talk to him, not at the equipment."

"Mama, I know how to behave."

"I'm sure you'll be fine," Celeste said, as if she wasn't sure at all.

They knocked and the night nurse opened the door.

"Well, come on in," Joanne said, tugging Maria's sleeve. "He's not coming to you."

Maria stepped into the room and faced the bed.

Mr. Ironwall's skeletal hands trembled on the bed-clothes, and his skin looked transparent. Wormy blue veins showed in his forehead and between his knuckles, and broken red capillaries laced his cheeks. Joanne hovered around straightening out blankets and pillows. On the nightstand was a newspaper, reading glasses, and a tumbler of water. There were no other personal items in the room. It was strangely like a hospital room in that regard, though it was here, in his home.

"Come closer," the old man said in a papery voice.

Maria didn't realize he was talking to her until her mother gave her a little push.

"Let Brutus off his leash."

Maria released the dog and held the leash uncertainly. Joanne took it from her and hung it on a hook beside the door. Brutus trotted, wagging, to the bed and gazed lovingly up at his master. Mr. Ironwall patted the coverlet and said, "Up-up."

Brutus leaped onto the bed, muddy paws and all. Maria heard her mother inhale sharply.

Mr. Ironwall seemed not to notice the dirt, or maybe he didn't care. He directed his gaze at Maria.

"Come here," he commanded. "So I can see your face properly."

Maria bent over the bed. The old man took her chin in his dry, knobby hands and peered at her face until she grew uncomfortable with the silence and scrutiny.

"Cheekbones like Hedy Lamarr." He finally released her chin. "Under that mop of hair and those glasses." He sank back into his pillows with closed eyes. After a few deep sighs, he seemed to have fallen asleep.

Maria wondered if she should leave. She looked around for her mother, who was pretending to resupply a tray with gauze pads and cotton balls.

"Should I go?" Maria whispered to Celeste.

Mr. Ironwall held up his hand. "There's one more thing. You have the run of the place, obviously, but please remember it is a very old place, and it's crumbling down about our ears. Doors that are shut must stay shut, for our safety." He looked at Maria with surprisingly clear eyes.

Maria held her face as steady as she could. She had the creepy feeling that he somehow knew about her visit to his movie room. Maybe Hattie had told him. She'd have to be more careful. She didn't really know Frank and Hattie well, and after all, they owed their jobs to Mr. Ironwall. Of course they'd be more loyal to him than to her. She'd have to keep her secrets close.

11

BICYCLES AND SAILS

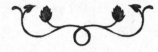

IN THE HALL OUTSIDE MR. IRONWALL'S ROOM, Celeste reminded Maria that she'd promised to have lunch with Hattie. "She's been cooking all morning. If you don't show up, she'll be very disappointed."

For lunch, Hattie laid a plate of fried chicken, beans, and fried potatoes in front of Maria. "Your mother tells me clam chowder 'isn't normal' for you, so I tried to make something you'd be familiar with." She put a basket of biscuits and a small dish of butter beside the plate.

Maria blushed. "I love fried chicken and potatoes and beans. I used to eat this same thing back home. Colony Fried Chicken was two blocks from our apartment. But actually, I really liked your clam chowder. I ate it all. You're a really good cook. And I could eat this chicken every day, except my mom says fried food makes you fat . . ." Her mother would probably think she was being rude. She scooped the beans with a biscuit to shut herself up.

"Don't look so worried. You could use a little fattening up," Hattie said. "How did things go this morning?"

Maria swallowed. "Fine. Mr. Ironwall is a little scary. But I don't think he's mean. Just really old."

"That's definitely true." Hattie put another chicken thigh on Maria's plate. "Can I get you anything else?"

"There aren't any computers in this house, are there?"

"No, and no TVs either," Hattie said. "That's why his last nurse quit. She was stone-cold bored, she said."

"Well, I need to look some things up."

"What sort of things?" Hattie asked.

"Just, well—" Maria hesitated. Hattie might have ratted her out about the movie room. So she couldn't ask her anything about Captain Murdefer or his map.

Hattie was staring at her, waiting, with a bowl of dessert in her hand.

"Who's Hedy Lamarr?" Maria finally asked. "Mr. Ironwall said I looked like her."

Hattie put the bowl down. "Well, that's a compliment. She was an actress in the old days."

"Oh." Maria took a bite. Apple crisp with whipped cream.

"You could go to the library in Edgartown," Hattie said. "They have free computers. It's not far, and there's a bike path the whole way, so no worries about cars."

"I don't have a bike," Maria said.

"Oh, there are quite a few in the Old West Shed. Mr. I kept them for guests—I'm sure there's one there that'll fit you. Ask Frank to help you. Now how's that dessert?"

"Amazing," Maria said.

Hattie looked pleased. "Well, there's more where that came from. I'll send it home with your mother. It's so nice to have someone appreciate what I do. Paolo never even says thank you. That boy just shovels it down and runs out the door. Did I tell you about the fight he got into at school? A week of detention. He's sure to fail . . ."

Maria didn't mind listening to Hattie's stories about her misbehaving son, if it meant a second serving of apple crisp. Besides, she didn't have anywhere else to go, and nothing else to do but eat, get fat, and solve the mystery of Captain Murdefer's treasure map.

* * *

She was peeking in the window of the Old West Shed when Frank came up behind her and asked what she needed.

"A bicycle," she answered. "Hattie said Mr. Ironwall kept them in here for guests, and I'm a guest, I guess. At least he said so."

"You're a guest, you guess." Frank smiled as if she had made a joke. "Well, in that case, I guess I can help you." He took a huge set of keys from his jacket pocket and unlocked the padlock. "Ah, they're buried way in back."

He moved a few lawn chairs, a large umbrella, and a huge canvas bag aside.

"What's that?" Maria asked.

"Sails." Frank disappeared into the rear of the shed. After a few moments he wheeled two bicycles out.

"Swing your leg over this one and sit on the seat." He steadied a rusty blue bicycle for her.

She did as she was told. Then she tried the other, a newer green one.

"Too big." Frank took the bikes back into the shed. "I'll be right back."

"What are the sails for?" Maria called after him.

"That old boat down on the dock. Here, try this one." He brought out a smaller red bicycle. It looked ancient. It had a moldy wicker basket on the front and no gears.

"*The Last Privateer*, right?" Maria asked, as she swung

her leg over and sat. It felt like a good fit, though she didn't know; she had never sat on a bicycle before. "Why aren't the sails on it?"

"Because no one's sailed it in years and they'd rot left out in all weather that long. Mr. I should have her hauled out," Frank said. "But then again, a boat that large is hard to find a place for in any of the local yards. And he's kind of sentimental about it, I think."

"Why?" Maria asked.

Frank shrugged. "It's a half-size replica of some old pirate ship from a movie he made."

"A pirate ship. Wow." Maria tried to balance on the bike. "I've never even been on a regular sailboat."

"Yeah, well, have you ever been on a bicycle?" Frank eyed her skeptically. "It looks like you haven't."

"No, not really. I couldn't have one where we lived. Nowhere to ride it."

"Oh, well, smart girl like you should be able to figure it out. Turn the handlebars in the direction you want to go, stomp backward on the pedal to brake. You'll have to practice, of course."

"Of course," Maria said.

"So that's your bike," Frank said. "I'll have to clean it up a bit."

Frank went again into the shed. Maria waited for

him. He came out a few minutes later with a bucket, an oilcan, and a rag.

"You don't have to wait," Frank said. "I have to soak the chain in a little gasoline to knock the gunk off." He pointed to the bucket. "And then I'll have to get you some new tires and tubes in town."

"Oh, no, I just had another question," Maria said. "About the boat, I mean."

He looked at her.

"It looks pretty okay," Maria continued. "Like someone's been taking care of it. I mean, it doesn't look like it might sink or anything. Like, from the outside. From standing on the beach."

She stopped talking. Maybe she was asking too many questions. Maybe he'd know she was up to something. Snooping about. Hattie probably told him, too, that she'd been caught in the movie room. She didn't want him to think she was sneaking around the property, getting into things she shouldn't. Even though she was.

Frank looked toward the beach. "My dad used to keep her fixed up for Mr. Ironwall, even after Mr. I stopped sailing. Pops said Mr. I could at least sell her if he couldn't sail her."

He flipped the bike over on its seat. Using a screwdriver from his pocket, he searched the chain until he found the link he wanted. With a quick movement, he removed the chain and laid it in the bucket. "Pops fell off a ladder a few years back—cracked a few vertebrae—and hasn't done anything with her since. I should probably check her out sometime. Shame to let her go."

"Yes," Maria said uncertainly.

Frank squinted at her. "Why all the questions about that old boat?"

"It would be nice to go for a sail. Get out on the water and see things."

"Yeah, well, no one's sailed that boat in years." Frank put down his oily rag. "You're pretty stuck here, aren't you? Hattie said you two don't have a car. You think you'd like a ride into town sometime? I could take you and your mom around the Island, show you the sights—help your mom get groceries."

"I don't know. You'd have to ask my mother." Suddenly Maria felt embarrassed, but she wasn't sure why. "I have to go."

"Well, I'll have this bike ready for you in a day or two. And ask your mom," Frank called after her.

"Sure." Maria hurried away. She wondered if her mother would be mad at her, bothering Frank like that. Maybe if she didn't say anything, he would forget he'd even offered.

12

OVER THE RAIL

IT WASN'T JUST THE MYSTERY ABOUT CAPTAIN Murdefer's map that bothered Maria. Every morning she walked Brutus on the beach and gazed at *The Last Privateer*, and wondered about it, too. What was it like inside? Did it still have things that used to belong to Mr. Ironwall, or was it empty? Could it still sail? What would that be like? Maria imagined sailing felt like flying. She pictured herself on the deck of a sailboat in a storm-tossed sea like the one in the painting over the mantelpiece.

But though she climbed the dock every morning, she never found a way on board. Someone had tied the canvas tent tightly, and it stayed tied. It was frustrating, but she couldn't complain to anyone. After all, she wasn't supposed to snoop.

But one morning she took Brutus on a slightly longer walk than usual. Though the wind was gusting and the sky looked a little dark, the air was so much warmer than it had been, and it smelled so good that Maria didn't want to turn around at the dock as she usually did. She walked Brutus past the boat to a narrow neck of land beyond the estate. On one side lay a saltwater pond and on the other was the ocean. Vacation homes dotted the far shore of the pond. The bridge between the pond and ocean had hydraulics to lift it so that the yachts of summer people could make it out to open water, but Maria had never seen the bridge in action. The houses remained shuttered for the off-season. She wondered what it would be like come July. She wasn't sure how she felt about the island filling up with summer people.

When she turned back toward the Great House she noticed an ominous black cloud in front of her. And as they were walking back, the skies opened up.

Brutus looked at Maria and whined.

"You *are* a big baby!" she told him. Then she pulled her sodden windbreaker over her head and they both ran, half-blind, down the beach.

The nearest shelter was the dock. Maria hoped they could crawl underneath the wooden planks, but when she reached it she saw the tide was so high there was no space between the sand and the boards. In fact, there was very little beach left at all.

She scrambled up onto the dock to get out of the waves, and raced to the floating dock at the end with Brutus pounding along the weathered boards behind her. Her glasses were useless, obscured by rain, so she felt blindly along the side of the boat for an opening between the canvas tent and the rail. There had never been one before, so she had no reason to expect there would be one now. But she was in something like a panic. Her heart raced and she repeated a nonsense prayer in her head: *oh, please be open, oh please.* She wondered if she would feel this way every time it rained. She told herself to calm down. After all, she was with Brutus and the estate was a safe place.

Something white flapped near the stern.

She inched herself toward the flapping white thing and touched it—it was a corner of the canvas tent. The wind must have blown it open.

Now she found a gap where the rope lacing had come loose. She reached her hand in, then her arm up to her shoulder. She popped her head in, then her other shoulder . . . she could just squeeze herself through.

She flopped onto the deck with a thud. It was very

dark under the canvas and it took a moment for her eyes to adjust. She stood and dried her glasses on her undershirt. The canvas stretched over her head was high enough that she could stand and walk around the deck with ease, but she did not take the time to look around. Poor Brutus, left alone on the stormy dock, was whining pitifully.

Maria stuck her head through the opening and called to him. He did an odd little dance on the dock and put one tentative paw in the space between the canvas and the rail. Then he poked his big snout in and sniffed.

"Come on, boy, you can do it." She grabbed his leash and tugged.

He pulled against it.

"Please, Brutus, just come. Come. Brutus!" She tried to sound firm, but he sat down and whimpered. Finally she clambered back out and pushed his big wet rump from behind. "I promise you lots of doughnuts," she said, as he placed one big paw, then the other, on the side rail. "But you have to go over. Up-up!"

He knew "up-up." It was the command Mr. Ironwall gave him to get into bed. With one hard shove from Maria, he vaulted over the rail and onto the deck. She scrambled in after him. They sat, wet and shivering, listening to the rain beating on the canvas.

"There has to be something here we can use to dry ourselves with," she said. And then she saw the cabin.

It looked like a little wooden shed sitting in the middle of the boat. It had round porthole windows and two swinging doors with a brass latch between. A lovely, unlocked latch. Maria opened the doors and peered in.

It was even darker below. She groped the wall for a light switch and found nothing. Maybe there wasn't electricity. She didn't have any idea whether sailboats typically had electricity. Other than the ferry that had brought them to the island, Maria had never been on a boat before. And even if there had been electricity back when Mr. Ironwall sailed it, it probably would not be working now. The boat looked as if it had been ignored for a long time.

A steep staircase, more like a ladder of four steps, led below. She started down, and Brutus whined anxiously behind her.

"I'm going to leave you up here while I go downstairs— okay, Brute?" She tied the dog to a rail. "Just be good."

The air below smelled stale and damp. It grew darker with each step. Once down, Maria stretched her hands in front and on all sides, feeling her way forward. Things scattered on the floor tripped her feet, and she brushed her elbow against something glass that fell and shattered. That stopped her. This isn't safe, she told herself. Mr. Ironwall had warned her. *Doors that are shut must stay shut, for our safety,* he had said.

But she didn't feel like she was in any danger. To her, people were danger; Bad Barbies were danger, not quiet abandoned places. And she knew she was completely alone.

Her hand brushed a set of wooden drawers. Inside, she found a stub of candle and an old metal cigarette lighter. After a few attempts she got her candle lit and used it to find three other candles.

The flames flared and settled, and then a soft yellow glow filled the small cabin. Everything in it looked old and unnecessarily fancy. A half-size replica of a pirate ship, Frank had said. A thick layer of dust coated every surface and cobwebs draped the corners. Along the wall, lanterns hung on pegs—clearly they were the lights, though they were empty of fuel. In the bunks, the cushions smelled of mildew and their lumpy-looking mattresses felt damp. In the forward area of the cabin, behind a curtain that crumbled in her hands when she moved it, Maria found a stained glass window. It depicted a similar boat under sail on Caribbean-blue waters, beneath an orange sun. Green islands framed either side. Behind the ladder was an area that contained controls of some sort: dials, gauges, buttons, and a fancy-looking radio with a handset.

Something glinted on the floor under the ladder. Maria picked up a key. A skull and crossbones wrought in silver adorned the key chain.

Maria figured it was the key to the engine, and indeed, the hole for the ignition looked to be the right size. But she didn't have the courage to try it. She knew nothing about engines—her mother didn't even drive, living all her life in cities with excellent public transportation. And so Maria had no idea what happened when you put ignition keys in ignitions, other than somehow engines started up—and that was the last thing she wanted to make happen. She turned the key over in her hand, and then, for some reason, she slipped it into her pocket.

Maria located the glass she'd broken—an old Coca-Cola bottle—and carefully picked up the biggest pieces and deposited them in a tiny steel sink. Beside the sink sat a wooden drain board. A sliver of dry soap caught her eye. Maybe Mr. Ironwall had once used that soap. Perhaps he'd drunk from that soda bottle.

Above the sink were rows of cupboards with ornate brass catches. She opened a few cupboards and found a whisk broom and dustbin. After she'd swept up the glass shards, she looked in the cupboards for a rag to wipe up the dust. She found a set of plates and cups of enameled blue tin, and a small caddy of silverware with an ornate *I* carved into the handle, but no rags. There were four knives and four spoons, but only three forks. She searched for the missing fork for a while—the silverware caddy felt disturbingly incomplete without it. The utensils were probably quite valuable; they were heavy, and after she'd polished one up with some spit and her T-shirt it shone like real silver. It bothered her to give up on the missing fork, but Brutus was whining again.

Right now she just needed a rag to dry off the Brute, and then maybe they could wait out the rain together on deck. He was probably frightened up there, alone.

"I'm coming, Brutus." She groped around, and then pulled a pillowcase off a bunk to use as a towel.

Maria looked once more at the overwhelming mess. She'd have to come back another day—perhaps many days in a row—to really clean it up. She could bring rags and cleansers, garbage bags . . . She blew out the candles and climbed to the dog.

Fixing up *The Last Privateer* would certainly keep her busy, though it was probably not what Hattie or Mr. Ironwall had meant when they said she needed something to do.

13

MR. IRONWALL, REVISITED

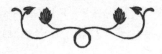

THE RAIN DIDN'T STOP. SO THEY HAD TO WALK back to the mansion in it.

By the time they reached Mr. Ironwall's bedroom, both Maria and Brutus were soaked and shivering. Celeste immediately rerouted them into a bathroom so they could drip on the tile floor instead of the carpet.

"That dog is sopping wet!" Celeste clicked her tongue and *la, la, la*-ed at Maria as she rubbed Brutus down with a fluffy white towel.

"I'm sopping wet, too." Maria sneezed.

"What's going on in there?" Mr. Ironwall called from his bed.

"They just got caught in the rain," Celeste said in an overly cheerful voice, as if getting drenched were some kind of fun. "I'm drying Brutus off now."

"Well, dry your daughter off first. She'll catch pneumonia!" he said.

"If he catches a cold from you . . ." Celeste handed Maria a towel. Maria sneezed again.

"What are you doing?" Mr. Ironwall said. "She needs dry clothes. Get her out of those wet things and put her in a bathrobe!"

"Well, do as he says." Celeste pointed to a robe hanging from the towel bar. "That one's clean."

Celeste took Brutus into the bedroom, and as Maria peeled her icy clothes from her shivery skin, she heard her mother apologizing. She couldn't hear what Mr. Ironwall said back, but he said quite a bit. Then the door to the bedroom opened and closed. Maria finished drying herself and wrapped up in the terry cloth robe. It was warm—the towel bar was heated, she discovered. She had never felt anything so comforting, and she let out a little involuntary sigh.

"Well, don't just stay in the bathroom all morning," Mr. Ironwall called to her. "Are you dressed? If you are, come out and keep me company."

Maria stepped into the bedroom. Brutus already lay upon the bed. Celeste had placed a fluffy towel under the damp dog and another on top of him like a blanket.

"I have sent your mother to find Frank so that he might get you dry clothes, start a fire in your cottage, and drive you there," Mr. Ironwall informed her. "Also, she was to tell Hattie to bring your lunch here—I believe she said something about chicken soup being on the menu today. And you need a hot chocolate, I should think. All those errands should keep your mother out of our hair for a good long time. Now, sit."

Maria sat at Brutus's rump. The dog harrumphed and settled against her.

"You're soaked to the bone," Mr. Ironwall said. "What were you thinking?"

"We tried to outrun the rain, but it came up fast," Maria said.

"Quickly. *It came up quickly*—adverb. *Fast* is an adjective," Mr. Ironwall said. He peered over his glasses at her. "And you were out in it for quite a while, for someone supposedly running quickly. I believe the rain started over an hour ago."

Maria didn't want to lie, so she said nothing. She wasn't sure what to say to the old man anyhow. Brutus looked quizzically at her, then at the old man, then back to her.

"He isn't used to me having company up on the bed,"

Mr. Ironwall said. "My nurses generally sit over there." He indicated an armchair in the opposite corner. "When they sit at all."

"Oh, I could move if you want me to." Maria started to stand.

Mr. Ironwall patted the air, shooing her back down. "There's plenty of room, if you can stand the smell of wet dog. Besides, it's easier to see you, my dear." He chuckled. "I promise I am not the Big Bad Wolf."

Someone knocked on the door. Maria answered it and found Hattie with a tray of covered dishes.

"It's soup and it's hot, so be careful," Hattie said to Maria. She sneaked a look at the bed. "Do you want me to stay?"

"We'll be fine," Mr. Ironwall said. "I gave up eating little girls ages ago. Shoo."

Hattie handed the tray to Maria. "His bark is worse than his bite," she whispered.

"I'm old. Not deaf!" Mr. Ironwall said.

After Hattie left, Mr. Ironwall directed Maria to set the tray on a small bedside table and to pull the armchair closer. He urged her to eat.

"Aren't you going to have something, too?" Maria felt awkward eating alone.

"Oh, I'll have mine later. Nasty pureed pablum. My lunch would put you off your food, and from the looks of you, you need to eat as much as you can."

Maria took a tentative spoonful. It was amazing, as always.

"I hear you've asked Frank for one of my bicycles," Mr. Ironwall said.

Maria looked up from her soup. "I'm sorry, if it's not okay—I mean, I know they belong to you . . ."

He held his hand up to stop her. "Do I look like someone who needs a bicycle anymore?"

"No," Maria said.

"Though your mother seems a bit concerned. She says you've never ridden a bicycle! What do you children *do* nowadays? Are you all such hothouse flowers?"

"There was nowhere safe to ride where I lived," Maria said.

"Safe!" Mr. Ironwall snorted. "It can't be healthy, all this staying indoors being safe. When I was your age, three hundred years or so ago, we would camp out in the woods overnight without any adult supervision. We played mumblety-peg with actual knives. A bow-and-arrow set was a perfectly acceptable toy for a ten-year-old—and we didn't have suction cups, we had real metal-tipped arrows. Now, children are supposed to pretend to camp via video game. How *will* you all survive when you grow up?"

Maria shrugged.

"And what will you do with your newfound freedom? Once Mr. Frank gets your wheels rolling, that is."

"I'll go to the library to research privateers," Maria said.

"Ah, the library!" Mr. Ironwall snorted again. "No wonder your mother is so worried. A lot of trouble can happen in libraries."

"Now you're teasing me," Maria said.

Mr. Ironwall ignored her comment. "Privateers. Why are you so interested in such scallywags?"

"Because Captain Murdefer was one." Maria watched his face closely for a reaction, but Mr. Ironwall didn't twitch.

"Captain Murdefer?" he said. "What a strange name. Sounds made up."

"There's an oil painting of his ship over the mantel in the cottage," Maria pressed. "And I bet that's his stuffed parrot, too. Isn't it?"

"I wouldn't know," Mr. Ironwall said. "I haven't been in the cottage in years."

"You should come over sometime. There's a lot of cool stuff in there. I wish someone would explain it all to me. Like why so much stuff seems to belong to this Captain Murdefer, and who is he."

"'And who is he'? My goodness, your grammar is atrocious. Anyhow, I have no idea who he may be." Mr. Ironwall closed his eyes.

"I think you do know something," Maria said under her breath. "But you're not telling."

The door opened and Celeste came in with a bundle of clothing in her arm. "Maria," she said in her don't-be-rude voice.

"Sorry," Maria mumbled to Mr. Ironwall. She took the clothes from her mother. "I'm going to change now," she said.

"Of course," Mr. Ironwall said. "You must get dry and stay healthy. Who would take care of me if your mother were busy with you?"

When she came out of the bathroom, Celeste told her Frank was waiting downstairs.

"Say goodbye to Mr. Ironwall," Celeste said.

"Goodbye, Mr. Ironwall." Maria held out her hand for him to shake. He took it, and pulled her toward him. She found herself bending close.

"If I could get out of this bed, I would investigate this Murdefer," Mr. Ironwall whispered in her ear. "See if he is real."

"Maria, come now," Celeste said. "Don't keep Frank waiting."

Maria wasn't sure, but as she pulled away, it looked as though Mr. Ironwall winked.

14

Stranger Danger

"IT'S A BEAUTIFUL DAY," CELESTE ANNOUNCED when Maria came down to breakfast the next morning. "No more rain."

Maria sat at the table. It was so nice to come downstairs and find her mother, instead of finding a note. And it was so much better to have breakfast with her mom in their quiet kitchen than eat it alone in the loud, smelly school cafeteria.

"And look! Muffins!" Celeste kissed the top of Maria's head and sat across from her.

Blueberry muffins—homemade by Hattie, with actual blueberries. Maria popped a blueberry against the roof of her mouth with her tongue. So, so much better than her old school's free breakfast. There, the muffins had tasted like the cellophane packages they came in.

"Mr. Ironwall doesn't get to eat Hattie's blueberry muffins," Maria said. "Right?"

"Yes," Celeste said. "Just smooth foods is typical after strokes. It is an issue with swallowing."

"Can he get better? Like, relearn how to swallow or walk?"

Celeste clicked her tongue and frowned. "It depends. But first he would have to want to get better. He would have to be willing to do certain therapies, and right now he says no to just about everything I suggest."

Maria had gone to bed thinking about Mr. Ironwall. Now she said, "I couldn't imagine living like he does, spending every day in one room, eating such nasty food."

"Well, it is pretty sad," Celeste agreed. "But you don't have to see him again."

"But maybe I should," Maria said. "You know, like hang out with him and cheer him up or something." She wasn't exactly sure how she felt about it even as she said it. On the one hand, he was old, sick, stinky, and cranky. On the other hand, he seemed to know something about Captain Murdefer, or privateers at least, that he wasn't telling.

Celeste nodded slowly. "At least you would be a change from me and Joanne."

"And I could give you a break. Like when I'm with him, you could leave the room, do whatever."

Maria thought that if she could get the old man alone, maybe she could get some information out of him.

"I wouldn't go far," Celeste said. "Just maybe get a cup of coffee from the kitchen. Usually I have to wait until he's asleep to sneak away, and then I worry he'll die on me."

Maria shoveled the last crumbs of the muffin into her mouth. "Maybe I can bring him some stuff from here. Like that parrot. You know, to look at."

"*La, la, la!*" Celeste's eyes widened. "Heaven forbid you break anything. Just keep everything as it is, please, please, please. We don't want any trouble." She squinted at Maria. "What is it with you and that parrot?"

"I just think it's weird, is all. Maybe he'd have some stories about it. Isn't that what old people do? Sit around telling stories?"

"How about maybe you just read him the paper? Or let him reminisce. I bet he has a million stories about the Golden Age of Hollywood . . ." Celeste glanced out the window. "Frank's here."

Maria grabbed a couple of muffins to go and slung her backpack over her shoulder.

"What do you need your backpack for?" Celeste asked.

Maria froze. She had planned on cleaning the *Privateer*. She'd packed two old T-shirts and three mismatched socks, a bottle of all-purpose cleaner, candles, matches, and supplies for herself and Brutus in her backpack. On a whim, she carefully added the leather tube with Captain Murdefer's map.

"I just thought it might be nice to read on the beach, and so I have, you know, something to read, some water—" It wasn't exactly a lie. The dock with the *Privateer* was technically on the beach, and if she studied Captain Murdefer's map it would be like reading.

"Okay." Celeste looked a bit puzzled.

Maria took Brutus's leash from Frank and ran with the dog down the shell drive before her mom could ask any more questions.

As soon as they reached the beach, Maria let Brutus off the leash. He trotted around her, sniffing at her backpack for the muffins inside.

"You're a good boy." Maria rubbed his big head. "You can keep a secret, right?"

Brutus licked her with a slobbery tongue, and then he bolted for *The Last Privateer*. Maria struggled to catch up. By the time she got there, Brutus was dancing on the dock, whining up at the boat.

"What's the matter? Is there something in there?"

Maria had a scary vision of some creepy animal, like a skunk, trapped under the tarp. Brutus whined and scratched at the rail. "Calm down—I'm sure we can chase it away." But she wasn't so sure. She'd never dealt with anything wilder than a pigeon or a squirrel. She wished she had a big stick.

She lifted the canvas slowly, and Brutus wriggled under it and onto the boat before she could peek underneath. In a flash he was down the cabin stairs, barking maniacally. Maria heard the skittering sound of Brutus's toenails on the floorboards. Then a few low tones, a scuffle, a thump, a few more barks. There was definitely something—or someone—downstairs.

Maria considered tiptoeing off the boat. But she couldn't just leave Brutus to deal with whatever was down there by himself. And she had to get him back to Mr. Ironwall. She couldn't just abandon ship.

She looked around the deck for something heavy. On the right side, along the rail, she found a small aluminum dinghy turned upside down, with two oars alongside. She picked up an oar and held it over her shoulder like a baseball bat ready to swing, and crept down the stairs.

"Whatever's down here better leave, before I beat it to death," she called into the cabin. She swung the oar in a wide arc, and it slammed against a bunk.

The intruder caught the oar and held it. "Careful with that thing!"

Maria yanked the oar free. A flashlight shone in her face, then moved down as if inspecting her. The owner then turned it so it lit the cabin instead.

It took a few seconds for her eyes to adjust. There, on the bunk, sat a scruffy, dirty boy. Brutus had jumped onto the bunk with him, wagging his tail so his whole backside swayed. The boy left off petting the dog and looked at Maria.

"So you're the one who's been messing with my boat," the boy said. He looked about her age, but he was taller and skinnier. His face was tan, despite the fact that it was the first week of June, and his fingernails were filthy. His black hair hung in tangled clumps over his eyes. His jeans had a hole in the knee, his shoelaces were frayed, and he wore a green army jacket that was much too large. A set of metal army tags hung from a chain around his scrawny neck.

"This boat belongs to Mr. Ironwall," Maria said. "It's private property. You're trespassing."

"Yeah, same as you."

"If you don't get off this boat right now I'll crack your skull open," she said.

"Don't get all crazy." The boy held up his hands as he stood. "It's not like the old guy's going to ever use his boat again."

"It doesn't matter. You have to go." Maria tried to look menacing.

The boy shrugged and climbed up the short ladder.

Maria followed him, brandishing the oar until he climbed back through the canvas and off the boat.

"I wasn't gonna hurt you," the boy said from the dock. "Besides, I found the boat first."

"No, you didn't," Maria said from the deck. "When I found it, it was obvious no one had been here for a long time. It was totally dusty. And before that it was always laced up tight."

"Well, how do you think you got in?"

He had a point. She'd visited the boat many times before, and she'd never seen a way in until yesterday. How had a hole appeared, just large enough for a child her size to squeeze through?

"You opened it?"

"Of course," the boy said. "What did you think? The wind untied it?"

Now she was annoyed with this boy who had invaded her boat and acted like she owed him something.

"I don't believe you," she said. "But even if you did, you shouldn't have anyhow. The whole estate is private property..."

But the boy didn't answer. When she looked through the hole in the tarp, she saw that he was gone. She climbed out and watched as he made his way up the dock. Soon he was on the beach, walking toward the salt pond. At least he wasn't heading toward the Great House. Then she would have to run and tell her mother or Hattie a strange boy was coming to mess with the House. Then they'd find out about the sailboat.

"That's right, get out of here!" she yelled after him. "Don't come back or I'll have you arrested!"

He waved her off without turning around. Maria watched until he was a small black dot by the hydraulic bridge. She took a few deep breaths to calm herself. "I hate other kids. They wreck everything," she said to Brutus. "Dogs are better."

The dog wagged and looked up the stairs at her. He put one paw on the first step.

"No, just stay there," Maria told him. "I'll be down soon."

She put her oar back beside the aluminum dinghy. The hull of the small boat looked and felt to be in good shape, and when she turned it right side up (it was lightweight enough for her to flip it easily) she saw it had two bench seats and two little metal fittings that slipped into holes and held the oars. After looking it over a bit more, she returned it to its original upside-down position. Then she walked the deck carefully, prodding for rotten boards as her mother had prodded the floorboards of the attic. Nothing creaked. She took her time, examining the cabin from the outside and checking the masts. Everything looked all right; there were no obvious cracks or breakage of any kind.

"Well, at least he hasn't trashed the place," Maria said. She looked down and saw Brutus had left his post at the foot of the ladder and made himself comfortable on the bunk where the boy had been.

"He better not come back," she said to the dog as she climbed down. But what could she do if he did? It's not like she could tell on him. He was right about one thing: she was a trespasser, too.

Brutus looked at her, sighed, and put his head back on his paws.

"Yeah, but he's a stranger," Maria explained to Brutus. "And you're a traitor."

The boy had forgotten his flashlight. It was a very nice one, shaped like a lantern with a loop on top for hanging it. She hung it from a hook on the wall, then pushed the curtains away from all the portholes. There'd been a storm the first time she'd seen the cabin, but on this bright day the sun filtered through the translucent tent and shone through the windows with a milky light. She wouldn't even need the candles. She left them in a kitchen cupboard, along with the matches, for other dark days.

She walked gingerly around the cabin, lifting the floorboards to see if there were leaks or obvious rot.

As far as she could tell, the area under the floorboards looked and felt completely dry. In fact, the boat seemed in far better repair than the attic she slept in. Clearly someone had once cared well for the boat. "Pops," Frank had told her.

But after such a long time abandoned there was a great deal of dusting to do. Maria quickly dirtied the T-shirts and socks she'd brought. She found some more old clothes in the drawers beneath the bunks, but she felt odd using things that weren't hers, so she took only what was blackened with mildew. The rest she refolded and tucked neatly away.

In one long flat drawer, instead of clothes, she found maps showing the ocean alongside various coastlines. These required careful inspection. She sat at the little table in the center of the cabin and unrolled each one.

Some, stored too long in unhealthy conditions, cracked and split. Others had little notes written in the margin: *Good picnic area. No moorage.* She wondered if Mr. Ironwall had written the notes, and if he had sailed these waters and picnicked on those islands. She wondered what *moorage* was. She unrolled the leather tube and laid Captain Murdefer's map alongside the others.

None of the maps matched. She sighed. Of course they didn't. Pirates buried treasure in faraway, exotic places like the Caribbean. These maps were all from the east coast of the United States and Canada. They were totally normal and totally useless. She rolled them up and put them back in their drawer.

The sun shining through the western portholes alerted her to the time—it was past noon, and she was supposed to get Brutus back. She hurriedly gathered her things, pushed Brutus up the ladder and off the boat, and ran him to the Great House.

* * *

Hattie opened the door to Mr. Ironwall's room with a finger to her lips. Celeste stood beside her. They both slipped into the hall.

"He's asleep," Hattie whispered, pulling the door half shut behind her.

"And you're late," Celeste said in a low voice. "We were getting worried."

"I'm sorry," Maria said. "I lost track of the time—it was such a beautiful morning we took an extra-long walk." She looked down at the dog, who looked anxiously back. He seemed confused that they were in the hall instead of the bedroom. He took a tentative step toward Hattie and sniffed her leg. She took his leash and made him sit.

Celeste looked at Maria and clicked her tongue. "How is it that you are so perpetually dusty?" She picked a cobweb from her shirt and showed it to her. "We're going into town with Frank. He said he told you about it, but you never mentioned it to me."

Maria combed her fingers through her hair. "Sorry."

Celeste turned back to Hattie. "I did all his meds and his bath. He should be fine for the next few hours—he usually sleeps most of the afternoon."

They all glanced through the half-open door at Mr. Ironwall. The sheet quivered slightly with his slow breathing.

"I hope you don't mind staying late," Celeste said.

"Actually, I prefer being here right now," Hattie said. "Pops called. Paolo got into another fight at school and ran off instead of going to the principal's office. Pops said I'm too easy on him, and we had an argument. He wants me to ground him again."

Of course, Maria thought. That stranger was Paolo, Hattie's wolf-boy son. That's why Brutus knew him. And he was hiding in the boat and making trouble for her after making trouble at school. She wondered how often he did that. He probably had been hiding in the boat forever. And he never thought to clean it. Typical. That boy was just trouble all over.

15

The Triangle Island

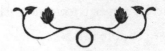

THEY SQUASHED TOGETHER IN THE CAB OF Frank's beat-up truck. Maria sat closest to the door, and she kept her nose pressed against the window, drinking in the sights. There were three major towns, Frank told them: Vineyard Haven, where their ferry had landed; Edgartown, which was the town closest to the Ironwall Estate; and Oak Bluffs, famous for its Gingerbread Cottages and crowded with day-trippers in the summer. Up-island had the farms of West Tisbury, the fishing village of Menemsha, and Aquinnah, where the Wampanoag lived.

"But that's pretty far. We can do that another day," Frank said. "Today we'll just drive through Edgartown, then swing through Vineyard Haven and into Oak Bluffs."

Edgartown was just a few blocks of stores and restaurants clustered by the waterfront, but it seemed full of people. Employees in blue-and-white uniforms bustled around the Harbor View Hotel, parking cars and carrying bags, while a couple of young women in red-striped aprons shared a cigarette in the alley beside an ice-cream shop.

"Edgartown is busy," Celeste said. "And it's not even summer."

"You should see Oak Bluffs in the high season. Come summer it's impossible to find parking. But I'll show you the lot behind Reliable Market."

After showing them Edgartown, Frank took a roundabout route through Vineyard Haven and Oak Bluffs. The outskirts of Edgartown had the cheaper Mexican restaurant that stayed open all winter; Vineyard Haven had the Brazilian buffet where all the shipyard employees ate. Oak Bluffs had the Flying Horses: the oldest carousel in the country. Up Circuit Avenue was the best ice cream—they even had lobster flavored. And if you didn't like ice cream, they had chocolates. And there, along the Oak Bluffs waterfront was Nancy's, where the president once got takeout.

"We should make an afternoon of it," Frank said. "They're open now. You want some clam strips?"

Maria looked at her mom. She could tell Celeste was thinking about it.

Celeste said, "I think maybe I just want to pick a few things up at the supermarket."

"Come on," Frank said. "In a couple weeks we won't be able to get a table. And if we ride the carousel now, it's empty enough that we stand a chance of catching the brass ring. You get a free ride if you do. I'll treat."

"Thanks, but no," Celeste said. "We really just want to shop and then head home for an early night."

"Well, maybe some other time." Frank pulled into the supermarket parking lot. "We have a little while still before the day-trippers start to come." He got out to open the door for Maria.

"I'll meet you back here in an hour," he said to Celeste. "I'm just going up the road to the hardware store."

Maria felt a bit sorry for him as he drove away. He shouldn't have said he'd treat. That made it like a date, and her mom never dated. In her whole life, Maria had never seen her go out with a man. She'd have to advise Frank to try a different approach. As she thought that, she realized she was kind of rooting for him. He was nice enough, and he made her mother smile.

In the supermarket, Celeste picked up a box of cereal,

tsked, and put it back. "Everything here is so expensive," she said.

"I don't know why you're even buying food," Maria said. "Hattie keeps cooking so much."

"I hate mooching off her." Celeste pushed the cart along. "She has so much on her plate."

"You mean with Paolo?"

Her mother looked at her as if she were trying to figure something out.

"What?" Maria asked.

"Nothing. I was just wondering—are you lonely, *chérie*?" Celeste asked worriedly.

"No! Why would you even ask?"

"Well, it's just because you mentioned Hattie's son, I thought—" Celeste interrupted herself. "Two dollars? They're crazy!" She put a can of chickpeas in the cart anyhow.

"I'm never lonely," Maria said. "And even if I was, I wouldn't want to hang around with some dumb boy who gets in fights all the time."

"Well, I'm glad to hear that," Celeste said. "I don't think you two would be a good match anyhow."

"Mama!" Maria said. "A *match*?"

"I meant as friends, of course. You're too young for

anything else." Celeste smiled apologetically. "It does sound like he gets in a lot of trouble."

Maria considered asking her mother what she'd heard about Paolo's trouble, if there was something other than fighting, but then felt weird. She didn't want her mom thinking she was obsessed with him or something. Because she certainly wasn't.

"This is nice, no?" Celeste said, picking up a head of garlic. "Shopping together like we used to." She smiled absently at Maria. "We could make chicken and rice tonight. And *hummus*. If I can find *tahini*."

At the end of the aisle, a large plate glass window opened up on the main street of town. Maria saw across the street a store with nautical things in its window. Maybe there was something she could buy for *The Last Privateer*. Anyway, she figured that if they were in town she should at least go somewhere more interesting than a supermarket.

"Can we go across the street when we're done?" Maria asked. "That store looks kind of cool. And I brought my dog-walking money."

"Why don't you go over now and I'll meet you later in the parking lot," Celeste said. She was distracted by the price of lemons. "Just don't be long, okay? I don't want to keep Frank waiting."

The store was mostly a cheesy tourist trap filled with fake pirate paraphernalia and corny T-shirts. Maria was about to leave when a book caught her eye. The lurid illustration showed a pirate straddling a treasure chest, flintlock pistols smoking. Blazoned in red calligraphy was the title: *The* Whydah—*A True Tale of Pirate Treasure*. She took it off the shelf and opened it.

"You like pirate stories?"

Maria turned to find a large young woman dressed in black lace and sleeved with colorful tattoos. She had a barbell pierce at the bridge of her nose and two rings in her lower lip.

"I don't know," Maria said. "I was looking for something about privateers. Do you know if they're some kind of pirate?"

The girl seemed not to have heard her. "It's true, that book. When the *Whydah* went down, it had like five tons of gold, silver, and jewels on board. Only two people survived." She smiled, as if this dismal survival rate made her happy. "And this guy, Barry Someone, found it like thirty years ago—right off the Cape."

Maria remembered they'd taken the ferry from Cape Cod. A prickle rose at the back of her neck. Maybe not all pirates buried their treasure in the Caribbean.

"It's really nearby," the tattooed girl was saying.

"There's a museum about it in Provincetown. That's such a cool town. Last summer, I went there with this guy . . ."

"So you know a lot about pirates in this area?" Maria interrupted. "Have you heard of Captain Murdefer?"

"I dunno. Maybe. New England was crawling with pirates; I can't keep them all straight. And witches. You interested in witches? We have some really cool Wiccan stuff. You should go to Salem—that is such a cool town . . ."

Maria looked back at the book. "Do you have any books about pirate treasure that hasn't been found? Like where it might be?" She didn't even want to admit to herself what she was hoping.

"Let me see." The salesgirl trolled the shelves. She wore a ring on every finger, and on some fingers two. Maria thought she looked a little piratey in all that jewelry and black lace. Maybe it was a job requirement.

"There's this one." The girl held out a slim paperback. "*True Pyrate Tales*. But if they knew where the treasure was, someone would have found it by now, right?"

"I suppose so. Still, it looks kind of interesting." Maria put the book on the counter.

"You interested in anything else?" the salesgirl asked.

"Just—" Maria stopped. "Well, do you have any maps? Like for sailing?" An idea was beginning to form. If she could find a map, a modern map, to compare with Captain Murdefer's map, one that *looked* like his map, instead of those useless ones on the boat, then she could tell where his treasure island was.

"They call them charts. Maps are for on land; charts are for at sea." The girl headed to the rear of the store and Maria followed. "You want framed? We also have these, this guy paints ships on them, people like 'em—I don't know, I think they're kind of weird."

The salesgirl gestured to a series of gilt-framed nautical charts with sailboats painted on the water. All were of the same triangular island. The same triangular island of Captain Murdefer's map.

Maria felt her cheeks burn. But the salesgirl didn't notice. She was riffling through a long drawer filled with colorful charts.

"Here's one. It's got the whole island, Nantucket, and part of the Cape." She held it out to Maria.

Maria stared at it. It was a crisp, detailed, modern rendition of Captain Murdefer's treasure map. There was the main triangle, and off in the northeastern corner the three smaller dots representing the tinier islands where the X was drawn.

At the top in black, block letters it said MARTHA'S VINEYARD.

"This is Martha's Vineyard?" Maria asked. "On this chart and in those paintings?"

"Yeah." The girl made it sound like "duh."

"I just got here." Maria blushed.

"Look, see?" The salesgirl pointed to the chart. On the northeast side was Oak Bluffs, and south of that was Edgartown, and at the very bottom Mr. Ironwall's private estate stretched between a "Great Pond" and the sea. It even said in small black letters: IRONWALL ESTATE.

It seemed an impossible coincidence. But the more she thought of it, the more sense it made. After all, the Vineyard had been Captain Murdefer's home. Of course he'd want to keep his treasure close.

"Can I have this? I mean, how much does it cost?" Maria had no idea how to judge the modern chart's quality. It seemed much more detailed than the captain's map, so that was probably good.

"Nineteen ninety-five."

"I'll take it," Maria said.

"You want anything else?"

"How much are compasses? One that works, but not too expensive." Maria pulled out her wallet. "I only have seventy dollars."

"Sounds like you're going sailing."

"No," Maria protested. "Not me. I can't sail. I've never been sailing. My dad does, though. Well, not really my dad, but—" She did not know why she was going through the effort of lying to this piratey girl whom she would probably never see again and who was not even listening. Already the salesgirl was leading her to another part of the store.

"Well, we've got some handheld compasses for around twenty bucks. They're in that case." The teen-pirate pointed.

* * *

When Maria returned to the supermarket parking lot, she found her mother and Frank already waiting.

"What did you get, *chérie*?" Celeste pointed to her bags.

"Just some souvenirs."

"Your mom tells me you're curious about Paolo," Frank said. "Well, you're going to get to meet him. You're coming to our house for dinner Friday."

As he went around to the other side of the truck, Celeste made a face at Maria, something halfway between a grimace and a goofy smile.

Ugh.

Maria liked Frank just fine, but she didn't feel like

hanging out with his nasty nephew. Maybe she could get out of it. She'd have to ask her mom when they were alone.

But when they got home, Maria rushed upstairs to compare her chart to the treasure map. And by dinner, her head was so filled with visions of pirate treasure that she completely forgot to ask if maybe her mom actually didn't want her to go to dinner at Frank's house after all.

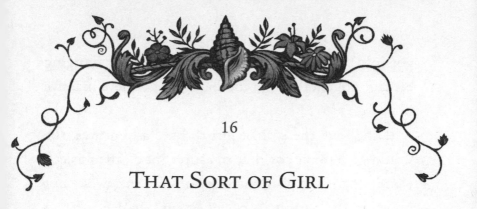

16

THAT SORT OF GIRL

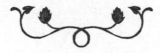

MARIA WOKE TO THE SOUND OF FRANK'S GOLF cart crunching to a stop on the driveway, just as it did every morning. Captain Murdefer's treasure map, the new chart of the island, and *True Pyrate Tales* were scattered across her quilt. She'd fallen asleep comparing the two charts, reading true pirate tales, and imagining her future.

Captain Murdefer's treasure would certainly buy them everything she ever wanted. She could already picture their house. Not too big—she and her mom didn't need to be cleaning a big house, and after all, it was only the two of them. But they could finally buy a nice car. She wondered if her mom even wanted to drive. They'd definitely have a pool—then she'd really learn how to swim. And she could go to any college she got into, a private university even, with ivy hanging off the stone walls, and football games, and a massive library.

If she were the sort of girl to have adventures, she would go looking for that treasure. She'd fallen asleep wondering if she were that sort of girl. She awoke not knowing the answer to her question. She'd never had the chance for an adventure before.

The morning sun was streaming through the porthole above her bed. The lovely smell of coffee, cinnamon, and sugar wafted up the stairs.

She had to get dressed and walk Brutus. She had to visit with Mr. Ironwall and eat lunch with Hattie. It wasn't as if she could just chuck it all and boat out to Treasure Island instead, could she?

Would she, if she could?

"It's about time, sleepyhead," Celeste said when Maria came down.

Frank and Brutus were standing in the kitchen. Frank held a mug of coffee.

Celeste gave Maria a look. "You woke up so late—are you sick?"

"No, just tired. I stayed up late reading."

"Brutus has been whining. He thought you forgot

him." Frank put his mug in the sink and tossed her the leash.

"We have to go." Celeste looked at the kitchen clock. She kissed Maria quickly on the forehead. "There's coffee cake from Hattie. See you tonight."

Maria waited until the noise of the golf cart faded. Then she stuffed three apples, four bottles of water, and a hunk of wax-paper-wrapped coffee cake into her backpack and ran off toward the beach with Brutus.

It was a beautifully sunny morning. Delicate wildflowers—yellow, blue, and purple—dotted the tall grasses on either side of the broken-shell drive. Small white moths fluttered about. Birds she didn't recognize sang songs she'd never heard. She wished she knew their names. Back home, in the empty lot on Rev. James A. Polite Avenue, there had been so few names to know: Queen Anne's lace, chickadees. Here, on this vast estate, there were so many things to know the names of. Birds and fish and shells and strangely shaped items that washed up with the bracken. She picked up interesting bits and put them in her pocket. Maybe she would show them to Mr. Ironwall later.

As she ran Brutus around the beach, her eyes kept cutting toward the sailboat. It bobbed at the dock, the morning sun glinting off the ripples around its hull. The tent looked like it hadn't been disturbed since she left it yesterday. Maybe she really had scared Paolo off.

* * *

After Brutus's walk, Maria offered to sit awhile with Mr. Ironwall so her mother could run down to the kitchen for a coffee break. Mr. Ironwall acted as though he needed to be convinced to allow Maria's visit.

"Well, at least she may be a diversion of sorts from my busy schedule," he said. He sniffed and waited for Celeste to shut the door behind her.

"Go ahead, make my day," Mr. Ironwall said to Maria.

"What?"

"Clint Eastwood, *Sudden Impact*." He frowned. "No? Never heard of it? I suppose you weren't born yet."

Maria shrugged.

"Fine then. What shall we talk about?"

"I found this." Maria showed him a peach-colored shell, delicate as a baby's fingernail.

"The Wampanoag call them jingle shells. I don't know the scientific name." Mr. Ironwall laid the shell aside. He folded his hands and waited.

"How about this?" Maria held out a black rectangle with four thin, curled appendages extending one from each corner. It felt strangely like leather and smelled of low tide.

"Mermaid's purse," Mr. Ironwall said. "An egg case for creatures like skates and dogfish."

"Dogfish?"

"It's like a small shark," Mr. Ironwall explained. "Now, I'm done playing the role of biologist. Entertain me with some scintillating news of the world beyond these walls." He waved his hand idly about.

"Um, we went into town yesterday," Maria said. "Frank drove us. I got an interesting book about pirates. Apparently they were all over around here, burying treasure, sinking . . ."

Mr. Ironwall gazed at the wall over her head. "When I was a boy, we often went looking for lost pirate treasure."

"Did you ever find any?"

Mr. Ironwall frowned as if she were ridiculous. "Of course not. But that didn't stop us from trying."

He closed his eyes and kept talking. "There was a slew of us—cousins from off-island, local children whose parents worked here. All ages. We would pack up supplies and sail off to the outer islands and camp for days at a time, digging around."

"What are the outer islands?" Maria interrupted.

"Guano-covered rocks," Mr. Ironwall said.

"Guano?" she asked.

"Bird poop," he said.

"Are they far?"

"No. Not really."

"Could you tell me about them? Like a story or something? A pirate treasure story?" Maria asked.

"I don't tell stories."

"But you just did. Well, you almost did—about you and your cousins hunting for pirate treasure."

Brutus lay on the bed between them, and Mr. Ironwall kept one hand on the dog at all times. Now he turned his focus to Maria.

"You should be outside playing. Instead of talking to me."

"I don't play," Maria said. "But I guess I should go. I'll call for my mom."

"Yes, do that." Mr. Ironwall put his hand over his eyes. "I want to be alone."

Maria stared at him.

He peeked through his fingers at her.

"Oh, come on," he scoffed. "I'm not that rude. Garbo, *Grand Hotel*. Your cultural education is severely lacking. Now, shoo." He waved her off.

* * *

After a quick lunch with Hattie, Maria headed back to the *Privateer*. On the walk over, she collected bouquets of milkweed, honeysuckle, and beach roses. If she found Paolo on the boat, she'd just turn around and leave. All the way there, she crossed her fingers and really, really hoped he wasn't there. And to her great relief she found the boat wonderfully, peacefully empty.

The bright afternoon sun shone through the tent and filled the cabin with soft light. Maria placed her little bouquets in the blue-enameled coffee mugs about the cabin. The sweet scent chased away the mustiness. She aired the cushions out on the sunny beach, then remade the beds and fluffed the pillows. She cleaned the windows with vinegar that she'd taken from the kitchen, then scrubbed the sink with baking soda (again, borrowed from Hattie's kitchen supplies) and seawater. Freshened and cleaned, the cabin felt quite homey.

Now she sat at the tiny table, reading. She liked the warm smell of the wood and the cool smell of the ocean, and she liked the gentle rocking motion. The noise was constant: creaking timbers and blowing wind, waves slapping the hull, but it was all good noise, calm noise. With all the noise, the cabin wasn't nearly so lonely as the empty cottage.

True Pyrate Tales told of many pirates, privateers, and

wealthy merchant vessels in and about these waters. Quite a few of them had wrecked, but only the *Whydah* had been found. There was an intriguing chapter about Captain William Kidd, who had started out as a privateer, but had turned pirate. Supposedly he buried gold at Money Head on Hog Island not too far away, and maybe another treasure on Nomans Land, an uninhabited island a few miles south.

She slid the book away and pulled Captain Murdefer's map from her backpack. She wondered if Mr. Ironwall and his cousins might have found the treasure if they'd had the chart. They had a sailboat, and the skills to sail it and permission to camp for days at a time, but no chart. She had the chart, but no boat or skills or permission to camp. And no helpful cousins.

> Twice twice two,
> Then twice that more.
> Take one from the first,
> The Queen treads upon the door.

What did it mean?

She sighed. The afternoon sun shone rainbows through the stained glass window. Maria packed up her books and charts and garbage. The treasure would have to wait for another day. Or forever, unless she found a way to get to the outer islands. Maybe Frank knew someone with a boat. But if she spoke to Frank, he'd tell her mom, and she'd say the treasure didn't belong to her and even if she did find it she couldn't keep it. No, it was definitely not something to get adults messed up in. She would have to do it herself. But how?

As she climbed over the *Privateer*'s rail to the dock, she saw the answer to her questions. The dinghy. It was the sort of boat that didn't require sailing skills. She'd already inspected it. It had both its oars; its hull was sound. It was small enough for one person to handle. There it lay, overturned on the deck, just waiting for her.

But it would have to wait some more. What had Mr. Ironwall said? It's not too far to the outer islands? She figured she would need a whole day to get there and back. And she needed to pack supplies: food, a shovel, warm clothing. She would do it tomorrow. She *would* be the sort of girl who had adventures.

17

A Boy Raised by Wolves

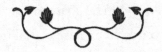

MARIA WOKE THE NEXT DAY READY TO ROW TO the outer islands. She'd packed her backpack with supplies the night before and ran out the door as soon as Frank arrived with Brutus. She made a lame excuse to her mom—she and Brutus wanted to take a long walk, so if she didn't come back before Mr. Ironwall's nap, she'd take Brutus to the cottage for the afternoon—buying nearly the whole day for herself. Even if she didn't have time to dig up the treasure, at least she could figure out which of the outer islands *held* the treasure.

But first Maria would have to get the dinghy in the water.

Flipping the dinghy onto its keel wasn't too difficult, but lifting the prow up onto the sailboat's rail made her legs shake. Then she tied a long rope from the dinghy to a post on *The Last Privateer*. The last thing she needed was the rowboat to float away when she dropped it over the side.

It splashed more loudly than she expected. Maria peered over the rail. The boat had landed in the water right side up—she hadn't been sure that would happen when she shoved it over the rail from behind—but there it was, bobbing against the hull of the *Privateer*. She untied the dinghy's lead rope and then climbed off the *Privateer*, onto the dock, pulling the little boat close. Brutus followed and sat patiently, awaiting further instructions.

"We just need to get in, Brute," Maria told him.

Brutus needed a lot of coaxing with dog biscuits to enter the rowboat without her, but she had to get him in first so she would have both hands free for the launch.

The boat rocked precariously when he jumped down. He looked up at her, panting. As soon as she climbed aboard, feeling a bit clumsy now that she was buckled into a life jacket she'd found on the sailboat, he licked her as if they'd been separated for days.

"You're such a chicken, Brutus," she told him. He licked her again, spun around, and lay down on the life jacket she had brought for him.

Maria tied her backpack tightly to the bench so it wouldn't go overboard if things got rocky. As a precaution, she'd put Captain Murdefer's map and the modern chart in plastic bags and then zipped them into another layer of plastic bags, inside the deepest compartment of her pack.

The tide was out and the water was calm, with only tiny waves breaking on the beach. She had figured the rowing part wouldn't be so hard. But rowing proved more difficult than it looked on TV. She hadn't realized how much coordination was required to keep the oars in those little metal U-shaped locks. They kept lifting up, slipping out and slipping in. She was about fifty feet from the dock, trying to stay close to shore, when she lost her left oar altogether. It floated just out of reach, and no amount of paddling with the right oar got her any closer.

"I'm just going to get the paddle, Brute. You stay. Stay!" She fixed him with a serious look and eased herself over the side and into the waves.

The cold water took her breath away, but her life jacket kept her afloat. Brutus stood on the bench, barking.

"It's okay!" she told him. "Just stay. I'm coming back. Stay!"

He didn't stay. He jumped in after her. And then, as if

he'd suddenly decided it was too cold, he tried to climb into her arms.

"Get off me, you big dummy!" Maria shoved him, but he refused to budge.

Her struggle to push him away pushed the boat away instead, and though Maria had a hold of the lead rope, she couldn't simultaneously pull the boat back, grab the oar, and deal with the increasingly agitated dog.

"Let go of me!" She grabbed at the side rail. The boat tipped and Brutus put his paws on the rail also, as if he could climb back in.

"No! Get away." Maria tried to hold the boat upright, but the dog was too heavy and too persistent. As he kicked her face with his hind paws and struggled to climb back in, water came in over the rail and the boat flipped over completely. Brutus fell back and began swimming in panicked circles.

"You total idiot!" Maria yelled. She grabbed at the rowboat's slick sides, struggling to hang on to the round hull, but there was nothing to hold on to. Brutus, too, tried to climb unsuccessfully onto the overturned boat, and then, when that didn't work, onto her shoulders. She felt herself being pushed under. She took a deep breath, held it, and—

Her feet touched the bottom.

It wasn't that deep after all. She'd been kept off the shallow floor by the life jacket. But the dog was still holding her under the water. She pushed his hairy bulk toward the shore and kicked off the bottom. As soon as she surfaced she grabbed the lost oar. Then she hunted for the other, found it, and grabbed that, too. But now Brutus was bearing down on her again—determined, it seemed, to climb back on top of her. She tried to swim away, but found it was too difficult with the oars in hand. She was about to let them go when someone whistled from shore.

Brutus abandoned her, swimming mightily for the beach. Maria watched as the dog reached the beach, shook, and went running to the figure who now knelt and rubbed Brutus's head with both hands. She realized it was Paolo.

Maria bobbed about alone, rescuing the boat and the oars. Brutus's new buddy watched without helping. He even looked as though he was laughing! Then he began throwing a ball for Brutus! And Brutus, the traitor, ran joyfully into the waves to fetch it. Suddenly Brutus, who was the biggest chicken when it came to swimming just moments ago, happily paddled after the ball, ignoring her.

And Paolo ignored her, too.

Though her soaked clothes weighed her down and the waves knocked her about, Maria finally dragged the boat onto the sand and threw the oars beside it. She untied her sodden backpack and laid it on the sand to dry.

Brutus came over and dropped the tennis ball at her feet. Relieved of his fuzzy green burden, he lifted his leg and peed on a hunk of seaweed.

"Thanks for nothing!" she yelled at Paolo when he followed. "You could have helped!"

"I did. I got the dog to lay off you." He picked up Brutus's ball and threw it again. The dog bounded after it. "Besides, you looked like you could handle it."

Brutus bounded up to him, dropped the ball, and wagged. He shook vigorously, and then danced around the boy.

"Brutus, come," Maria commanded. "Come!"

The dog ignored her, jumping and fawning at Paolo. She'd been walking Brutus for ages! And now the beast acted like she was not even there!

"He wants to play more," Paolo said. He threw the ball into the water. Brutus plunged happily back into the ocean up to his neck, turned, and paddled after the floating ball.

"Stop doing that!" Maria said. "What if he drowns?"

"He swims better than you," Paolo said. "Why were you stealing that rowboat?"

"I wasn't stealing it," Maria said. "And it's certainly none of your business."

"Well, it's *certainly* not your rowboat. And you were taking it. Kinda like stealing."

"What are you doing here?" Maria said.

"I'm fishing." The boy jutted his chin at an ancient fishing pole lying on the sand.

"So?"

"So, you can be on any beach on this island between the high tide and low tide line if you're fishing." He picked up the pole. It didn't have any fishing line in it. "What's your excuse?"

"I was walking my dog."

"In a rowboat?"

Maria shrugged.

"And that's your dog like that's your boat," Paolo said. "I've known Brutus for years. He just wants to play. That's why he was climbing on you in the water. He thought it was a game. If you knew him better, you'd've known that."

When Brutus returned, Paolo took the ball from the dog's mouth and held it to Maria to throw.

"That is disgusting," she said.

Paolo shrugged and put the ball in his pocket. Brutus tilted his head and looked disappointedly at his empty hand. Paolo rubbed the dog's ears and got a slobbery lick in return.

"You'll need help getting that rowboat back on board," he said.

"Well, I don't want *your* help." She didn't like his tone. And she didn't like him.

"Fine." He looked around the empty beach. "Go ask someone else for help."

Maria grabbed the prow of the boat and began dragging it toward the dock. She didn't get very far until Paolo lifted the stern. She marched angrily toward the dock as if she didn't notice he was helping her. But together, they walked the dinghy out the length of the dock to *The Last Privateer.*

"You know, I'm just trying to be nice. You're really impossible to be nice to." Paolo raised the canvas tent wider to make space for the dinghy. "Lift it over the rail, so it doesn't scrape."

"I know. I'm not an idiot." Maria carefully held her end off the rail and climbed aboard. Paolo followed with his end and together they laid the rowboat gently on the deck.

"Anyhow," Maria said, "I don't need you to be nice to me."

"I bet you have, like, no friends," Paolo said.

"I have a ton of friends back home," Maria said.

"No, you don't."

"How would you know?"

"'Cause I have no friends and I know what it looks like," Paolo said, matter-of-factly. "You should get some dry clothes on. You're going to get sick."

"I don't care." Maria felt embarrassed and stupid, and very, very cold. She would have to go home to put on dry clothes. And Paolo stood between her and the cottage.

"You're weird," he said. "First you steal the old guy's rowboat, then you act all snotty. What's your deal?"

"I don't have a deal."

"I'm really, really not dangerous," Paolo said. He climbed back under the tent, jumped onto the dock, and jogged back to the beach. She followed behind, a good distance off. Poor Brutus, confused, did not know who to follow, so he bounded back and forth between them.

"Anyhow, you don't need to worry about me telling the old guy," Paolo hollered back at her.

"Why do you keep calling him 'the old guy'?" Maria said. She clipped Brutus to his leash.

"'Cause he *is* old. He's going to die soon," Paolo said over his shoulder. "And leave you high and dry."

"What does that even mean?" Maria said.

"It means your mom better be good at keeping him alive. Or she's out of a job, and you guys are homeless." He picked up his fishing pole and headed toward the mansion.

Brutus pulled against the leash, as if he wanted to follow Paolo. But Maria tugged back. There was no way she'd let him anywhere near that jerk again.

18

CAPTAIN MURDEFER, REVISITED

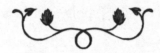

THE NEXT MORNING, FRANK BROUGHT THE BI-cycle and a brand-new helmet to the cottage.

"Sorry it took so long," Frank said. "I decided she needed a lick of paint."

"No, it's beautiful," Maria said, staring at the gleaming red machine. "I can't wait to try it."

Anything would be easier than rowing a boat, she figured.

But after an hour, Maria had scraped her right knee and the palms of both hands and torn her pants. She'd also caught her right sock in the bicycle chain, crashed into a tree, skidded out several times on the clamshell driveway, and bruised her elbow. And still, she could not ride without wobbling and falling over.

She gave up. Then tried again. And gave up all over again. Maria figured she was the only twelve-year-old in the world who couldn't ride a bike. It was humiliating. She felt as though she'd been trying all day without improving.

That evening, by the time Frank and her mother pulled up in the golf cart, Maria was covered in dirt, scabs, and grease.

"Maria, *habibti*!" Celeste clucked worriedly over her. "What happened to you?"

"I'm trying to learn how to ride this beast." Maria gave the bike an angry kick.

"Maybe it would be better to just walk?" Celeste suggested. "Or ask Frank for a ride."

"I want to do things by myself! I'm sick of being a hothouse flower!"

"A hothouse flower?" Celeste said. "What is this hothouse flower?"

"A canned string bean. A wimp! I want to be normal. Normal kids go places by themselves. Normal kids ride bicycles!"

Celeste sighed. "Well, okay. Show us what you can do."

Maria approached the bike with trepidation. She swung her leg over the center bar. Then she remembered the kickstand, and she tried to kick it up with the bike between her legs. Big mistake. She fell sideways onto her already-scraped knee, with the bicycle on top.

"Why do this to yourself?" Celeste asked.

"She'll survive," Frank said. He helped Maria up. "You just have to get moving in order to balance. You need momentum. Here—you get on and I'll help you balance." Maria climbed on again. "Now push off the ground—kick with your foot and then bring it onto the pedal. Keep your handlebars straight—don't turn until you're really moving. And then just a tiny shift on the handlebars to start your turn."

He held the seat while Maria began to pedal.

She felt wobbly and scared, but then suddenly she straightened out and was going.

"I'm doing it! I can ride!" She took a wide turn around the beetlebung tree. "Look at me!"

"I can't," her mother said. But she was looking, and almost smiling. "If you're going to stay out here and help her kill herself," she said to Frank, "I'm going in to see what Hattie left in the fridge. She always gives too much food. You can stay for dinner if you want."

Frank's neck reddened. "Well, I guess I could stay a little while and teach Maria some more."

"That would be nice," Celeste said as Maria coasted

to a stop in front of them, at the last moment putting her foot down to stop herself from tipping over. "Instead of leaving her alone to die. I'm just saying." Celeste's eyes twinkled.

Maria had never seen her mother laugh, but sometimes she did kid a little, like she was kidding now. It meant she was in a good mood. She'd been in a lot of good moods lately. Definitely more often than back in the Bronx.

Frank spent the rest of the evening helping Maria ride, until she could mount, turn, brake, and dismount all by herself. They quit only when it became too dark to see. Then they sat around the tiny kitchen table, sharing Hattie's lasagna, green salad, and peach cobbler.

"That poor guy has to drive all the way up-island," Celeste said after Frank left. "That was very nice of him to help you like that."

"He *is* very nice," Maria said.

"Yes, maybe." Celeste gathered up the dirty dishes and took them to the sink. "Tonight he definitely went beyond the call of duty."

"So I can ride the bike off the estate now, right?" Maria asked. "Frank taught me everything I need to know, and Hattie says the bike path is perfectly safe."

"Yes, fine, fine, all right, as long as you wear your helmet," Celeste said. "But if you kill yourself, don't come crying to me."

* * *

The next morning, after she had discharged her dog-walking duties, Maria ran back to the cottage and packed for her first day of bicycle freedom. She stuffed the leather-bound map, a bottle of water, and a chocolate bar in her school backpack. Then she found her mother's cell phone and threw it in, just in case. Her mother didn't take it with her to the Great House because there was no reception there, or anywhere on the estate. Celeste complained that she had to walk halfway down the long drive to make a static-filled call. Though Maria wasn't sure whom she would call if she needed help. She had no idea what the Great House phone number was, and she didn't even know if Frank or Hattie had cell phones. But at least she could dial 911 if she had to. And the screen could function as a watch.

Her tires crunched over the crushed-shell drive. Then the bike path began where the private road ended, and it ran parallel to the main road all the way to town. A nice wide margin of grass separated Maria from passing cars.

The route *was* easy to follow—a straight shot most of the way, with few hills, and signs at every turn. Clearly the island had been set up for tourists.

After a couple of miles, she stopped being afraid and began to enjoy the ride. It seemed summer was nearly here. Green washed the fields, and the trees had leafed out. Even the air smelled fresh and warm.

She pedaled past sweet summer cottages and glorious mansions. She passed a school, but all the children were inside and the building was quiet. Maria felt relieved as she slipped past, unnoticed. More than a few farms had horses or cows that looked up as she whizzed by. A heron fished in a salt pond, and a man in hip-high rubber boots stood in the shallows dragging a long pole through the glassy water. She stopped briefly to watch, and saw an osprey being harried by three crows.

She found the library easily enough, and neither the librarian nor the few patrons asked why she wasn't in school. Maybe this, too, was a function of a tourist-centered town—maybe they just assumed she was on an early vacation with her family. The librarian simply smiled and handed Maria a slip of paper with a password and a computer cubicle number.

"We'd like you to keep it to half an hour," the librarian said. "Unless no one is waiting."

Maria quickly located a useful website about privateers. Apparently they *were* like pirates, only they worked for the government, raiding enemy ships. But then she decided it didn't really matter. What was more important was figuring out about Captain Murdefer, why all his stuff was in her cottage, and which outer island he'd visited. Perhaps it was best to start with something concrete. Like Captain Murdefer's boat, *Le Dernier Corsair*. But she got too many results and they were all in French. Though she didn't speak or read French, she knew enough from the snippets her mother said to recognize the language.

She went to a translation website, typed in the boat's name, and selected "French to English." The translation box read *The Last Corsair*.

She dictionaried *Corsair*. The definition came up: "1. a pirate; 2. a privateer [from Old French *corsaire* pirate, from Medieval Latin *cursarius*, from Latin]."

So *Le Dernier Corsair* meant "The Last Privateer." It was the same name as Mr. Ironwall's sailboat, but in French. She sat back and considered what that meant. It definitely meant that Mr. Ironwall had been playing her when he said he had no idea who Captain Murdefer was, because he'd named his sailboat after Captain Murdefer's boat.

Out of curiosity, Maria typed: *Murdefer, French to English.*

Do you mean mur de fer? the computer asked. The cursor blinked at her.

Maria replaced *Murdefer* with *mur de fer* and hit Enter.

The English box said "wall of iron."

Maria sat back in the chair and stared at the screen. Wall of Iron. *Iron wall.*

Murdefer was French for Ironwall.

* * *

On the bike ride home Maria thought about her discovery. Something Hattie had said on that first day—what was it? All of Mr. Ironwall's ancestors had been captains: whalers, merchants, maybe even pirates. Captain Murdefer must have been an ancestor of Mr. Ironwall's. That was why the cottage had an oil painting of Captain Murdefer's ship, and his old treasure map. That's why Mr. Ironwall and his cousins went out looking for pirate treasure. They'd hoped to find their ancestor's secret cache. But he said they never did find any treasure. So there must still be a secret cache out there to be found. Which brought her back to her original problem—how to get to the outer islands?

Maria was so lost in thought she didn't notice that she'd ridden back to the school until she heard the loud voices. A pack of wild children spilled out the open doors and into the parking lot, laughing and screaming.

Maria slowed her bicycle and stopped beside a bus shelter. It hid her from the crowd, but she could watch them. If they stayed, if her mother kept her job, she would have to join that pack next September. They seemed as wild as the kids from back home, with their yelling and shoving. She wondered if Paolo was in that crowd. She pushed off and pedaled quickly away, before any of them could reach her. She didn't stop pedaling until she was safely at the estate.

19

UP-ISLAND

MARIA HAD COMPLETELY FORGOTTEN THEY'D promised to go to dinner at Frank's house that evening, and by the time she got back to the cottage, her mother and Frank were already sitting outside waiting for her.

Now Frank drove Maria and Celeste up-island in his old truck. Maria dreaded the whole thing. Paolo would be there. Maybe if she stuck with her mother and didn't say anything to him it would be okay. But her dread grew as they turned down one dirt road after another, each more potholed and narrow than the last, until they came to two tire tracks between a stump and a mailbox. They rattled down that for a bit, then the track abruptly ended. An old woman appeared and grabbed Maria as soon as she tumbled out of the truck.

"I'm Ella Newcomb, but you can call me Grandma—everyone else does." She looped her arm through Maria's.

The old lady was nearly as round as she was tall, and she wasn't very tall at all. She looked like a cartoon grandmother. She wore a cotton dress with an apron overtop, and her gray hair was in a bun. She had a homely round face, as if made of dough, and her ocean-colored eyes sparkled.

Maria's mother introduced herself, putting out her hand. "And this is my daughter, Maria."

"I know! I've heard all about you from the boys! They can't stop talking about you two—so that's why I made them invite you." Grandma Newcomb winked at Frank. "Now I know why you keep going on."

"I brought you *arak*." Celeste held out a bottle-shaped package.

Grandma Newcomb unwrapped the paper and inspected the blue bottle with unreadable gold script. "Well, isn't that interesting."

"It's a special Lebanese drink," Celeste explained. "It tastes like licorice and you have to put the ice in first, then when you pour it over, it turns white."

"Well, we'll have to try it at dinner." Grandma Newcomb guided them up a slate stone path. "Pops's still napping. Those pain pills he's got for his back knock him out—then he doesn't sleep well at night. I wanted to ask you about that, Celeste, what you think of them. I wonder if he's getting too much. He cracked some vertebrae falling off a ladder a number of years back, but he can still get around just fine."

Before them spread the Newcomb compound—two cedar shake houses and a handful of weathered sheds. The buildings looked ancient, with their shingles silver and their rooflines sagging. Chickens ranged through the vegetable patch, bees buzzed around a couple of wooden hives, and starlings swarmed the apple trees that were just beginning to show little green apples.

"Those birds are a nuisance—they got all my blueberries last year, so I had to chicken-wire them. We'll see what we get this year." The old lady gestured to some bushes covered in wire mesh.

"Grandma and Pops make nearly all the family's food from what they grow and hunt," Frank explained.

"Oh, now that's an exaggeration," Grandma Newcomb said. "Pops hardly hunts anymore. Harry—that's my eldest, he won't be home till the five o'clock ferry—Harry brings home a deer or a turkey now and again. Pops just fishes and rakes oysters. You want to see them? Bet you city gals have never seen oysters like these. We can have some for supper." Grandma New-comb led Maria and Celeste to a patch between two raspberry bushes.

"Got to keep a stone on the lid or the raccoons get in." The old lady bent with a grunt to lift a rock off a wooden cover set in the ground.

Underneath, dug into the dirt, was a white plastic bucket. Grandma lifted a batch of seaweed, then a damp sponge, and revealed a pile of living oysters.

"They stay cool and fresh for weeks this way. Paolo, get us about— Where'd that boy go?" She looked around the yard, and then turned to Maria. "He was here right before you arrived. You like oysters?"

"I don't know, I've never tried them," Maria said. Maybe Paolo was avoiding her, too. Good.

"Oh, well then, we've got Pops, me . . ." She counted on her fingers. "We'll need about fifty or so. Frank can get them, can't you, Frank? I'm taking these ladies in. Hattie's baking and she'll want to see you."

Maria looked warily about for Paolo, but he was nowhere to be seen. Grandma Newcomb bustled them into the kitchen. It was a tiny room with a low-hanging ceiling made even lower by the exposed beams hung all over with bunches of dried herbs, ropes of garlic, and strings of chili peppers. Maria pointed at the chilies and garlic—clearly *someone* in the family cooked with spices—and Celeste shrugged.

Like their cottage on the Ironwall Estate, the kitchen, living room, and dining room were all one space, with the separate areas defined and divided by counters and handmade furniture. A large woodstove took up a great deal of the room, and it was not only their source of heat, but also their cookstove and oven. A kettle steamed on top, and something fragrant simmered in a cast-iron pot.

Hattie was rolling out biscuits on the sideboard and she waved Celeste over to keep her company. Maria found herself alone with Grandma, who busily swept papers and magazines off kitchen chairs and onto the already-crowded floor.

"Pops's a big one for reading. And he won't throw anything out. Would you like some tea? I have some of last year's honey still, and the mint is nice—it held its flavor well."

"Yes, please." Maria peeked through a door. She didn't want to be surprised by Paolo.

"Go on and look around if you like while the water boils," Grandma said. "You can't get lost. It's a straight line."

Maria considered the invitation. Then her curiosity

overwhelmed her dread and she said, "Could I use the bathroom?"

"Sure. It's to the back and up the stairs." Grandma pointed through the series of rooms toward the back of the house.

It seemed all the other rooms led off this main area, one after another like cars on a train. Maria went through a small room lined with bookshelves straining under the weight of books, and another in which paintings covered every inch of wall. Another room held glass globes brimming with African violets. It was as if each time a new person had joined the family, they'd just added another room off the back of the old one, with no thought to hallways or privacy. If you wanted to get to your bedroom, you walked right through someone else's. She wondered where Paolo slept. And his mom. Did they share a room? And where did they put Frank? And apparently there was that other son, Harry, also.

Maria was so used to her small family of two, she couldn't imagine living with so many people so close up against each other.

She slipped into the next room and bumped into a gnarled old man. He was short and round like Grandma, but more bent. His hair rose from his head like white smoke, and he wore a trim white beard and glasses. His legs bowed out as if he'd been straddling barrels his whole life, and as he shuffled across the room he rolled from side to side as if he were on board a ship in a storm. Maria figured this was Grandfather Newcomb, or "Pops."

"You must be the company," he said in a gruff voice. "Ma said you'd be here." He shuffled out toward the light and cheerful noise of the main room.

Maria crept through two more rooms, filled with fascinating things but empty of people, until she came to the last bedroom. There, a steep staircase with no railings led to a loft. She went to the bottom of the stairs and peered up.

"Hello?"

No one answered. She climbed up the steep stairs and found herself in a loft room similar to her attic loft. It ran nearly the length of the house, but there were a couple of dividing walls. She could see a bed behind a half-open door, and tile on the floor of another—the bathroom. The rest was covered with drawings, paintings, and colorful works of art in various stages of completion. A drafting table took up one corner, and an easel another. Through the skylights she could see the garden and beehives out back. After inspecting all the pictures, she decided to check out the bedroom.

She took one step in, then stopped.

Paolo stood in the corner with his back to her, rummaging through the drawers of a wardrobe. He looked much the same as he had before, except perhaps a bit dirtier. She wondered if he'd even washed his hands after that dog-slobbery ball.

"I'm not going to tell on you, so you don't have to keep staring holes in me like that," Paolo said without turning. How did he even know she was looking at him?

"I'm not staring at you," she said. "I just came up to use the bathroom."

"Go ahead."

She passed behind him and closed the door. Now she stood at the sink, wondering what to do. She didn't want to go—and she couldn't with him out there, possibly listening. She pretended to wash her hands—running the water, rattling the soap dish around. She listened to him walking around the bedroom, rummaging through drawers.

She stared at herself in the mirror. Her cheeks and the bridge of her nose were pink from the sun, and her normally boring brown hair had streaks of red highlights. She polished her glasses and put them back on. She wondered how she would look without them, but when she took them off she couldn't see her own reflection.

When she came out he was still there, as if he'd been waiting for her. They looked at each other. Maria couldn't help but remember him saying, quite accurately, that she had no friends, and then admitting that he didn't either.

"These are beautiful," Maria finally said of a series of pictures that hung from a wire strung along the wall. They were of the same forest path, but the colors had been printed differently in each version. "Did you make them?"

"They're Frank's," Paolo said. "This is his bedroom and that's his studio in the other room. Those woodcuts are the nature preserve. It's not far from here."

"I didn't know he was an artist," Maria said.

"He's not. He's a gardener," Paolo said. "He just likes to make art, too." He held a strange blue plastic stick out to her. "Here—I found this for you."

"What is that?"

"It's so you don't have to touch the gross dog ball. You scoop the ball up in the cup end when he drops it." He demonstrated scooping an imaginary ball from the floor and flicking the stick over his head.

"Is it Frank's?"

"He said I could give it to you." He held it out to her again. "Take it."

Maria took it. "Thanks."

"Why were you stealing that rowboat anyhow?" Paolo asked.

"I wasn't stealing it, I was borrowing it."

He shrugged. "Same difference. But why?"

"I needed to get somewhere."

"Why didn't you just ask Frank to take you? You obviously don't know the first thing about rowing, and he could've borrowed Harry's lobster boat."

"I can't tell adults about it." She fixed him with her fiercest gaze. "So don't you say anything, okay?"

"Okay," Paolo said. "I already said I wouldn't tell."

"You better not." She started down the stairs, careful to stay in the exact middle of the steps. Paolo bounded past her. Four steps from the bottom, he jumped off the side and landed in the last bedroom with a thump.

"Paolo, if you break anything I will kill you!" Hattie shouted from the kitchen.

"Nothing broke!" he yelled back. He turned to Maria. "You know, I can get you a boat if you want. If you still need to go somewhere. A sailboat."

"I don't sail." She started through the string of rooms back to the kitchen.

"I do." He bobbed along behind her.

"Yeah, right."

"My dad used to take me sailing on his boat all the time," he said.

"You have a sailboat?" Her curiosity made her pause.

"Ma sold it after he died."

Now Maria turned to face him. He wasn't actually scary, after all. "I'm sorry, you know, about your dad," she said.

"It's not your fault."

They walked through the painting room and the book room in silence. Then Paolo whispered, "But I *could* get a sailboat to take you where you want to go."

"It's something I have to do by myself," Maria said.

"You need help," Paolo said.

"I don't need *your* help," Maria answered.

"I need help!" Frank called from the main room.

Maria shushed Paolo. He glared back at her and they both walked in together.

Frank stood at the sink, shucking oysters. "Why don't you two stop arguing and start shucking?" He handed Paolo a blunt knife.

"Here." Grandma Newcomb handed a stack of plates to Maria. "You can help me set the table. We'll be eating outside if the bugs aren't too bad—we don't all fit inside."

As they set the places, Grandma Newcomb kept up a steady string of explanations and complaints about the food, bugs, birds, tomato rot, skunks, tourists, summer people, and anything else that came to mind. Maria couldn't get a word in edgewise. Other people kept walking in, various cousins and spouses of cousins, children of cousins and nieces and nephews, and she couldn't keep them straight. They all seemed busy: cleaning fish, slicing bread, fetching beers, bouncing babies. All those people in one place chatting and laughing: it was simultaneously confusing and wonderful. Maria wondered if it was like this every night.

It was only when the whole family sat down together at the groaning table, and Grandma's mouth was full of oyster stew, that Maria could turn her attention away from the old lady and to this strange new food. Oysters weren't all that different from clams, she decided. Maybe a bit bigger. They tasted okay once she got past their boogery texture.

Her mother said a familiar name. She was asking about Mr. Ironwall, when he was younger.

"What was he like?" Grandma Newcomb lifted her eyes to the apple tree as if remembering. "Oh, he was a wild one—loved to throw parties."

"I used to help with the clambakes," Pops Newcomb interrupted. "Do you remember, Ella, how we could throw a clambake for a hundred people with one day's notice?"

"Oh, Pops, no one wants to hear about that—" Grandma patted the old man on the hand.

Pops Newcomb went on as if she hadn't said anything. "He was Mr. Moneybags, that Mr. Ironwall! And he loved to spend it—practically gave it away. Not like he is now, all shut up and stingy."

"He's been very generous to our family." Grandma smiled apologetically at Celeste. "Hattie and Frank are well paid."

Pops went on. "I remember one time I'd raked up all these fat, fresh oysters and he said, 'You know what we should do, Bo? We should hide pearls in them.' I thought he was nuts, so I just shucked 'em and iced 'em, and what do you know, he came back with, honest truth, a whole box of pearls. Real ones! He had me hide them under the flesh. You know, to surprise the guests. We had to ruin the surprise though, when one lady cracked a tooth." He chuckled to himself.

Maria looked across the table at Paolo. He didn't seem to be listening. He kept his eyes on his plate and shoveled the stew in like he was a machine built for eating.

"That party did get out of control." Pops chuckled.

"Most did," Grandma said.

"What were the parties for?" Maria couldn't help but ask. She couldn't imagine that pale old man throwing out-of-control parties with entire boxes of pearls.

"Oh, all sorts of reasons," Grandma said. "Holidays, friends' weddings, movie releases."

"He loved to throw parties when his movies were coming out," Hattie explained. "*To Have and to Hope*— everything had to be French because the film took place in Paris. And *The Last Privateer*—all pirate things."

"What do you know?" Pops said. "You can't have been more than a baby."

"Yeah," Hattie said, "but you've told that pearl story a thousand times. *Privateer* was the party with the pearls in the oysters."

"Well, it's still a darn good story!" Pops thumped the table.

"Time for pie," Grandma interrupted. "I had some canned apples left over from last fall."

Celeste and Hattie stood and helped to gather the dirty dishes.

"It's a shame he never had children," Grandma said to Celeste as they went into the house. "That whole place for nothing. He's going to die with no one to hand it off to."

"And leave us all high and dry," Hattie said. "Just you wait."

Paolo caught Maria's eye and nodded once, as if to say he'd told her so. Then he stood and picked up his plate. Maria started to clear hers, but he took it from her and said, "You sit."

Maria strained to hear the rest of their conversation, but the kitchen door slammed shut.

Mr. Ironwall was going to die and leave them high and dry.

It was the second time she'd heard that, and she was starting to believe it. After all, what would they do when Mr. Ironwall died? Return to the city? Return to that scary apartment building crawling with Bad Barbies? She would do anything before she would do that.

20

THE DREAD PYRATE PAOLO

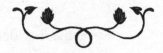

THE NEXT MORNING DAWNED BRIGHT AND sunny, but Maria was too lost in thought to notice. She was trying to figure out her next treasure-hunting move. If Mr. Ironwall was going to leave them all high and dry, then she needed to find that treasure quickly, before her mother lost her job and they lost their home.

"He's going to leave you high and dry, too," she grumbled to Brutus on their walk. She let him off his leash and he disappeared over the dune as swiftly as if he'd caught the scent of a rabbit. Maria ran after him.

As she came over the dune, she saw a small sailboat tied up to the dock behind *The Last Privateer*. It was white, about twelve feet long, and had one mast. A large number 32 was painted in red on the hull. Then she saw that Paolo was aboard, waiting for her. Maria's stomach squeezed. She wasn't sure if she was glad or scared to see him.

But Brutus was already on the dock, wagging and turning joyful circles. Paolo threw a tennis ball far into the water. Brutus bounded into the waves after it.

"You bring the ball chucker?" Paolo called out.

Maria held it up. She'd even brought her own tennis ball.

"Told you I could get you a boat," Paolo said.

"Told you I didn't want your help," Maria said. But she stepped onto the dock to look at the boat anyhow. "Did you steal it?"

"No." He sounded annoyed. "I *borrowed* it from the yacht club."

"You did steal it!"

Brutus swam to the beach, and then scrambled back to the dock and ran down the ramp to drop the ball at her feet.

"He's gotten used to the ramp and dock," Maria said. She scooped the ball up with the tennis ball–size cup and flung it back into the ocean. Brutus dove off the end of the dock, into the chop, and paddled after it.

"Do you like it?" Paolo asked. He sounded as if he actually cared what she thought.

"Yeah, it works well." It was much easier this way; she

didn't have to pick up the disgustingly drooled-on ball. She found herself smiling at him and he smiled back.

"I meant the boat," he said. "Climb aboard."

He held out his hand to help her. She climbed on without taking it.

The boat was very different from *The Last Privateer*. It looked brand-new and everything was metal or plastic. No wood or glass or charm at all. It had barely any deck. Most of it was a hollowed-out hull with molded plastic benches on either side where you could sit and handle the sail and the tiller. Paolo whistled and Brutus swam to the beach, clambered onto the dock, and ran down the ramp. He pranced his forepaws on the floating dock and gazed at them sitting in the boat. After a few attempts, the boy maneuvered the dog onto the boat.

"We could get in so much trouble," Maria said.

"No one will know. We'll bring it back in a couple of hours," Paolo said. "It's not like anyone needs it. They've got, like, a million of them, and no one's using them right now. Sail camp doesn't start till July eleventh."

"What if someone sees us?" she asked.

"Like who? We'll stay away from Edgartown."

"It's not safe."

Paolo pointed to a couple of life jackets. "Come on,

Maria. Did I really go to all the trouble of stealing this for nothing?" He looked at her a long time, but she did not know how to answer.

"Besides," he continued, "I brought us a really nice breakfast." He held up a wax-paper bag of the sort Frank always brought her mother. "The best doughnuts ever."

She did think they were the best doughnuts ever. And she loved Hattie's fritters, muffins, and croissants. She couldn't believe she'd spent her entire childhood eating mass-produced cardboard junk from mass-produced cardboard boxes when there was such home-made deliciousness in the world.

"Hot chocolate, too," he said. A thermos was propped in the corner of the hollowed hull.

Maria looked around. No one else was on the beach. And it really was a beautiful day. It was sunny and warm, and the breeze was light. And she'd never been sailing before. And ever since she'd seen *The Last Privateer* bobbing on the dock she'd wanted to go sailing.

"Oh, all right," she said. "But you'd better be safe. If you do anything scary, I get to say turn around and you can't argue. Promise?"

"Promise."

* * *

Within a few minutes they were under way. Paolo had launched them expertly. He quickly loosed the line with one hand and steered with the other. He raised the sail as they drifted from the dock, and pointed them toward the mouth of the bay.

"Where are we going?"

Maria opened her backpack and handed him the modern chart and pointed to the three tiny islands in the northeast corner. "There."

"Why? There's nothing on those rocks except bird poop."

"I just want to go there," Maria said. "No questions."

Paolo shrugged. "Okay. No questions. But you can't just sit there like a landlubber. You have to work for your passage. I'm going to teach you how to sail on the way over."

"Okay," Maria said.

"Okay," Paolo said. "This kind of boat is the simplest kind. One sail, small, easy to handle. It's called a catboat for some reason, although maybe it should be called a dogboat." He nodded at Brutus, who lay curled at their feet.

Maria smiled and Paolo continued. "Where we're sitting is starboard. The other side is port. You can remember because 'port' has four letters and 'left' has four letters, and when you face the bow—the front—port is left. The back is the stern. This stick is the tiller, it's for steering, and you just push it opposite the way you want to go. The rudder is attached to the tiller underwater, and when you push the tiller left, it goes right, and vice versa, so we can steer. Try it."

Maria put her hand on the tiller. She was surprised by the force she felt pushing against it, and let go. Paolo quickly took it again.

"It felt weird, like it was going to jump out of my hand," she said.

"That's because of the force of the wind on the sail," Paolo explained. "The wind pushes the sail in one direction, but the centerboard, which is an underwater keel, keeps us from sliding sideways in that direction."

Maria nodded. She was already lost in all the new vocabulary.

"This is the boom." Paolo whacked a metal pole that ran along the bottom of the sail with his hand. "Remember 'boom,' because it hits you with a boom in the back of your head if you aren't paying attention when we come about. It goes from one side of the boat to the other like this."

For the next few minutes, Paolo demonstrated how he controlled the angle of the sail by moving the boom from side to side with ropes and pulleys—sheets, he called them. Every time he moved the sail, he moved the tiller, and the boat zigzagged back and forth across the bay.

"What we're doing is tacking," he explained. "You almost never have the wind directly at your back, so you have to tack back and forth to move forward toward your heading, which is the direction you want to go. Now, if you want to turn completely around, you jibe. You yell, 'Coming about,' so no one gets hit. That's when it's important to remember the boom and duck."

He completely loosed the sail, gave the boom a shove with one hand, and pulled the tiller all the way over with the other. "Coming about! Duck and come to port!"

Maria hesitated and he pushed her head down and pulled her over to the other side of the boat. As she slid across the bench, the sail swung completely across the deck and reached the end of its lines with a shuddering stop. Brutus raised his head and sniffed. The boat swung in a wide arc and suddenly they were facing in a completely new direction.

"You have to switch sides because our weight matters in a boat this small," Paolo explained. "See how we are tipping over? Even big boats heel because of the wind pushing on the sail. But on something larger, you don't need to switch sides."

As a gust of wind caught the sail, the boat heeled closer to the water, but Maria found that she wasn't scared by all the strange movements.

"It does feel like flying!" Maria said. "I thought it would and it does!"

"Here, put your hand on the tiller with mine and just try to get a feel for what I'm doing," Paolo said.

Maria put her hand near Paolo's so it wasn't quite touching his, but almost. The tiller vibrated under her palm like something alive and buzzing.

Paolo steered them out of Ironwall Bay. "You do realize there's no way you could have rowed out to those rocks. I mean, it's really far." He adjusted the tiller.

Her cheeks burned. "I know," she said, though she hadn't known at all.

Paolo pulled on the sheets and pushed on the tiller, and took them around a promontory to the neighboring cove. The mansions along the shore were mostly still shuttered, but here and there Maria could see signs of life. Housekeepers hung rugs over the porch railings of one large mansion, and next door a stable hand exercised a horse. Teams of gardeners pruned, clipped, and mowed this yard, while painters painted that house, and at one estate they sailed past, workers were setting up a large white party tent.

"Maybe we should go back. There are a lot more people out than I expected," Maria said.

"The summer people are coming, the summer people are coming!" Paolo said, as if he were Paul Revere announcing the British invasion. "Don't worry. The workers won't tattle. Most of them can't speak English anyhow."

"What do they speak?"

"Portuguese." He cupped his hands around his mouth and yelled, *"Olá! Bom dia!"*

"Bom dia!" a worker from the tent-raising crew called back.

"You speak Portuguese?" Maria asked.

"Not really. Just food and curse words, mostly," Paolo said. "It's kind of like Spanish. You speak Spanish?"

"No. I can read signs, and I know some words from kids at school." Maria looked out at the brilliant water.

"What's your mom?" Paolo asked. "I mean, it's just that she has a little accent."

"I'm supposed to lie and say it's French. Most people believe that. Anyhow, she did go to a convent school in Paris, before she met my dad and followed him to New York. But she was really born in Lebanon."

"You speak Lebanese?"

"Arabic, you mean. Not really. I was born here. And my mom wants me to be American, so she only speaks

English at home. The only time I ever hear her speak Arabic is at the grocery store or when she loses her temper. There really isn't anyone else for her to speak Arabic to anyway—my grandparents are still in Beirut and I'm never going to meet them."

"Why not?"

"'Cause they're always blowing each other up over there, my mom says." The wind caught her hair and whipped it across her face. Maria pulled it back and tied it in a loose knot. "But really it's because her family disowned her for getting pregnant with me."

"That's harsh," Paolo said. "I can't imagine not having my grandparents."

"It's okay. I mean, the lady in the grocery store was kind of like a grandma."

The sharp, sudden memory of Tante Farida caught Maria off guard. She wondered what Tante was doing now. Who visited her? Was she lonely? If you didn't have family, a big family like the Newcombs, you ended up alone.

She shook her head. "Is your whole family Portuguese?"

"No," Paolo said. "My dad was from Brazil. But everyone you met last night, my mom's side, is all longtime Island. So we always just spoke American. I just learned a little Portuguese from listening to my dad and the guys he worked with."

"You have a huge family," Maria said, "in that tiny house."

"Yeah. I guess. Back when my dad was alive though, it was just him, me, and Mom in our own house. I mean, we saw everyone at holidays and stuff, but we didn't live with them like we do now." Paolo looked away. "Let's tack. You do it this time. Loose this sheet and haul that one."

Maria did what Paolo said and miraculously the boat turned. "Do you miss your dad?" she asked.

"Yeah," Paolo looked back at her. "Do you miss yours?"

"I never knew him," Maria said. "He went back to Puerto Rico before I was born . . ."

He shrugged. "I guess you can't miss what you never had."

"I used to think that, too. It's weird, though. Since moving here, it's not that I actually *miss* having a family, it's just that I'm kind of *noticing* I don't have one . . ." Maria paused. "Mr. I tells these stories of growing up with his cousins, and you have all those people around . . ."

"Come on," Paolo said. "Grab the tiller. I want you to try to jibe."

They spent the next hour tacking back and forth,

working their way around the tip of the island. Maria loved the soaring feeling she got when the boat came around and the wind filled the sail.

On the eastern side of the island the wind came close to their back, so they could both take a break from the constant tacking. Paolo kept his foot on the tiller and his eye on the heading, and Maria lay back on the tiny deck. She was almost falling asleep when she heard the roar of a close engine. Brutus leaped to his feet, barking. A small powerboat whizzed by them, splashing spray, then circled back and cut the throttle.

"Attention!" A boy called from the boat. He stood straight and saluted. "It's Major Dirt!"

His friend next to him laughed.

"You can tell by the smell that he isn't washing well!" They chanted in a military cadence. "Sound off! One, two! Sound off! Three, four!"

Maria froze. She felt the same sick sinking in her stomach she'd had when the Barbies attacked. She glanced at Paolo. "Can we go?"

"Yeah." His eyes looked fierce, and he was pushing the tiller over to turn the boat around.

Maria adjusted the sheets. It was a small comfort. Even if their sail was ruined, at least she knew what to do with the lines. Slowly they began to move in the opposite direction, but they were going largely against the wind, and the powerboat puttered alongside easily.

As they made their way back toward the Ironwall Estate, the two boys jeered and hurled insults.

"Where'd you get that boat?" the taller and blonder boy said.

"Yeah, you steal it?"

"Looks an awful lot like a yacht club boat, doesn't it?"

"His mom certainly didn't buy it for him."

"She can't even buy him new clothes!"

"Yo, Major Dirt!"

Maria winced for Paolo. They ignored the boys as best they could and headed for the promontory. When they were nearly there, the boys in the powerboat turned away and roared off in a cloud of foul smoke. Maria felt tremendous relief now that Ironwall House was in sight.

"Who were those guys?" Maria asked.

"Taylor Bradford and his jerk friend." Paolo steered the boat toward the dock and let the sail down so that it slowed.

"Do you know them from school?" Maria asked.

"Taylor got me suspended for fighting. Twice." He jumped from the boat with the bowline in his hand and looped it around a cleat. "Throw me that line," he said.

She tossed the stern line. "I don't even know how to fight."

"Well then, aren't you little Miss Perfect?" He didn't look at her.

"No. That's not what I meant."

But Paolo kept looking down at the cleats. He finished securing the boat and whistled Brutus off. "You and Brutus go on without me. I'd better get this back before one of them says something."

"I'm sorry, Paolo," Maria tried again. "Those guys were real jerks."

"Yeah, I know." He packed the remains of their picnic breakfast into the bag and handed it to her, still without meeting her eye. "Sorry I couldn't get you where you wanted to go."

"Paolo—wait—"

But Paolo had already pulled the lines back aboard. He pushed the boat off the dock and pulled up the sail.

"I'm sorry—" Maria moved to the end of the dock trying to get him to look at her, but he steered away.

She walked slowly back to the Great House with Brutus, kicking sand and chucking shells. She felt terrible. She hadn't helped Paolo at all, and he probably was getting in trouble right now for helping her.

21

HIGH AND DRY

"'THE BLANK SPOT,' FIVE LETTERS," MARIA WAS saying a short while later. She sat beside Mr. Ironwall on his huge bed, the *New York Times* crossword puzzle spread on the blankets between them. Brutus, still damp and sandy, had been relegated to a towel on the floor.

"Your heart is not in this," Mr. Ironwall said. "What is distracting you?"

Maria couldn't tell him about sailing or the horrible boys who may have been, at that very moment, turning Paolo in for a thief. She struggled for something relevant to say.

"I went to the library and looked up privateers," Maria finally said.

"And?" Mr. Ironwall raised his brow.

"And I found out that a privateer is like a legal pirate," Maria said. "And Captain Murdefer was an ancestor of yours, wasn't he?"

Mr. Ironwall's eyes widened. "And how did you discover that particular skeleton in my closet?"

"Well, Murdefer is actually *mur de fer*, which means 'wall of iron' in French," Maria said. "So someone in your family changed the name. Probably to hide the fact that you all are descended from pirates."

"Aha, you're a regular Sam Spade."

"Who?"

"Famous detective? Dashiell Hammett wrote the novels, Edward G. Robinson did the radio shows. Humphrey Bogart, *The Maltese Falcon*; any of this ringing a bell?"

"I've heard of Humphrey Bogart."

"Thank heavens for small blessings. I was about to give up on you entirely." Mr. Ironwall took a deep breath. "So now that you know my bloody ancestry, I suppose you won't respect the great name of Ironwall anymore." He put his hand dramatically across his eyes, as if he were too ashamed to look at her.

Maria could tell he was kidding. "I just think it's exciting. Do you know any stories about him?"

"Stories about him? Legends, I should say." Mr. Ironwall furrowed his brow. "He was a blackguard. A thoroughly unprincipled person. They say he betrayed more than a few governments, and spent time in many a jail. He fought on both sides of the war on both sides of the ocean—he was a gun for hire who changed his loyalties as frequently as he changed his striped socks. It was only the love of a fine Island maiden that made him settle down here on Island soil. He moved into her homestead—the cottage where you are now—and set about having little Murdefers. Somewhere along the line we Americanized the name."

"So did he get actual treasure?" Maria bounced with excitement. "Is that why you're so rich?"

"Hasn't your mother ever told you that discussing other people's money is rude?"

"I'm sure she would have," Maria said. "But we never knew anyone with money before."

"So let us change the subject." He folded his hands like a prim old lady. "How was the party at the Newcombs'? It must have been delightful. Ella was my favorite cook—don't tell Hattie. Her clam chowder was ambrosia."

"Mrs. Newcomb is still a good cook," Maria said. "We had oysters, which I thought I'd hate, but I kind of liked." That reminded Maria of the previous night's conversation. "The Newcombs told me about *your* parties. They sound like they were wild."

"I have never been 'wild' in my life." Mr. Ironwall looked away as if he were insulted. "I have always been the epitome of decorum."

"I don't even know what that means." Maria laughed. "Okay, your parties weren't wild, but they sound like they were fabulous. Pops said you once put pearls in all the oysters!"

"He exaggerates. I put a few pearls in a few oysters . . . maybe three at the most." The corner of his mouth twitched. Maria supposed that was as close as he ever got to a smile. "But I did throw fabulous parties once upon a time."

"Where did you get the pearls?" Maria said. "Were they leftovers from Captain Murdefer?"

He tapped his finger on the side of his nose. "My secret."

"Where are they now? Your pearls, I mean."

He waved his hand. "Somewhere. I don't know. Doesn't matter."

"Of course it matters!" she said. "You *have* to know where they are."

"Why? They're just round white oyster spit."

"Well." She thought for a moment. What Grandma had said while clearing the dishes came back to her. "It matters to your family. They might want them someday."

"I have no family."

"So what about all this?" Maria swept her hand through the air. "The mansion? The estate? The cottage?"

"When I shuffle off this mortal coil, the estate and all it holds can fall into the sea for all I care. I am the end of the great Murdefer line!" Mr. Ironwall closed his eyes for such a long time Maria thought he'd fallen asleep. She looked around for her mother, but Celeste had taken Maria's visit as a chance for a coffee break with Hattie. Then the old man opened one eye.

"You're still here," he said.

"Of course I am," Maria said. "You can't just say let it all fall into the sea! Think of all the people you'd be leaving high and dry. Frank, Hattie, my mom, me . . ."

"Ah." Mr. Ironwall opened his other eye. "Now we get to the real point. Selfish girl."

"No!" Maria protested. "It's not just about us. It's that you don't realize how lucky you are. How beautiful this place is! How can you not love it? I love the cottage, and the beach, and—" She almost said *the boat*, but stopped herself.

"Perhaps I would feel as you do if I ever ventured from this room. But I never do, and so I don't care about much beyond these four walls. I've become a self-centered, whiny old curmudgeon."

"I don't believe you're a whiny old whatever you said," Maria told him.

"We really must work on your vocabulary," Mr. Ironwall said. "I shall give your mother some useful literature to further your education. At any rate, I will turn to dust in this very bed without having enjoyed for decades the splendors you enumerate." He waved vaguely about, as if to indicate all the splendors outside the room.

"Then get out of bed!" Maria said. "My mom said some people can get better if they really want to. If they try."

"I can't. I'm too old." He stuck out his lower lip like a petulant toddler.

"That's ridiculous. You don't have to give up just because you're old."

"But I am also sick. And tired. And alone and waiting to die."

"That's a horrible thing to say," Maria said.

"But it is true. I have no children, no family, and there is nothing that distinguishes one day from the next. I have become one of those parasitic old people who can't even go to the toilet themselves. There!" He pointed at Maria. "Now I've shocked you. But it's true."

"It doesn't have to be like that," Maria said. "You can still have parties. You can have a Fourth of July party. That's the next holiday coming up. I'm sure it would be fun."

"What am I going to do? Invite all the people I know for fireworks and a backyard barbecue?"

"Why not?"

"Because I've outlived them all!" Mr. Ironwall frowned.

Maria frowned back. "Well, I want to celebrate the Fourth this year, even if you don't."

"You don't need me to throw you a party," Mr. Ironwall said. "Just go into town. You can have it all: parade, fireworks—a real all-American extravaganza."

At that moment Celeste walked into the room with a tray covered with paper cups of pills and a small dish of applesauce. "Enough, Maria. You can continue your conversation on another day. Now it's time for Mr. Ironwall's meds. And we are doing those range-of-motion exercises whether you like it or not, Mr. I. 'Use it or lose it,' as Dr. Singh says."

"Yes, sir, ma'am sir." Mr. Ironwall saluted Celeste as if she were a general in the army. To Maria he said, "Do you see how your mother bosses me around?"

* * *

Maria spent the rest of the afternoon in her attic, half-heartedly working on a jigsaw puzzle of cartoon cats. But her mind kept drifting back to the disturbing conversation she'd had with Mr. Ironwall. Sometimes, she couldn't tell if he was kidding or not. He said the saddest things as if he were making a joke. But it wasn't funny.

Though she was no closer to getting a boat, at least she could try to decipher the cryptic message at the bottom of the treasure map:

> *Twice twice two,*
> *Then twice that more.*
> *Take one from the first,*
> *The Queen treads upon the door.*

She rolled over on her back and stared at the sloping ceiling. The strange carvings on the beams held no clues either. *JM 1689, 1230, FH 1718, SI 1812.* So many people had lived here and left their marks down through the years. And now Mr. Ironwall was the end of the line, waiting to leave them all high and dry.

* * *

The door downstairs slammed and Maria startled awake from a nap. Of course, it was nearly five-thirty—her mother was coming home. She slid the charts under her bed.

"*Chérie?* You up there?" Celeste called from the bottom of the stairs.

"Yeah, Mama. I was just doing a puzzle." Maria started down. Her mother was already pulling off her scrubs and heading for the bathroom.

"Could you start the stove? I need to take a shower—I'm going out to dinner with Frank. He's taking me to that fried fish place. He wouldn't take no for an answer. Do you mind? Hattie sent me over with food for you—maybe I shouldn't go."

"No, you should go. Really."

"I hate leaving you alone all evening after you've already been alone all day."

"I'll be fine, Mama." Maria twisted up paper and loaded some kindling and a few logs into the woodstove, and lit it all with a long match. "It'll be a few minutes before the water heats up. I haven't had a fire today."

"Did Hattie tell you about Paolo?" Celeste called back. "Frank said he got caught stealing a boat from the yacht club."

An icy knot twisted in Maria's stomach.

Celeste popped her head out of the bathroom. "He

sailed it up to the yacht club around lunchtime today—
in full view of the security guard and everything—as if
he wasn't doing anything wrong."

"At least he brought it back . . ."

"But still, *chérie*." Celeste shook her head in disbelief.
"That poor Hattie."

Obviously Paolo hadn't told on her, or her mother
would be mad at her right now. He had said he wasn't
going to tell and he didn't.

"He's not a bad kid, Mama," Maria said. "He's just a
little confused. You know, because of his dad."

"That excuse is only good for so long. You grew up
without a father and I don't see you going all crazy."
She disappeared into the bathroom. "Water's probably
hot enough."

Maria listened to her mother's shower water. The tinfoil packages of food that Hattie had sent sat on the
kitchen counter. They smelled good, but Maria wasn't
hungry. It didn't feel like dinnertime yet. These were
the longest days of the year. It would be hours before it
was dark—she wondered if her mother would be back in
time to tuck her in. She'd kind of gotten used to it.
Celeste and her reading together, or playing cards or a
board game, then her mother climbing up the winding
stairs to make sure she was comfortable and safe.

She thought about Paolo and how miserable he must be right now. She wondered which bedroom was his—the books one, or the African violets? Did anyone tuck him in when he was in trouble? Or was he too old anyhow?

The shower turned off and Celeste stepped from the bathroom in a terry cloth robe, comb in hand.

"You look like you maybe just lost your best friend," Celeste said.

"No, it's just . . ." Maria poked at the fire. She couldn't talk to her about Paolo or the treasure map. Suddenly it seemed there were so many things she couldn't talk to her mother about.

"What is it?"

"I don't know," Maria said. "It's just—do you think Mr. Ironwall is going to die?"

"But of course," Celeste answered. "Everyone dies."

"No, I mean soon."

Now Celeste stopped combing and stood still. "Well, he's very old. And he's had a stroke."

"But what will happen to us?" Maria hung the poker up. "When he dies you won't have a job anymore. We'll be left high and dry."

"High and dry? Where did you hear that expression?"

"You know. What Hattie said last night—"

Celeste put the comb in her pocket and sat on the couch near Maria's feet. "Is that what is bothering you? Don't worry, *chérie*, I can always find a job. People always need experienced nurses."

"Here, though? On this island?"

"If not here, somewhere else." Celeste took hold of Maria's ankles and gave them a squeeze. "Come. Let us see what Hattie cooked for you."

Maria didn't move. "I don't want to go somewhere else. I like it here."

Celeste patted her knee and stood up. "I'm glad you like it here. I like it here, too. But I don't want to make you any promises I can't keep. If Mr. Ironwall were to die, we maybe could go back to the city and stay with Tante Farida until we got back on our feet. She said we could if things didn't work out." She laid a plate and silverware on the table.

"Why would we have to stay with her? She's not even related to us."

Celeste sighed. "Maria, you know we don't have family we can go to."

Maria shuffled over to the kitchen table. "I'd rather be homeless here than move back with Tante Farida."

"Well, we don't always get what we want. And we are very lucky to be in this place right now. And perhaps we'll be lucky enough to be here a good long time." Celeste put the tinfoil packages on the table. "But I can't promise we will stay here forever. That would just be unrealistic."

"I hate being realistic." Maria opened the first package. Fried chicken again. It was still warm.

"Being realistic is part of growing up. My apologies, but we all have to do it sometime." Celeste looked at the clock. "Frank will be here any minute."

After her mother left, Maria carried her dinner over to the sofa. Fried chicken, biscuits, sweet potatoes, and greens. It smelled lovely. But she kept thinking about what her mother had said.

She wished Brutus were here, or even Paolo. She really didn't want to be alone after all. But Frank had finally gotten her mom to say yes to a dinner. Her mother never went on dates. And she'd actually looked happy, getting ready for it. Maria stared into the dying fire. She was thinking of Celeste combing her hair, smiling into the mirror, getting ready for a date with Frank.

A date.

Something sparked in Maria's brain. She put the plate down and raced up to the attic. With shaking hands she took the chart from under her bed and unrolled it.

Twice twice two,
Then twice that more . . .

It was a date. One was a day and one was a month. Two times two times two equaled eight, and twice that more was sixteen. Maria scribbled the math on a scrap of paper. Eight came first, so it must mean eight, then sixteen. But take one from the first, so the first number was actually seven. The seventh month was July. July 16. On July 16 the Queen would tread upon the door. And probably only on that date. If she didn't figure it out by then, she'd have to wait a whole year more. It was nearly July! How little time she had! She needed a boat before July 16. She needed a plan. She needed help.

22

Help from Major Dirt

THAT MONDAY, HATTIE MENTIONED THAT Paolo was finishing his last final exam. As soon as she was able to get away, Maria biked over to the school. She hid behind the bus kiosk and peered at the quiet building. She worried that she'd already missed him. But after a few minutes' wait, a bell rang and kids poured through the double doors.

She hadn't really planned it well. Paolo didn't know she would be there, and he wouldn't be looking for her. She wasn't sure she could find him in the enormous and chaotic crowd. Then, as the last stragglers exited, his familiar shape appeared in the door. He headed for the bike path, his skateboard in hand. Maria pedaled over to him.

"What are you doing here?" he asked. He didn't sound exactly pleased to see her.

"I wanted to say thank you for not telling on me."

"No worries." He took a few running steps and dropped his skateboard, then hopped on it and skated away from her as if their conversation were done.

Maria pedaled after him. When she caught up she said, "I hope you didn't get into too much trouble."

"Not too much." He coasted without looking at her. "Just if I ever borrow a boat from the yacht club again, I'm going to juvie. The only reason they didn't haul me off right then and there is Pops is an old fishing buddy of the security guard."

"I'm sorry," she said. He still didn't stop.

"Yeah, and the only reason I'm not in lockdown at home is today was my last final. But Pops has me doing crazy chores. He says I have to learn responsibility. And I'm going to have to go fishing with my uncle Harry, too. Because I obviously want to go messing around in boats, Pops said." He made a face that showed he clearly did not want to fish with his uncle.

"I'm so sorry." She pedaled alongside him. "Is there anything I can do? What if I said it was my idea?"

"No one would believe you," he said. "And anyhow, it

wasn't." He stopped and kicked his board up into his hand. "Besides, I've got other, worse problems."

"What?"

He looked down. "I failed English and nearly failed Social Studies. I got a C minus in Science. The only A I got was Math. I'll have to go to summer school or get left back."

"Do they even have summer school here?" Maria asked.

"I'm supposed to do it online. They gave me textbooks and stuff, but I have to log on for assignments and tests, which totally sucks 'cause we don't even have a computer."

Maria felt terrible for him. School had always come so easily for her.

"It probably won't be so bad the second time around," she said. "You probably already know most of it and maybe just need to try harder. I'm sure it's just because, you know, your . . ." She was going to say *dad died*, but stopped herself. ". . . because you've been distracted and stressed out, you know, with things. I bet you're really smart. And I could help you. We could use the computers at the library. I know how."

A group of walking girls caught up with them and passed by. Two of the girls turned and looked back at them, whispered, and giggled. Maria couldn't help but think they were making fun of her and Paolo in some way.

He didn't say anything for a moment. Finally he looked up. "Yeah, well, what do you want in return?"

Maria suddenly felt awkward and didn't know where to look, so she focused on her feet. "It turns out I still do need your help. Getting to those islands."

He didn't say anything. She looked up and saw he was staring at her, waiting. She met his eyes. "I was a jerk about it before," she said. "Sorry."

"Okay, but now you have to tell me why you want to go to the islands. I won't do it unless you make me a full partner. No secrets."

"Okay. No secrets. Promise." Maria pulled her bike off the path. "Come here and I'll show you."

She slid Captain Murdefer's map from her backpack and unrolled it carefully.

He stood beside her, close enough for her to feel his breath on her cheek.

"I don't think it's real, do you?" She tried to sound dismissive, in case he thought she was crazy.

"I don't know." He touched the paper lightly. "Where'd you find it?"

Maria told him about the attic in the cottage, how

the map was hidden in the insulation behind a carved eave, and what she'd found out about Mr. Ironwall's privateering ancestor.

"I've heard of Captain Murdefer," Paolo said. "Everyone has."

"I never heard of him before I moved here. It's not like he was totally famous—like Blackbeard or something," Maria said.

"Well, all *Islanders* have heard of him," Paolo said. "Mr. Ironwall made a big movie about him in the 1950s."

"The Last Privateer," Maria said. "Like the boat."

"Yeah. A lot of the movie was filmed here. There even used to be a theme restaurant in town with pictures from the movie." Paolo paused. "But it would be nuts if the story was true, and this was really his treasure map."

"Yeah, well, maybe I'm nuts," Maria said.

A shadow fell across the treasure map. Maria looked up and saw two boys standing on either side of them.

"What do you have there?" The taller boy snatched the map from Paolo's hand. Maria recognized him from the motorboat. Taylor Bradford.

"Oooh! Major Dirt has a map! Is it a treasure map?

Does X mark the spot?" This came from the shorter friend.

"Maybe we should call you Captain Dirt!" Taylor said. "Ya be searchin' fer pirate gold, me hearty?"

"Aargh!" The friend squinted and danced a hornpipe.

Taylor tossed the map to his friend, who caught it easily, one-handed.

"Give it back," Paolo said. "It's not mine. It belongs to her."

"Is that your girlfriend?" The friend tossed the map back to Taylor. "She isn't very pretty."

Taylor had a long reach, and he easily kept the map from Paolo. "Though I suppose that's the best you can do, dirty monkey like you. Jump, monkey. Jump for your map."

Maria was relieved to see that Paolo did not jump. He just waited. He was watching someone approaching on the bike path. Maria figured he was a teacher, with his tie and the fancy bicycle clips holding his chino cuffs away from the greasy chain.

The man stopped his bicycle. "What's going on here, Mr. Silva? Fighting again?"

"No, Mr. Smith," Paolo said.

"That paper belongs to me," Maria said, pointing to

the map. "They took it and Paolo was trying to get it back."

"Is this true, Mr. Bradford?" Mr. Smith turned to Taylor.

"We were just playing." Taylor handed the map back to Maria.

"Well, I suggest you move along now," Mr. Smith said. "Enjoy your summer, boys."

"Yes, sir," Taylor said.

Paolo didn't say anything. He dropped his skateboard on the path and pushed off. Maria stuffed the map into her bag and pedaled after him. The troublemakers, without wheels, couldn't keep up. Maria and Paolo went as fast as they could until they reached the Ironwall Estate.

"So you think it's a real treasure map and you want me to help you get a boat," Paolo said, walking now with his skateboard under his arm. He kept his eyes on the clamshell drive.

"Yeah," Maria said. "For a cut, of course." If he didn't want to talk about Taylor Bradford, then she wasn't going to bring him up.

"We can't use a yacht club boat again," Paolo said. "And it's too far to row."

"We do have another boat . . ." Maria said.

Finally Paolo raised his head. "Last time I went on it you threatened to beat me with an oar."

"Well, I won't hit you if you're my crew," Maria said. "But do you think we could really sail it? I mean, it's so big."

Paolo shrugged. "It's a pretty simple setup—we could just use the foresail, mainsail, and maybe staysail."

Maria had no idea what he was talking about, but he seemed to know a lot.

"Skip the gaff topsail, the fisherman—"

"But it doesn't have sails," Maria said. Then she remembered the big canvas bundles in the Old West Shed. "No, wait, it does. I know where they are. I don't know which ones are which, or what shape they're in, and I don't know how to put them up."

"I know how to rig—I told you, my dad had a sailboat. I used to help him with it all the time."

"The sails are in the shed. It's always locked, but your uncle has the key. Can you get it from him?"

"Are you kidding? He doesn't trust me as far as he can throw me." Paolo kicked a large shell.

"His keys are always in his jacket pocket," Maria said. "Maybe you can *borrow* them without him knowing."

"Maybe you can," Paolo said. "I'm sick of getting busted."

"Maybe it's unlocked." Maria grabbed him by the sleeve. "Let's at least check it out!" They ditched her bike and his board at the cottage and ran to the shed.

But of course the shed was locked. They both stood, hands cupped to their faces, noses pressed to the glass, staring at the unreachable sails.

"Anyhow, wouldn't Frank notice if the sails weren't in the shed?" Paolo said. "And wouldn't he notice if the boat suddenly had sails?"

They fell silent again.

"Maybe we could just drive it with the engine?" Maria suggested. "I found the key." She rummaged in her bag and brought it out. The silver skull and crossbones glinted in the afternoon sun.

"We should see if the engine even works," Paolo said. "Let's go now. I'm in no hurry to show my mom my report card."

* * *

When they entered the cabin, Paolo whistled.

"I cleaned it up," Maria said.

Paolo nodded appreciatively. "You want to try the engine?" He headed for the control panels under the companionway.

"You do it," Maria said, following. "I'm too scared."

Paolo tried to slip the key in the ignition, but it didn't fit.

"That's weird," she said. "It was the only key in here. I cleaned everywhere."

"Maybe it goes to a lock in the house or something. Anyway"—he tapped a gauge—"see this? There's no fuel. We'll have to sail."

"Then we'll have to find a way to get the sails," Maria said.

"That'll be impossible," Paolo said. "Frank never lets those keys out of his sight."

"Well, we have a *little* time," Maria said. "We don't have to leave until July sixteenth."

"What?" Paolo asked. "Why?"

Maria took the map out of her backpack and spread it on the table. She pointed to the note at the bottom.

"'Twice twice two, then twice that more . . .'" Paolo began.

"That's a date, see? July sixteenth." Maria took a pencil from her backpack and showed him the math. "But I don't know what the rest means. About the Queen treading on the door. I mean, I know treading is like walking, so we're talking about something with feet . . ."

Paolo stared into space. "Maybe the modern chart will help. Put them next to each other."

Maria laid the charts side by side.

Paolo traced his finger on the map. "These little islands"—he pointed to the three islands with the X off the northeast coast—"they're all part of a nature preserve. For birds and seals. Which is a good thing, because there hasn't been any building, so no one would have dug the treasure up accidentally, digging a cellar or something."

"Oh," Maria said. She was amazed at how much he knew, and how silly she'd been, trying to figure it out herself. "But how do we know which is the right island? The X kind of covers all three."

"Something will point to it on that date. Something that has to do with a queen." Paolo lay back on one of the bunks. "It's from a pirate's point of view. From a boat. What looks like a queen?"

"Maybe it's a special rock," Maria suggested.

"But a rock is always there. So why would it have to be seen on that particular date?" Paolo sighed. "What changes by the date?"

"The moon?" Maria said.

"The moon," Paolo said. "That's good."

"But what do queens have to do with the moon?"

Maria said. "I always thought it was a man in the moon, or green cheese."

"Maybe a planet?" Paolo suggested.

Maria thought about it. "The planets were named after Greek or Roman gods. But all I know is Mars is for a god of war and Venus is for love. I'd have to look up the others."

Paolo thought some more. "Venus is visible in the summer. Was she a queen?"

"Not really," Maria said. "And anyway, how does a planet tread? They're round. Nothing sticking out like feet."

"You're right. A planet doesn't tread. It orbits or rotates or something."

"What else is in the sky?" Maria said. "Clouds, the sun, stars."

"Stars!" Paolo sat up. "Stars make constellations! Constellations are pictures of things like people or animals . . . they could tread. Like Orion—you can see his shoulders and his belt and his sword. So he would have feet if the constellation had more stars."

Maria smiled. "So on that date, maybe a constellation of a queen will line up with the right spot, and that's where we dig!"

"What constellation is a queen?" Paolo asked.

"You're asking the wrong girl," Maria said. "I don't know anything about constellations. You couldn't even see stars in the city."

"Well, that's what you're going to have to figure out while I'm doing summer school work," Paolo said. "You said you know how to use the library computers."

"But figuring out the queen won't do us any good if we can't get those sails," Maria said.

"Okay, so whoever has the first chance to steal the key from Frank's pocket, takes it. Agreed?" Paolo stuck out his hand.

Maria had never stolen anything in her life before the rowboat. Now she was an accomplice to the theft of the yacht club sailboat and was signing up to pick Frank's pocket.

"Come on, Maria. You can't expect to get pirate treasure without being a bit of a pirate yourself," Paolo said.

"Okay," Maria said. "But that's the last thing we steal."

"Except this boat," Paolo reminded her.

"Except this boat." She stuck out her hand and shook.

23

ONWARD . . . ONWARD!

THE NEXT MORNING, MARIA WOKE UP EXPECT-
ing to see Paolo down at *The Last Privateer*, key in hand.
She walked Brutus to the beach and played fetch the ball
for as long as he would stand it. But Paolo never showed.

Maria didn't go onto the boat. It felt a bit lonely
without Paolo. Which was strange, because when she'd
lived in the city and had no friends, she'd rarely felt
lonely. Or at least she'd never noticed she was lonely.

Mr. Ironwall pretended to be cranky about her coming back from the dog walk so late, but in fact her later
arrival was better for him. He was more awake and already cleaned up and ready for company. Maria tried to
bring him something every time she visited. Today she
had a purplish shell, a blue flower whose name she did

not know, and a strange object that looked like soft vertebrae on a spindly spine.

"Ordinary clam—the Wampanoag made wampum from them—cornflower, and a whelk's egg case." One by one he identified her offerings and had her line them up on the windowsill beside his bed.

"You know a lot about nature and stuff," she said.

"Not really," Mr. Ironwall said. "I've just been alive for a long time and one picks things up."

"Do you know about outer space? Like stars and planets?" she asked.

"A little. Why?"

"Well, for instance, do you know if there is something with a queen? Like a star, or a planet, or maybe a constellation?"

"What makes you ask about the Queen?" He looked at her through narrowed eyes, as if he were trying to figure something out. "That's a rather obscure way to refer to Cassiopeia."

"I don't know; just something I heard someone say." She got up quickly and opened the window so she would not have to face him. Mr. Ironwall sounded suspicious. Perhaps, as Paolo said, all Islanders knew about Captain Murdefer—and maybe some, like Mr. Ironwall, knew about the message on his map. After all, he was

214

his great-great- (no one knew how many greats) grandson. She would have to be more careful not to give too much away.

"Smell the beach roses!" she said to change the subject. "They're blooming all over the dunes. I could bring you a bouquet."

"No, leave them for the bees," he said. "But I'll take some hydrangeas."

"You should come outside," Maria said. "You can see the roses from the back patio. It's so sunny and lovely out."

"Perhaps tomorrow."

"How are we going to get you to the Fourth of July celebration if we can't get you out the door?" Maria said.

"You have a point. And perhaps I should see it one more time before I die," he said. "Or at the very least, the town should see me. After all, rumors of my demise have been greatly exaggerated." He gestured to the newspaper on his nightstand. "Now read to me about the festivities they are planning."

But after she read the newspaper to him for a few minutes, she looked over and saw that he'd fallen asleep. She sat with him until her mother returned.

* * *

After lunch, Maria hunted the grounds for Frank. She found him in the garage, cleaning the mower. His jacket was slung across the tool bench; the keys to the Old West Shed bulged in the right breast pocket. She did not have the courage to pick his pocket with him right there.

"Whatcha up to?" he asked her.

"I was just wondering if there was a way to get Mr. Ironwall out of the house. You know, like I could take him around the yard in his wheelchair or something?"

"That would be really nice, Maria." Frank wiped his oily hands on a rag. "But I'm not sure he's up for it."

"Maybe he could become up for it. If we took it slow."

"I'll talk to your mother and Joanne. See what they think."

"Okay. Thanks." She cast one more look at the jacket, but there was still no way to reach the keys without him seeing.

She swung past the shed, and it was locked as usual. The sails, two white bundles in the back, sat on the other side of that locked door.

Maria spent the rest of the day in a comfortable notch she'd discovered in the beetlebung tree, reading *True Pyrate Tales*. Black Sam Bellamy captained the

Whydah, which sank off the Cape with the largest treasure ever found in modern history. Edward Teach, also known as Blackbeard, terrorized New England. Apparently he buried a large treasure off the coast of New Hampshire—not too far away. It was never found. Maybe if they couldn't find Captain Murdefer's treasure, they could go for Blackbeard's. But she didn't have Blackbeard's treasure map.

Maria laid the book in her lap and looked over the golden lawn. It was definitely summer now. June was nearly done, and soon it would be the Fourth of July—and then July 16, when the Queen would tread upon the door. At least now she knew who the Queen was—Cassy O'Pee-a.

Maria climbed down and headed for home. The late afternoon sun baked the beach roses and spread their scent throughout the estate grounds. Butterflies fluttered in the milkweed and honeysuckle. When she let herself into the cool, shady cottage, Celeste was already in the kitchen, chopping onions. The smell of freshly baking pita filled the small house and made Maria's stomach rumble. She hadn't realized it was so late, but her mother didn't question where she'd been.

She took glasses down from the cabinet over her mother's head.

"What are we eating? Do we need bowls or plates?" Maria asked.

"Tonight, we have a *meze* with *hummus*, *tabbouleh*, and *mujadarah*." Celeste exaggerated the rolled *r* and smiled triumphantly. "So, plates."

"Yay!" Maria did a little dance. Tante Farida had sent a big box of Lebanese food: real Turkish coffee and cardamom pods to flavor it, brown lentils, red lentils, bulgur, *za'atar*, *halwa*, *halloum*, and a bunch of other things they couldn't find on the island.

"How'd you get Hattie to let you cook?"

"I told her you'd requested your favorite dish. Actually, I think Hattie was insulted."

"Uh-oh." Maria put the glasses on the table and went for plates.

Celeste stopped chopping. "Maria, we have to talk about something."

"What?" Maria set the plates on the table and went back for silverware.

"I want you to stop bugging Mr. Ironwall about the Fourth of July," Celeste said.

"I'm not bugging him. He wants to go."

"He doesn't. He just wants to make you happy."

"Why would he want to make me happy?" Maria said.

"He likes you. You talk to him. You're probably the

only person in the whole house who isn't paid to, and you still do it. It's very kind of you, Maria. Don't think I haven't noticed."

"Well then, let him come with us!"

Celeste shook her head. "Frank says he hasn't gone out in years. I can't even imagine how we would get him out of that room, much less into town."

"We could anchor his wheelchair in the back of Frank's truck. I could ride in back with him."

"And what if, heaven forbid, he gets hurt?" Celeste asked.

"And what if he insists on going?" Maria answered. "He's your boss. You have to do what he says."

"We'll see." Her mother dumped the onions in a frying pan. "Now move your *taztouz* and stir these onions. It's about time you learned how to make this."

* * *

Paolo wasn't on the beach or the boat the next morning either. After taking Brutus for an extended walk, Maria delayed as long as she could before she headed over to Mr. Ironwall's room.

To her surprise, she found Celeste and Frank struggling to get Mr. Ironwall from the bed to his wheelchair. Maria joined Hattie, who stood in the corner, worriedly watching. The old man dangled midair in the canvas seat of the Hoyer Lift. But the transfer wasn't going well. Mr. Ironwall had turned an odd shade of green. He vomited violently into a pink plastic basin held to his face by Celeste, while Frank wrangled the wheelchair in the narrow space allowed by the bed. Sweat beaded Frank's red face. Maria noticed his sleeves were rolled up and his jacket was nowhere in sight.

"Don't worry, child. It happens when we get him out of bed," Hattie whispered, jutting her chin at Mr. Ironwall. "Before your mom came, I once helped Joanne get him up. He had to see a doctor off-island. He puked up a storm. All that movement—he's not used to it. It's kind of like he gets seasick."

Frank said, "We've got to get him back to the bed."

"No!" Mr. Ironwall shouted. "I've gotten this far. It can't get any worse!" He paused to retch into the basin. "Oh, just lower me already."

Celeste lowered him into the wheelchair. After a few moments of shifting him about and cleaning him up, she said, "There, that wasn't so bad!"

"That was a train wreck," Mr. Ironwall said. He rinsed with some mouthwash Celeste offered and spit in the basin one more time. "But it is done. Wheel me out," he ordered Frank.

Frank pushed the chair and Mr. Ironwall down another hall Maria had never noticed, to an ornate elevator. It announced its arrival with a "ding," just as if it were in an apartment building. They all crowded in and dutifully faced front.

"Well, isn't this cozy," Mr. Ironwall said.

Frank turned a key and the door shut. Soft, wordless music came from a speaker in the corner.

Maria looked down at Mr. Ironwall smiling in his chair. He looked up at her. "'Girl from Ipanema,'" he said. "I thought it would be funny to have an elevator that played elevator music in my own home."

"It kind of is," she agreed.

Ten minutes later, when he and his chair were parked on the back patio and Maria was seated beside him, Mr. Ironwall took her hand and patted it. "Don't worry, I have nothing left to lose. I am completely empty inside."

"Why were you so sick?" Maria asked.

"Orthostatic hypotension," Celeste answered for him. She placed a shawl around his shoulders, despite the hot sun.

Mr. Ironwall waved his hand dismissively. "A fancy way of saying if you lie down too long, you can't get back up. Let that be a lesson to you." Mr. Ironwall fixed a steely eye on Maria. "Pursue your dreams! Your destiny! Onward . . . Onward!" He lifted his fist as if he were urging his wheelchair into battle.

"Are you okay?" Celeste asked him.

"Yes. Now go inside and gossip with Hattie. Your daughter and I have gossip of our own and we don't need nosy parkers listening in."

After a few backward glances, Celeste left them.

"I didn't realize it would be so difficult . . ." Maria began.

"Before you start to worry"—Mr. Ironwall held up a belaying hand—"rest assured. The good Dr. Singh told your mother she is to get me out of bed and into the chair every day. We spoke to him this morning. Best thing to prevent blood clots and further strokes." He closed his eyes and took a deep breath. "The air is lovely out here. You were absolutely correct. Now read me that paper."

Maria opened the *Vineyard Gazette* and read him a story about a proposed roundabout at some contentious crossroads. By the time she got to an article on hidden beach plum trees, he had fallen asleep.

She put the paper down and gazed out over the roses to the ocean beyond. Because of the swell of the hill, the beach and the dock were hidden, but the masts of *The*

Last Privateer showed over the scrub. If she hadn't known it was there, she might have mistaken it for two very tall, very bare tree trunks.

Maria closed her eyes and turned her face toward the sun.

Then she heard a hiss and opened her eyes—Paolo was peeking over the stone balustrade of the patio.

"I got them," he whispered. Frank's keys flashed in his hand. Suddenly, he ducked. Celeste was coming.

"He fell asleep again," Maria said to her mother. She was careful not to look where Paolo was hiding.

"I hate to wake him," Celeste said. "But I should take him inside before he gets too much sun." She frowned. "Anyhow, the doctor says it's good for him, even though it's difficult. Though perhaps it will get better as he gets used to it."

"Do you want me to help?" Maria asked.

"No. I can call Hattie or Frank in. Frank got us walkie-talkies." Celeste swung her hip so Maria could see the black box clipped to her waistband. "You go find something fun to do. I'll see you tonight."

As soon as Celeste and Mr. Ironwall had gone, Maria jumped over the wall.

"Where have you been?" she asked Paolo. "I thought you wanted to help me!"

He flinched as if he expected her to swat him. When she didn't, he relaxed. "I was grounded."

"For what?"

"Failing. But it's okay. I got Pops to understand that I can't pass if he doesn't let me out of the house. So I can help now, as long as we go to the library, too. But look—" He held up the keys proudly.

"You really did get them!" Maria swatted his shoulder now. "You are such a pirate!"

"I just borrow things!" Paolo protested. "I always return them!"

As they headed to the Old West Shed, Maria filled Paolo in on the constellation.

"Cassy O'Pee-a sounds like an Irish girl who can't make it to the toilet in time," Paolo said.

"I'm not sure how it's spelled," Maria said.

"I don't know either," Paolo said. "But I do know it's shaped like a W. One of the lines must be her legs and feet."

"How do you know about it?" Maria asked.

"I don't know much—like I didn't know she was a queen. But it's one of the easy ones, like the Big Dipper. My dad showed me."

Paolo stopped talking as they reached the shed.

Frank was nowhere to be seen, Hattie was in the kitchen, and Celeste would be busy till evening. The coast was clear.

They had to try five keys before the padlock opened. Maria ran inside and tried to lift the smaller sail bag.

"How are we going to get them to the boat? They're so heavy," she said.

Paolo turned the bundle over. "We need wheels."

"Like the golf cart?" Maria said.

His eyes lit up. "Like the golf cart."

They found the golf cart behind the old greenhouse, plugged into a recharging cord.

"And we have the key." Paolo dangled Frank's big key ring from his finger.

"What if Frank comes back and finds the cart missing?" Maria asked. "What if he sees us driving it?"

"Onward . . . Onward!" Paolo said, with a grin.

"Were you eavesdropping on me and Mr. Ironwall?" Maria said. "I'm sure this isn't what he meant."

But Paolo had already pulled the cord out and turned on the ignition switch, so Maria hopped in beside him.

Paolo hit the gas pedal and they lurched away. They bounced hard over tree roots and rocks, and Maria's head hit the roof a few times.

"Do you even know how to drive this thing?" she said.

"It's not rocket science." He took a sharp right that nearly tipped the cart, and let off the accelerator, which brought the cart to a halt at the door of the shed. "Come on!"

Maria sprang out and grabbed one end of a sail bag and Paolo grabbed the other. They strained to lift it, and failed.

"We're going to have to roll them," Maria said. She joined Paolo on his side, and together they managed to wrestle the unwieldy bag onto the back seat of the cart. The second, smaller bag was only slightly easier.

Once they both were loaded, Paolo drove close to the forested edge of the estate, as fast as the burdened cart would allow, while Maria steadied their stolen cargo and kept lookout from the back.

Paolo came to a stop at a footpath that led from the estate to the beach. "We can't take the cart down to the sand. I am pretty sure it will get stuck," he said.

They wrestled the sails off the cart and drove it back to the greenhouse and plugged it in. Then they ran back to the beach.

Maria kicked the sails. "They're so heavy! I don't want to roll them all the way to the boat."

"Yeah," Paolo said. "And the sand will make it even harder."

"Couldn't we use the dinghy?" Maria said. "Roll them down to the water and then row them over?"

"I guess," Paolo said.

They worked hard for the next hour. First they rolled the boom tent to the mainsail mast. Then they got the dinghy off *The Last Privateer*. This time, Paolo insisted they rig up the davits and lower it off the stern properly, instead of just heaving it over the rail. He said it was just dumb luck the rowboat had landed right side up the day she'd tried to take it out.

They rowed the small boat to the beach by the footpath, heaved the sails aboard, and rowed back. Maria watched Paolo handle the oars. She realized she'd been facing the wrong direction when she'd tried to row herself out to the islands.

"You face backward?"

"Yeah." He scrunched his face. "You looked kind of crazy, trying to row facing forward that day. I wasn't going to mention it because you were already so mad."

Paolo held the rowboat steady while they hooked up the dinghy to the falls. Then he helped Maria climb aboard, and once he'd joined her, they hauled everything up. After unloading the sail bags, they stowed the dinghy back on deck—someone would surely have noticed it if they left it dangling off the stern of the *Privateer.*

Maria lay on her back beside the dinghy, exhausted but exhilarated. The sails were finally on board.

"Well, come on." Paolo kicked her feet gently. "We're not done yet."

Maria turned over, groaning. But she got up. Together, they spread the sails on the deck to inspect them— unrolled, the canvas filled nearly all the walking space. Maria took hold of the smallest one.

"This must be the one that goes in front," she said.

"That's the jib. The other two are the mainsail and foresail," Paolo explained. "I guess we don't need the topsail. We couldn't handle that much sail anyhow, just the two of us. These aren't in such bad shape. Just a couple tears and missing grommets in the cringles."

Maria laughed. "It's like you're speaking a foreign language. Jib. Cringle."

"The holes are the cringles and the grommets are the metal circles inside the holes. That's where the rope goes."

"Oh. To kind of sew it to the—the—whatever that is." Maria pointed.

"Don't worry about the names. I'll teach them to you while we rig," Paolo said, inspecting the sails.

"These old lines are all rotten. We're going to need to buy new line. Rope to you landlubbers."

"I've got my dog-walking money. We should go buy some tomorrow."

"We could say we're going to the library for my summer school."

"We *should* go to the library for your summer school," Maria said. "When's your first test?"

"You sound like my mom." Paolo kicked at an empty sail bag.

"Oh no!" Maria looked at Paolo, horrified. "What if Frank goes in the shed?"

Paolo looked blankly at her.

"He might notice the sails are gone," she explained. "We need to rearrange the shed before he sees." The wind was picking up, as it always did in the evening. It was getting late.

"We should put the boom tent back on first," Paolo said.

As they tied the tent to the rail, Maria noticed the silhouette of a motorboat at the mouth of Ironwall's cove. The glare of the sun made it hard to see details.

"Do you think they're watching us?" she asked.

"Probably just some tourist fishing." Paolo tied a

loose but convincing final knot. "Come on. We have to get back before the adults finish for the day." He began jogging up the beach.

"Sure." Maria trotted alongside him. "But what if it isn't just a tourist?"

"I know what you're thinking," Paolo said. "But even if it was Taylor, there's nothing we can do about it."

"Right."

They both looked back, but the motorboat was gone.

24

An Old-Fashioned Fourth

"YOU FOUND YOUR KEYS!" CELESTE SAID. SHE slid into the front seat of the truck, next to Frank. She looked pretty: she wore a sundress splashed with big bright flowers, and a lacy cardigan on top. She'd even put on eye makeup and lipstick.

"It was the darndest thing," Frank said. "I swear I checked a hundred times yesterday—you know I had to call a cab to get home last night—but then I found them in my jacket pocket this morning. As if they'd been there all along!"

Paolo looked down as Maria climbed into the back seat without meeting his eye.

"The old man's not coming?" Frank asked Celeste now.

"Maria is pretty disappointed," Celeste said. "Though I told her not to expect it."

Maria leaned her head against the window. She *was* disappointed. Because she *had* expected Mr. Ironwall to come. He'd been getting out of bed every morning for the last three days. He'd even gotten out of bed this morning. But when the time came, he said he'd stay home with Joanne.

"You can tell Mr. DeMille that I'm not ready for my closeup," Mr. Ironwall had said. Only Joanne seemed to understand.

"Gloria Swanson, Norma Desmond, *Sunset Boulevard*," Joanne said, as she ushered Maria out the door.

* * *

Frank parked the truck on the outskirts of town and they walked along the bike path the rest of the way. Other people with the same idea crowded around—they all streamed toward the center of town like a pre-parade parade. It seemed everyone on the island was gathering on the Old Whaling Church lawn: cooking, serving, or eating the barbecue. Everyone except Mr. Ironwall.

Blankets were spread across most of the grass, and a long line snaked from the tent where the volunteer firemen grilled burgers and hot dogs.

Frank led their group to an empty patch and spread their blanket.

All along Main Street, little children held empty buckets they hoped would soon be filled with candy thrown from the floats. Bigger kids zoomed around the traffic-free street on scooters, skateboards, and bicycles, until the police came through and told them to settle down.

Then a policeman straddling a wide motorcycle cleared everyone to the curbs, and as a brass band began playing "Stars and Stripes Forever" a cheer went up from the crowd.

Paolo looked at his mother. Hattie waved her hand. "Go ahead—we'll watch from back here."

"Come with me." Paolo dragged Maria by the hand to the sidewalk. "If we stand here, we might get candy."

Maria looked back at Celeste, who waved and smiled as if she wasn't worried about the crowd that separated them at all. She waved back to her mother and sat on the curb beside Paolo.

The parade was just as wacky and fun as Maria had hoped it would be. When the giant blow-up rat from the exterminating company got caught on a tree and deflated, Paolo high-fived her, and when the campers from Camp Jabberwocky rolled by in their souped-up wheelchairs dressed like gangsters and gun molls, Maria cheered crazily with the rest of the crowd. There were stilt walkers, ballerinas on roller skates, and colonial re-enactors firing muskets into the air.

A team of miniature horses sporting patriotic ribbons was trotting by, much to the delight of the smallest children, when an ugly voice broke through the music.

"Hey, if it isn't Captain Dirt!"

Maria looked up to see Taylor and his friend standing over them. It was the friend who had spoken. They were dressed nearly identically, in white polo shirts and red-and-blue madras shorts.

"Hi, we weren't introduced properly when last we met." Taylor came closer and held his hand out to Maria to shake.

Maria did not take his hand, but he kept talking in a friendly voice, as if she had.

"I'm Taylor Bradford, and this is Josh." He gestured to his sidekick.

"We saw you fixing up the old man's sailboat yesterday," Josh said.

Just as Paolo said, "What sailboat?" Maria said, "Oh, that was you."

"So you *are* fixing it up!" Josh gloated.

Paolo glared at Maria.

"I don't know what you're talking about," Maria said, too late.

"It's all right," Taylor said. "We aren't going to tell."

"For a cut," Josh said.

"Let's go," Maria said to Paolo.

"Come on, now." Taylor stepped in front of her and smiled. "Can't we all just get along?"

Maria stopped. He looked like an actor from a TV teen drama. Boys didn't look like him where she came from. Blond and tan with straight white teeth.

"Listen," Taylor said to Paolo now. "Josh and I did see you fixing up the old man's boat yesterday. Don't bother denying it. I'm guessing those bundles you worked so hard to bring aboard were sails. And your girlfriend just confirmed it."

"I'm not his girlfriend," Maria said.

Taylor ignored her. "The only reason I can figure you'd risk doing something that crazy is you think you've found a *real* treasure map."

"Captain Murdefer's map," Josh said.

"Think what you want. Doesn't make it true," Paolo said.

"Come on now, buddy," Taylor said. "Everyone on this island knows the old man has a thing for Captain Murdefer."

"We don't know what you're talking about," Maria said again, lamely.

"That's 'cause you're a wash-ashore." Josh snorted dismissively. "But all Islanders know. The old guy made a movie about Murdefer! Doesn't surprise me he'd have the treasure map, too."

"And now you've somehow found it," Taylor said.

"Probably stole it," Josh said.

"But I can't believe you'd steal *another boat*." Taylor put his hand on his chin like a TV detective. "Not after the yacht club incident. You'd be sent to juvie, and we wouldn't want that."

"I was caught 'cause you called security before I got there."

"Why would I tell on you?" Taylor spread his hands as if their emptiness proved his innocence. "I don't want to make trouble for you, buddy. In fact, I want to offer you my services. You have a treasure map; I have a boat. We could do business together."

"I wouldn't do business with you if you had the last boat on the Island," Paolo said.

"Come on," said Taylor. "I can help you."

"Yeah, just let us see the map," Josh said.

"We don't have it," Maria said.

"I bet you have it right there." Taylor smiled at her bag. She'd never seen someone whose smile could mean so many different things.

"I don't."

She didn't. It was safe in the cottage. Still, she clutched her backpack to her chest.

"What are you gonna do?" Paolo said. "Snatch her backpack in front of all these people?"

Maria looked over her shoulder at their adults. Hattie was eyeing the boys warily and saying something to Frank. Celeste was blissfully ignorant, watching a gaggle of skateboarders doing tricks behind a banner that said MV SKATE CAMP.

Taylor stepped back. "We're not here to make trouble."

"Yeah, you are," Paolo said.

"Just think about our offer." Taylor directed this at Maria, with another brilliant smile. Then he turned and walked down the street. Josh followed.

Paolo waited till the two were a block away. "Way to give up our secret, Maria."

"I didn't mean to," Maria protested. "He saw us with the sails anyhow."

"But you didn't need to confirm it. Now they know the map is real," Paolo said. "That we're serious. I bet this isn't the last we hear from them."

Maria watched the retreating boys. "I wonder how long they've been spying on us."

"Taylor may have been watching us for a while. He lives

in the big mansion next to Mr. Ironwall's." Paolo looked directly into her eyes. "You have to keep the map safe."

Maria thought of the map hidden under her mattress. "He wouldn't break into the cottage, would he?"

"I don't know. I don't know what he'd do," Paolo said. "Let's go back to the blanket. The last part is all fire engines and it's too loud by the road."

Paolo plopped himself down on the quilt between Hattie and Celeste. Maria sat on the other side of her mother.

"What happened?" Hattie asked anxiously.

Paolo shrugged. "Nothing, Mom."

"What did they want?"

"They just wanted to invite me to a sleepover," Paolo said.

"They wanted to invite you?" Hattie sounded incredulous.

"We're not enemies, Ma. They apologized a long time ago. In fact, we're starting a sailing club together next year, and they wanted to begin planning for it, so Taylor—the big one? He's invited me and a few other guys to his house for a birthday sleepover on July sixteenth. I can go, right?"

Hattie looked surprised. "That's nearly two weeks from now. We'll see."

Maria leaned behind her mother's back and glared at Paolo. She understood that he had to lie about the conversation they'd just had. But July 16 was the night *they* were supposed to sail for the treasure. And he said he didn't want Taylor's help. Was he going to do business with Taylor after all?

She turned her back to him. All around them on the lawn, families sat on picnic blankets, drinking from red plastic cups and chatting. Maria focused on two children, a brother and sister most likely, dressed in matching blue-and-white-striped seersucker. What kind of parents let their kids play on grass in such expensive clothes?

After the last fire truck had passed, Frank took a twenty from his wallet and handed it to Paolo. "Why don't you kids go ahead and get some ice cream? We'll meet you on the beach."

"I don't really like ice cream," Maria said.

"Of course you do." Celeste wore her don't-argue-with-me face. Maria had no choice but to go with Paolo.

"They just want to get drinks at the Harborview," Paolo said once they were out of the adults' earshot. "They probably won't even make it down to the beach for the fireworks."

Maria trudged along in silence.

"I think my uncle likes your mom," Paolo tried. He came around and stood in front of her. She lowered her gaze and he ducked himself down to meet her eyes. "How do you feel about that?"

"Great," she said, in her blandest voice.

"What is your problem?" he asked.

"You. Having a sleepover with Taylor. On July sixteenth. And you just said you didn't want his help! How'd you change your mind in thirty seconds like that?"

She tried to walk away from him, but the lawn was too crowded to satisfactorily storm off. Instead, she found herself tiptoeing around lawn chairs. She made it to the street and stomped across. Then she found herself caught in a stream of revelers headed for the beach and her pace was slowed again.

Paolo bobbed along beside her, trying to catch her eye. "Will you just stop walking for a second and let me explain?"

"Explain what? That you'd rather go with that preppy jerk than a loser girl? You don't need to explain that! It's very clear." She wished she could get away from him.

"No!" Paolo grabbed her elbow. "That's not it at all."

She stopped and someone bumped her from behind.

"It's like a stampede. Keep going or you'll be trampled," the person behind her said.

Paolo and Maria were swept along with the crowd till they reached the beach and the people fanned out. Suddenly there was space. Paolo led her to an empty spot and sat down facing the ocean. She stood beside him, her arms crossed.

"We were supposed to get ice cream," he said.

"You had the money," she said back.

"It was too crowded," Paolo said. "Sorry. Do you want me to go back for it?"

"No." She looked across the dense sea of people. "How are we going to find our moms and Frank?"

"We can meet them in the parking lot at the truck." He pulled her shirttail. "Will you just sit down and listen to me?"

Maria sat, but she did not look at him. She looked out at the ocean instead. It was nearly black, and the sky overhead held only the faintest gray light. Kids danced around, twirling neon glow sticks.

"I just said I was sleeping over at his house to give me an alibi," Paolo said. "You know, to explain why I'm not home that night. But I won't be with them—I'll be with you. We're still going on the boat just like we planned. Together. Us. You and me."

"Oh." Now she felt like a jerk. "So you still want to sail with me?"

"Of course." He looked steadily at her until she felt a blush creep over her face. She was grateful it was dark.

"Why would I want to sail with anyone else?" he said. "That's *our* treasure."

A small smile tickled the corners of her mouth. Then she remembered. "But what's my alibi?"

"We still have to work on that," Paolo said. "But don't worry. We'll come up with something."

Maria looked at the lighthouse. She'd been inside it—Frank had taken her and her mother up for the view. A long spiral ladder wound to the viewing platform, very like her own spiral staircase to the attic. But at the bottom of her stairs slept her mother. No way could she sneak through the living room.

"If only I had a fire escape," Maria said.

"A what?"

"It's this kind of metal staircase on the outside of apartment buildings in the city, so you can escape through the window if there's a fire and you can't get out the door."

"Oh, yeah," Paolo said. "That would be great."

Suddenly the first firework shot into the air, exploded, and a hundred tiny sparks fell like silver rain.

25

TUNING THE RIG

THE FOURTH OF JULY SEEMED TO MARK THE true beginning of summer. After each ferry arrival, cars stuffed with families and beach equipment joined a long line of other cars stuffed with families and beach equipment, heading toward weeklong rentals, summer homes, hotels, and friends' houses. Maria felt a local's superiority, zipping by on her bicycle while frustrated tourist kids sat red-faced and bored in the back seats of minivans. She and Paolo went everywhere on the wonderful bike paths. He had a bicycle even older than hers—a rusty beach cruiser that rattled over bumps. She insisted they go to the library at least an hour every day— Paolo had to start passing his exams. While he struggled through his summer assignments, Maria read up on navigation. She found star charts for July 16 on the

Internet and located the position of Cassiopeia at each hour of the night.

"Why do you need so many?" Paolo asked.

"The problem," she explained, "is that depending on what time of night it is, the position of her feet changes. According to the legend, the god of the sea, Poseidon, got mad at her for boasting that she was more beautiful than the sea nymphs. So to punish her he threw her into the sky and made her spend half her time in an upside-down position—to make her look stupid or something."

Maria drew a W on a scrap of paper.

"So even though you said Cassiopeia was a W, throughout the night she could be an E, an M, or a 3 depending on which way she's rotated." Maria drew three figures:

"Okay—let's say the night of the sixteenth starts at midnight," she continued. "So at midnight, this part is her head." Maria pointed to the top of the 3. "And this is her feet, at the bottom. But she circles counterclockwise around this star, Polaris, throughout the night. So by four a.m. the 3 is now nearly an M." She pointed to the M. "Then the feet are totally in another direction. And we have to consider that the 'night' of July sixteenth is really two of our nights."

"What?" Paolo frowned as if completely confused.

Maria drew two crude clocks:

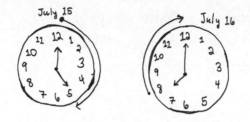

"Well, it could mean the second part of the night that begins on July fifteenth. The night of July sixteenth officially starts at midnight on that night and continues to sunrise at about five a.m.—that's one. But then we have to consider the night that begins with sunset on July sixteenth and ends at midnight. So what we really need to know is what *time* Captain Murdefer meant. Not just the date."

"He probably didn't want to make it easy," Paolo said. "In case the chart got into the wrong hands."

"I just wonder if there's something we're missing," Maria said. "Like maybe these other illustrations have something to do with it?" She pulled the chart from her backpack and examined the sea monsters and the compass drawing. But no matter how closely she looked, she didn't find any clues as to the time the Queen would tread on the door.

"Maybe you should just print all those star charts, in case," Paolo said. "And then if you figure it out, you won't have to look all this up again."

Maria hit the print icon. "You know, you are pretty smart after all."

* * *

After their required time in the library, Paolo often took Maria swimming. Though they could have swum off Ironwall beach, Paolo insisted they ride their bikes to all the different public beaches so Maria could get a real feel for the island. Then he showed her the secret swim spots in kettle ponds visited only by Islanders. But what Maria loved best was their visits to the towns. Every store was open and packed with beautiful, useless things. The ice-cream shops had lines out the door, and the smell of fried clams and hot dogs filled the air. Using her dog-walking money, Maria and Paolo splurged on all the arcade games, all the different flavors of fudge, all the matinee movies, and anything else that struck their fancy.

But their favorite stop was the marine supply store. They browsed the aisles and bought grommets, seine twine, canvas for patching the sails, and rope for rigging. This came in large spools that they balanced precariously on the back racks of both their bicycles—then they walked their bikes side by side, sharing the load between. The one drawback to bikes was their inability to carry much in one trip, so they found themselves returning to the marine supply again and again, nearly every day, much to the shopkeeper's amusement. When he questioned whether they were building a boat from scratch, Paolo mumbled something about a tree house.

The one dark spot in Maria's otherwise sunny summer was Mr. Ironwall's health. Though he sat on the patio with her each morning, he seemed thinner, paler, and more tired each day.

"It's my legs," he told her. "It is as if they are perpetually cold."

She tucked the wool blanket tighter around his bony knees. "Have you told my mother? Or Joanne?"

"I don't want to worry them. And I forbid you to

worry them, also." He smiled at her. "It is not unusual to have poor circulation at my age. Don't fret."

But Maria did fret. She tried to keep him warm with extra blankets and hot water bottles. But despite her efforts, he did not improve.

Paolo was no comfort, saying only, "He's old, what do you expect?"

Maria did not know what she expected, but she knew what she wanted. She wanted him to get better.

They had made great progress with the boat. They'd repaired the mainsail and the jib and attached them to the mast and jib stay. They rigged all the various lines and halyards, and oiled all the blocks so the lines ran easily. Still, at the end of every day, the new sails and rigging had to stay carefully hidden under the covering tarp, so that no one else would know *The Last Privateer* was ready to sail.

"I wish we could do a shakedown sail," Paolo said when he'd coiled the last line. "Just to make sure we rigged it right."

"What's a shakedown sail?" Maria asked. They were sitting on the deck of the *Privateer*, the morning sun already blazing hot. Brutus worried the tennis ball, tearing at the green fur with his teeth. He could denude a ball in ten minutes flat if they didn't pay attention, and then he pooped neon-green tennis ball fuzz for days after.

"Kind of like a practice," Paolo said. "If we weren't trying to hide it, we'd take her out in the bay and sail around a little to see that everything runs right. But I can't figure out how to do that without getting us caught."

"I can't figure out how we're going to go for the treasure without getting caught," Maria said. "Or how I'm even going to get out of my room in the middle of the night without my mom noticing. You do realize our whole plan is crazy."

"Yeah, I know," Paolo said. "But it won't matter how crazy it was after we find the treasure. Then everyone will just be congratulating us and spending money."

"We're running out of time," Maria said.

"I know," Paolo said. "But freaking out isn't going to help. And I'm tired of worrying about it." He lifted the corner of the tarp on the ocean side of the boat. "Last one in is a rotten egg!" He disappeared over the side with a splash.

Maria dove in after him. Her swimming had been gradually getting better. Though she had the basics from her long-ago lessons at that awful, overcrowded city pool, Paolo had shown her new tricks: how to exhale through her nose when she jumped off the dock to keep the water out, how to dive under waves, and something he called "elementary backstroke," which made Maria feel like a frog on its back. She paddled over to him now.

"You know, I agree with you," Maria said, treading water. "It's pretty crazy for us to go out without a what-do-you-call-it sail." She turned toward the beach. "Come on, I can't swim as long as you."

Maria rode a gentle wave in and sat in the shallows, facing the boat. Paolo swam up beside her. The waves billowed his swim trunks around his legs, showing the pale white of his upper thighs in sharp contrast to his tanned knees.

"It's too risky," Paolo said.

"Risky or not," Maria said, "we'll have to be ready to grab whatever chance we get."

26

SHAKEDOWN

MARIA WAS SURPRISED TO FIND THEIR CHANCE came the next evening. She was sitting in the beetle-bung tree behind the cottage, as she often did in the afternoon to read and wait for her mother to come home. Sometimes Celeste walked up the clamshell drive, sometimes Frank gave her a ride. This time Frank drove her up in his truck. Hattie was with them. They were all going to head up-island to Menemsha for lobster and steamers, and to watch the sunset from the beach.

"You're welcome to come." Celeste squinted up at Maria, one hand a visor over her eyes. "We won't be back till after ten and Hattie didn't make you any food because we thought you'd join us."

"No, thanks. I'm kind of tired. And there are a ton of leftovers from last night. I'll be fine. Really."

"Well, okay." Celeste looked a bit doubtful. "I'll just go in and change, then we'll go. If you maybe change your mind."

But of course Maria didn't change her mind while her mom changed her clothes. She waved as the adults drove off, then leaped from the tree and ran into the cottage to pack food. She'd just wrapped everything up in plastic bags when she heard Paolo's bicycle skid on the drive. Maria met him at the door.

"Did you hear? They're all gone!" He threw his bike on the grass.

"I packed food." Maria showed him the bag. "What about your grandparents?"

"I told them I was coming over to study. And I'd catch a ride home later with Frank and Mom." He took the bag from her and started trotting toward the beach.

Maria jogged after him. "What are we studying?"

"Phoenicians."

"Okay. I'll be sure to quiz you later."

"Don't bother," Paolo said. "I got them down. Invented the alphabet. Big on sailing. Purple dye made from snails. Established Carthage. Defeated by Alexander the Great."

"And they're Lebanese," Maria said. "Or at least they're who the Lebanese came from."

"Yeah. Your people."

They crested the dune and ran up the beach.

* * *

"Sail first, eat second," Paolo said when they reached the boat. He unlaced the line that held the canvas to the rail. "We'll have to get all this out of our way."

"And we'll have to put it back up like it was when we're done," Maria said. She ran across the deck and pulled the line from the other side. They met each other halfway and laid the tent on the deck. Then they folded it longways and rolled it tightly till it resembled a giant white cigar. Paolo did a fancy thing with the lace-line and secured it to a deck cleat.

"The next part is going to be a little tricky," Paolo said. "We have to get the sail up first, I think, then untie her from the dock. Because we need power to get off the dock and we can't risk being washed up on the beach while we're hoisting sail." He was readying the various halyards as he spoke, running the lines back toward the wheel and leaving them in neat coils. "But the problem is, if the wind catches the sail while we're still attached to the dock, the lines might pull too tight and we won't be able to undo them. And whoever's on the dock might get left behind."

Maria tried to picture it. She could see the problem. Wind pulling them off the dock while the ropes held them to it.

"We could maybe take all the lines off except one, and then run that last one around that thing." She pointed to a short, thick post.

"Bollard," Paolo said.

"Yeah, run it around the bollard but tie it off to a cleat on the boat. Then, as the boat starts pulling away let it go real quick."

"Yeah. Yeah!" Paolo jumped off the *Privateer* and began untying docklines and tossing them aboard. Maria caught and coiled them down.

Finally he loosed the stern line. But he left it running around the bollard and carried the rest back aboard and secured it to a deck cleat. With no sails yet up, the boat's nose swung gently away from the dock, her back end tethered by the stern line, till she was nearly perpendicular to it.

Together, they hauled up the mainsail and the jib. As the evening wind filled the sails, the *Privateer* started to pull away from the dock.

"Hold this!" Paolo unwrapped the stern line from the cleat, leaving only one loop on. He handed the line to Maria. It felt alive, as if it were trying to jerk away from her. She leaned back and dug her heels in.

Paolo spun the ship's wheel. "Slowly let it go."

Maria loosed the line. It slipped around the cleat and the *Privateer* pulled farther from the dock, and the bow swung more toward the mouth of the bay. The sails made a luffing sound as the wind bellied them.

"Let it go completely!" Paolo yelled.

Maria unwrapped the line and tossed it over the rail. The rope fell in the water. The *Privateer* was truly under way now, heeling starboard and picking up speed. The wet end of the stern line flew out of the water and whipped around the bollard, spraying the dock with sparkling droplets before it dropped back in the ocean again and trailed behind them like a tail.

"Haul it up! Haul it up!" Paolo shouted.

Maria hauled the heavy rope onto the deck. She looked up and saw the mouth of the bay just ahead and the open ocean beyond that. "We did it!"

"We did!" Paolo looked as surprised and happy as she felt.

Maria slid over the wet deck to him. "Now what?"

"I don't know. We sail around a little, then eat."

They sailed out of the bay. *The Last Privateer* bucked

and bounced on the larger ocean waves. It felt like that first time they'd sailed in the yacht club catboat, only stronger, as if the wind was a giant hand pushing the canvas. The air felt crisp and smelled clean. Far off in Edgartown harbor a fleet of white sails scudded about.

"You're a natural," Paolo said. "I can't believe this is only your second time out."

"It's 'cause I'm half Phoenician. It's in my blood." She was joking, but she felt free and happy. She lifted her arms and ululated.

"What the heck was that?"

"Just, like, cheering. Like 'whoo-hoo!' In Phoenician."

He laughed. "Whatever. It's good, though, right?"

"Yeah, it's good."

Paolo spun the wheel and the boom came across the deck. Suddenly they were pointing back toward the bay.

"Do we have to go back so soon?" Maria cried.

"We know it works, and we can't risk getting seen." They were closing quickly on the mouth of the bay. Soon they would be back at the dock, doing the boring hard work of sewing the canvas tent back to the rail.

"You're right." Maria sighed. Already she could see the enormous house in the cove beside theirs.

"Is that where that guy lives?" Maria said. "Taylor what's-his-name?"

"Bradford."

"He's super rich," Maria said.

"Yeah." Paolo stared at Taylor's mansion. The sleek motorboat and a couple of jet skis were tied to its dock.

"And that's just his mom's house. His dad's got a bigger house in Newport and a massive condo in Boston. And a ski lodge in Maine."

As they neared the shore, they dropped the sail and coasted in. Paolo handed Maria the wheel and jumped onto the dock with the stern line. He quickly wrapped it around the bollard and stopped the boat. Then he secured the rest of the lines.

"Our parents are getting their sunset picnic," Maria said. "We can at least have our sunset picnic, right?"

"Yeah," Paolo said. "We can put the tent up after."

Maria sat at the stern and laid out corn bread, deviled eggs, and tomato salad. Paolo sat beside her and they dangled their legs over the water as they ate. The sun was large and low and turning the waves copper.

"My dad told me if you keep your eyes on the sun, you'll see a green flash as it disappears over the horizon," Paolo said.

"We'll have to put the tent up before that." Maria held the jar of Hattie's homemade pickles out for him. "Have you ever seen it?"

"No." He was staring at the horizon. Then he took a deep breath and held it so long Maria put the jar down and looked at him.

"My mom was really messed up after my dad died," he finally said.

Maria didn't know how to answer. She watched him close his eyes, then open them. She'd never had anyone die on her. She couldn't imagine it.

"I mean, it was so unexpected it was ridiculous! She just kind of lay there on the sofa, and she wasn't doing laundry, or cleaning, or anything. I guess I smelled pretty bad for a while there."

"I'm sorry," Maria said.

He went on as if she hadn't interrupted. "And I was wearing my dad's old army stuff—his dog tags and coat—because that was the only thing I had of his. I don't know, I guess it made me feel like he was still out there somehow. So that's the Major part: Army Major. And I was like majorly dirty—ha, ha. And now everyone calls me it. The whole school. All the time. And I can't do anything about it because I already got busted twice for fighting."

"It's okay," Maria said. "It doesn't matter what people call you. Everyone calls me ugly. And I don't care, because I know I am."

"No you're not," Paolo said. "You look . . ." He squinted at her. "Normal."

"Gee, thanks," Maria said.

"Anytime," Paolo said.

"Do I look normal now?" Maria crossed her eyes and fattened her lips.

"Very normal," Paolo said.

"How about now?" She rolled her eyes back till the whites showed and flared her nostrils.

"Even better," Paolo said. "But really, I prefer this look."

He shoved a hard-boiled egg into his mouth so it pushed his lip out like a chimpanzee's.

"Oh, that's pretty," Maria said. She shoved an egg in her mouth the same way.

Paolo swallowed his egg whole, rather disgustingly. "Gorgeous," he said.

27

SQUARE ONE

AFTER HER MORNING VISITS WITH MR. IRON-
wall, Maria generally found Paolo in the kitchen with
his mother. Hattie would feed them something (which
Paolo would wolf down so quickly he could barely have
tasted it), and then they would either go off on their
bicycle adventures or head over to the boat to make re-
pairs.

But the next day Paolo wasn't in the kitchen with
Hattie.

"Where's Paolo?" Maria tried to sound casual, but
she felt nervous. Maybe she'd been too weird or something last night. She cringed, remembering the faces
she'd made.

"Oh, Harry took him fishing. Pops decided Paolo had

too much time on his hands if he was going around stealing boats. It's time he learned a useful trade."

Maria remembered Paolo saying something about that. How he would have to go fishing as punishment for stealing the yacht club catboat.

Hattie set out a plate with steamed mussels, sliced bread to mop the sauce up with, and an empty bowl for shells. "He certainly isn't going to be a rocket scientist with grades like he got, despite your efforts, Maria. Which I do appreciate."

"When is he getting back?" Maria asked.

"You won't see him for a couple of days. But he told me to tell you: *You know what to do.*" Hattie turned back to the sink. "Whatever that means. Is it something for school? Because I don't want you doing his schoolwork for him."

"No. No. We were just, you know, just building something . . . a clubhouse." Maria stopped talking by digging into the food.

"Well, I hope you two aren't making a mess. And don't use anything from the shed. Frank says things have been moved around. He still swears someone stole his keys and took the golf cart for a joyride. I just hope it wasn't you two."

After she was done eating, Maria wandered over to the boat. If Paolo had been with her, they might have taken Brutus along—he liked to swim off the beach—but since he was gone, she figured she'd just hang out belowdecks and read.

But when Maria climbed through the gap between the tarp and the rail, something was wrong. Her foot came down on a round object; it rolled underfoot and she heard the sickening sound of breaking glass. She'd stepped on the glass chimney of a kerosene lamp. The lamps usually hung on the wall of the cabin below. It made no sense that she should have stepped on one up here, on deck.

She looked about. Nothing was where they'd left it. Nothing was the *way* they had left it. The lines had all been pulled from the pulley blocks, and all the pulley blocks lay scattered about. Whatever could be taken apart had been taken apart, and more than a few things looked smashed—as if whoever had done the damage had taken whatever heavy thing lay at hand and banged it about indiscriminately.

Had they secured the boom tent properly after their sail last night? Maria couldn't remember. They'd been having so much fun; maybe they'd been careless. Or maybe someone saw them out sailing; maybe someone saw them come back into the bay. Maybe Taylor.

Maria wandered the deck, stunned and heartsick. The dinghy had a dent, the sails had been unstrung from the stays, and the deck was littered with objects previously stored below. She didn't even want to go into the cabin to see the wreckage there.

But she forced herself down the ladder and gazed, nauseated, at the destruction. All their weeks of work—undone. The drawers had been pulled from the cabinets, upended, and their contents thrown all over. The books pulled down from the shelves lay broken-backed on the floor. Whatever cushions and pillows hadn't been thrown up onto the deck lay trampled and muddy. Someone had even taken the bouquets she had made, torn the petals from the stems, dumped the water, and shattered the vases.

Maria brushed her sleeve across her eyes. She would not cry. She would clean. She had done it once before, she could do it again.

She found the whisk broom and dustpan and began sweeping. It seemed so pointless. They were back to square one. There was no way she could repair all this damage without Paolo's help. And she had no idea when he'd be back.

28

FIRE ESCAPE

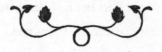

THE MORNING AFTER THE DESTRUCTION, WHEN Maria walked Brutus on the beach, she felt as she had back in her old neighborhood, walking home from school watching out for Bad Barbies. Afterward, she paid a quick and distracted visit to Mr. Ironwall, in which he'd become frustrated by her "lack of conversational skills" and insisted she needed books, "good books, to improve your mind." He dismissed her with a cranky wave.

She decided to spend the afternoon repairing what damage she could. When she slipped under the tarp, her heart pounded. What if Taylor and his buddy Josh were back on the boat undoing all the work she'd done the day before? They could come back anytime and wreck everything again. If the boat was trashed, then she and

Paolo couldn't use it for the treasure hunt. And they'd have to either forget about it or come crawling to Taylor for his boat.

She resented cleaning and fixing things a second time, but mostly she resented the creepy feeling she now had. It was as if she'd had something special, something she'd worked really hard on and felt really good about, and Taylor Bradford had snatched it from her and thrown it in the mud. The boat had been her chance to change her future. With it, she could get the treasure, buy a house, and never have to move back to the Bronx. They could stay on Martha's Vineyard forever. Without it, what could she really do?

Be realistic, her mother would say.

Maria did her best to put aside her worries and concentrate on fixing things. Cleaning below and putting things back in their proper spots—that wasn't so hard. It was just like the work she'd done before. But the rigging! She consulted the mildewed books she'd brought up from below. Whatever she didn't understand, she left for Paolo's return.

She tied the tarp tightly and hoped it would stay tied till she returned the next day.

Maria kicked at clamshells as she walked home. It was now July 10—just days before they had to sail. And still Paolo was not back. And the boat was not finished. And she still didn't know what time the Queen would tread upon the door, so she had no idea which island the treasure was on, or whether they should leave early in the morning on the sixteenth or late at night. And she was no closer to figuring out how she'd sneak past her mother.

She entered the cottage and sighed. There was just one door, and that was so close to the sofa where Celeste slept; there was no way Maria could slip out without waking her mom. It was hopeless.

Maria gave up and went to the kitchen for some dinner. As usual, the refrigerator was full of gourmet leftovers Hattie had cooked far too much of. She helped herself to some chicken pie, and was working on a slice of zucchini bread when her mother burst through the door, talking as if she and Maria were already in mid-conversation.

"Mr. Ironwall says you have a real interest in history." Celeste dumped a cardboard box on the table. "Apparently you are the only one who appreciates Ironwall Estate and all it has to offer. He wants to know if you would like to borrow some old books he has."

Maria opened the box. A plume of dust wafted up and made her sneeze. The top book had a gray bloom of mildew on its plain maroon cover. *Prominent Island Families, 1500–1900.* She looked at the books beneath—a history of the Wampanoag tribe, a book on *Historic Vessels and Their Captains,* a glossy compendium of the films of *Hollywood's Golden Age,* and a thesaurus.

"Frank spent all afternoon in the library, finding them. Mr. Ironwall's library, not the town's. He has an entire room filled with books!" Celeste stripped off her scrubs and changed into sweats as she spoke. "Pretend you like them, even if they are really boring."

A knock on the door interrupted Celeste. She looked at Maria with raised eyebrows. Maria shrugged. She hadn't expected any visitors. Her mother opened the door and there stood Paolo, holding a big canvas rucksack and a large dead fish wrapped in wax paper.

"You better get this on ice," he said, handing the fish to Celeste. She looked at the wet package for a moment and then dumped it in the kitchen sink. Then she looked at her hands and excused herself to the bathroom.

"You've been gone for two days!" Maria told him.

"I couldn't help it," Paolo said.

"I've got to show you something," Maria said. She meant the boat. Though it wasn't as bad as it had been at first, he had to see, as soon as possible, all the work that remained.

"I got to show you something first." He swung the rucksack to the floor.

"Do you want some zucchini bread?" Celeste came back in, wiping her hands. "Your mother made it, it's very good."

"No, thanks, Ms. Mamoun. Frank's waiting for me in the truck."

"Invite him in, too."

"No, we've got to be going. Gram's expecting us. I just wanted to drop this off for Maria." Paolo nodded at the rucksack.

"What is it?" Celeste asked warily. "Not more fish, I hope."

"Just books," Paolo said. "You know—summer school?"

"Oh yes, how is it going?" Celeste moved to the sink, stared at the fish, and then turned her back to it.

"Really well." Paolo smiled. "We're doing a social studies project on the history of fire escapes." He winked in a way that only Maria could see.

Maria grabbed the bag. It didn't feel or look at all like books. It was so heavy she almost dropped it.

"Can you help me carry it upstairs?" she said to Paolo. "It's really heavy—"

Paolo grabbed one end and she followed with the other. They dumped it on the floor beside her bed.

"What the heck is this?" She opened it up and brought out a handful of rope.

"Shh! Your fire escape. I kept thinking about it while I was fishing. It was a great idea you had. See?" He pulled out a bit more to show her.

"It's a rope ladder," Maria whispered.

"Yeah! I made it. You can tie it to your bed—as long as you put your bed right up against the wall under the window—and climb down!"

"Oh," Maria said.

"You don't seem very excited," Paolo said. "I worked really hard on it."

"It's not that," Maria said. "It's the boat. Someone trashed it. I think Taylor."

Paolo's face reddened. "What do you mean trashed it? Can it still sail? Did he mess with the hull?"

"The hull is fine. He didn't sink it or anything. But he undid all the rigging and messed with everything else." Maria felt tears prick her eyes. She shook her head. "I've been working on it the whole time you've been gone . . . but I don't know if we'll be ready."

"We have to be."

"How? You haven't seen it. It's awful."

"We'll just work till it's done. I'll get started tomorrow while you're walking Brutus."

Maria shook her head. "And what if he comes back and tears it all up again, right before we go? I'm such an idiot. I can't believe I gave away our secret to him."

Paolo put his hands awkwardly on her shoulders and bent a little so he was looking directly into her eyes. "You're not an idiot. You're the smartest girl I know. And the nicest. The only thing wrong with you is that you just didn't realize what a jerk that guy could be." He paused and stared over her shoulder. "But that gives me an idea."

"What?"

"Maybe if we tell him he can come, he'll stop messing with us."

"But we aren't going to let him, are we?" Maria asked. "I mean, you said—"

Celeste popped her head into the attic and interrupted. "Frank's cleaning the fish after all."

Paolo and Maria turned at the same time, and he dropped his hands from her shoulders.

* * *

After Frank and Paolo left, Celeste and Maria sat on the sofa eating *bizir*, salted pumpkin seeds, sent by Tante.

Frank had taken care of the bluefish for Celeste, and now it sat chilling in the freezer, safely wrapped in cellophane. He'd even taken the head and tail away and left a recipe Celeste could use if Hattie ever stopped cooking for them.

"Let us play Go Fish." Celeste dealt hands for the game. "In honor of our first bluefish."

Maria sat on the opposite end and took up her cards.

Celeste took a deep breath, held it, then exhaled slowly as she did when she had something important to say.

"What?" Maria started putting her cards into pairs.

"I don't want to worry you," Celeste finally said, "but Mr. Ironwall is not doing as well as you hoped."

"He didn't seem sick when I visited him this morning." Maria kept her eyes carefully on her cards. But he had been unusually cranky.

"He didn't want to worry you," Celeste said. "And sometimes it happens fast."

"*Quickly*. Mr. Ironwall says it's the adverb. *Fast* is an adjective." Maria put down a pair of twos. She could feel her mother looking at her, but she didn't look back.

"Fine, Maria. It happened quickly. Right now, his ankles are swollen and his breathing sounds bad. We've got him on diuretics, but if they don't work by tomorrow, I can make no promises."

Swollen ankles. Bad breathing. Diuretics. Her mother

had told her about these symptoms before, with other patients. Something to do with the heart not pumping hard enough.

"Is he going to be okay?" Maria met her mother's eyes.

"Well, *chérie*, we're doing the best we can." Celeste folded her cards into her lap. "I don't like that he's giving things away, though. Like the books he sent you."

"Why don't you just take him to the hospital?" Maria asked. "Tonight. Call an ambulance."

"Joanne thinks the one on the mainland is better. The emergency room here, at least in the summer, is overrun with tourists. The only thing is, we need to decide before he gets too bad—"

"Then why don't you just take him now? Isn't there some kind of rescue helicopter or something? Why are you waiting?" Maria felt her face getting hot.

"Calm down, Maria." Celeste fixed her with a stern look. "It is not a Medivac emergency at this time. If he needs to go, he can go in an ambulance on the ferry. But he doesn't want to leave the house, and we can't make him go against his will. You need consent. Sometimes people get tired, and they don't want to keep trying."

Maria threw her cards down. "Are you serious? Are you saying what I think you're saying?"

"Maria, *habibti*, it's going to be okay," Celeste said in

her soothing-mommy voice. "No matter what happens, it will be okay."

Maria stood. "It will not! It is *not* okay for him to die! You have to take him to the hospital. If you won't make him go, I will! I'll go talk to him right now!" She headed for the door.

"Maria! I absolutely forbid it!"

Celeste stood. She moved to block Maria. Maria feinted right, then went left. Her mother grabbed her from behind. Though she wasn't much taller, Celeste was still stronger, and she whipped Maria around to face her.

"You don't get it!" Maria yelled.

"No! *You* don't get it!" Celeste yelled back, louder. She hardly ever yelled, but the few times she had were frightening. "This is not up to you!"

"Who is it up to then?" Maria said. "Joanne? If it were up to her, he'd never even get out of bed! She gave up on him a long time ago."

Celeste closed her eyes and took a breath. "No. It is not up to Joanne either. It is up to Mr. Ironwall. He gets to decide. We don't get to decide for him."

"Can I at least talk to him? Can I see him?" Her voice came out scratchy and choked. She should be able to see him after the dog walk as she always did. "I still have to walk Brutus, right? No matter what?"

And if she got to talk to Mr. Ironwall she could convince him to go to the hospital. There was medicine there that could save him.

"If he is well enough," Celeste said. "We'll see."

* * *

Later that night, Maria couldn't sleep. She lay in bed gazing at the carved beams above her head. Though she could barely see them in the dark, she had the carvings memorized. *JM 1689*—Captain Jean Murdefer. Her privateer. But she still did not know who *FH 1718* or *SI 1812* was or what *1230* meant . . . or anything else, it seemed. Too much was going on, and it was all too confusing.

She turned her mother's words over in her head—people get tired and don't want to keep trying. That wasn't fair. People shouldn't get to stop trying just because they want to. Not if other people care about them.

Maybe he'd just been alone so long he didn't realize that was a rule.

He just needed her to explain it to him.

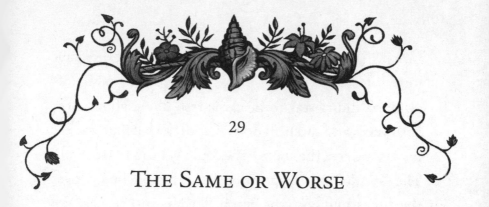

29

THE SAME OR WORSE

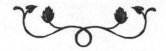

THE NEXT MORNING, MARIA STOOD AT THE front window waiting for Frank. When she saw his stony face, her stomach sank.

"Don't jump to conclusions, *habibti*," Celeste said.

"You only say *habibti* when you're really worried." Maria stared out the window.

"I'll find out how Mr. Ironwall is doing when I see him," Celeste said. "How about you maybe bring Brutus to his room as usual, and if he is doing well, you come in?"

"But he isn't doing well," Maria said. "Or Frank wouldn't look so serious."

"We don't know that." Celeste opened the door to Frank and the dog.

"He's the same," Frank said, by way of greeting. "Or worse."

Maria didn't stay to hear the rest. She grabbed Brutus's leash and ran him down the driveway. The sooner he was walked, the sooner she could get to Mr. Ironwall. They sprinted through the break in the rose hedge, over the dunes, and onto the beach. She was surprised to see Paolo waiting for her. He was throwing stones into the water, skipping them two, three, four times.

"I already checked out the boat." He skipped one last stone and fell into step beside her. Brutus ran in and out of the waves, looking expectantly up at Maria. She'd forgotten to bring a tennis ball.

"Just go swim." She tossed a piece of driftwood into the water. He trotted in, pointed his nose toward the floating stick, and paddled steadily toward it.

Paolo was still talking. "It's really not so bad. I mean, they didn't *destroy* anything—and we have enough line left over on the spool to rerig that jib."

Maria stared at him. She hadn't even thought of the boat since her mother told her about Mr. Ironwall.

"Are you okay?" Paolo asked.

"No." Maria suddenly realized she wasn't okay. "I'm really worried about Mr. Ironwall."

"Yeah, he's pretty sick, my mom told me," Paolo said.

"I have to get him to go to the hospital," Maria said. "As soon as I'm done walking Brutus, I'm going to make my mom let me see him. I can make him go. He'll listen to me."

Brutus was swimming about in circles. She wished he'd get out and take care of business so the walk could end.

"Maria?" Paolo said her name as if he'd already said it a few times. "Will you?" He touched her arm.

"Will I what?"

"Will you come with me to see Taylor?"

Maria headed toward the water. "Come on, Brutus. Go already."

Prize stick in his teeth, the dog dutifully came out, shook, and peed on a hunk of seaweed.

"But we're not really going to take him . . . we're just going to let him think he's coming. We'll tell him a different date." Paolo trotted along behind her. "You have to come with me. I'm banned from the yacht club, and that's where he works. Maria!"

Maria was too focused on Brutus to pay attention to Paolo. Now the dumb dog was eating crab legs. The gulls took the meat from the bodies and left the legs rotting on the beach, and Brutus loved them.

"No crab cookies!" Maria hooked up the leash and pulled him away. "We have to get going!"

Paolo jogged after them. "Maria, are you going to help me or what?"

Brutus was finally circling a promising patch of wrack in the way he did right before he went number two. Maria waited till he squatted, then she turned back to Paolo. "What do you want?"

"Just meet me in the kitchen for lunch, okay? I'll tell you then." He sounded exasperated.

"We always meet in the kitchen for lunch," Maria said.

"Whatever. I'm going to go work on the *Privateer*."

As she watched Paolo heading for the boat, Maria realized she had no idea what he'd been talking about.

"Finally!"

She scooped the dog's mess into a plastic bag. "We have to go see Mr. Ironwall!" She dragged the insulted-looking animal toward the house.

* * *

Maria wouldn't take no for an answer. Celeste met her at Mr. Ironwall's bedroom door and tried to take Brutus without letting her in.

"He's exhausted, *chérie*," Celeste whispered. "Just breathing makes him tired. If he has to talk he will only get worse, heaven forbid."

"He doesn't have to talk. He just has to listen," Maria said.

"Let her—!" Mr. Ironwall called. Then he began coughing.

"See?" Celeste hissed. She let her daughter in anyhow.

Maria waited by the door until Mr. Ironwall's coughing stopped. Celeste scurried forward to replace the oxygen mask that he had pushed off. He wheezed with each inhale, but he looked alert enough. He patted the bedspread beside him.

Maria sat on the bed by his feet. "Don't talk. My mom says it makes you tired."

He made a fist of his hand on the coverlet and bobbed it up and down.

"That means *yes*," Celeste told her.

"What's *no*?" Maria asked.

Mr. Ironwall made a beak out of his thumb and first two fingers and tapped them together.

"How are you doing?" Maria asked him. Then she winced—that wasn't a yes or no question. Still, he nodded his hand *yes*, and she took it to mean *good*.

"It's okay, Mama," Maria said. "You can take a break."

Celeste looked at her warily, but Mr. Ironwall nodded his hand.

"Okay, *chérie*. But I'm going to leave my walkie-talkie. I'll just be down in the kitchen with Hattie, so you can call me there—it is already on the right channel. Just push that button on the side and talk into it. And don't come down to get me, call me and I will come up. I don't want Mr. Ironwall alone for one second. *Compris?*"

"I understand," Maria said. She looked at Mr. Ironwall. He nodded his hand again.

She waited till her mother was gone a few seconds before she said, "Mama says you won't go to the hospital. Is that true?"

His hand nodded.

"You're really sick this time though, aren't you?"

His hand made the tapping beak. *No.*

"Don't lie to me. I know you're sick," Maria said. "And you're not going to get better unless you go to the mainland hospital and get the best help you can."

He tapped the beak, *no.*

"But why not? Don't you want to get better?"

He rolled his eyes toward the window.

"Listen." She took his hand in hers. It felt cool and

dry and fragile. "I know you're sick of being sick. But we need you. *I* need you. I don't want to go back to the city *ever*. So if you give up and leave us high and dry you're just being selfish. You are!"

Mr. Ironwall looked at her and wheezed. He pulled the mask from his face and Maria saw he was smiling.

"And your insistence"—he wheezed—"that I get better"—wheeze—"so you can stay here"—another wheeze—"is not selfish?"

"Well, I guess it kind of is," Maria admitted. "But I don't care!"

Brutus heard her raised voice and looked up from his spot on the carpet.

"And Brutus needs you, too!" She reached for Mr. Ironwall's mask. "Now put this back on or my mom'll kill me."

He pushed her hand away and kept the mask off. "Why"—he began his halting, wheezing talk again—"would a young girl . . . want to stay . . . in this rotting carcass . . . of a place?"

She looked steadily at him. "Well, I love the cottage, and all the weird, old-timey things in it. I love your dog. I love the beach and the things I find on our walks. I like bringing things to you and you explaining them to me, and you telling me old Island stories . . . Put your mask on!" She took the mask firmly from him and placed it back over his nose and mouth. "I just like hanging out with you." She felt suddenly shy. "You know what I mean."

He tapped his fingers *no*.

"What do you mean, *no*?" She pushed him lightly on the shoulder. "Now you're just messing with me, pretending you don't know what I'm saying."

His eyes twinkled, and she figured he was still smiling under the plastic mask.

"Don't you dare leave us high and dry," she said, swiping her eyes. Her hand came away wet. She hadn't realized she'd been crying.

Mr. Ironwall laid his hand on top of hers. He patted her knuckles.

"Will you go to the hospital or what?" she said in a quieter voice.

He reached up and pulled the oxygen mask from his face again. "Call your mother." He put the mask back on.

"I'm not calling her unless you say you'll go." Maria stood and held the walkie-talkie in her hand.

He nodded his hand *yes*.

Maria grabbed his nodding hand and held it close to her face. "You have to come back. Promise."

Mr. Ironwall curled his fingers so they brushed her cheek.

* * *

The household scurried to get Mr. Ironwall ready for his trip to the hospital. In the kitchen, Hattie told Maria she'd have to stay with them till her mother returned from the mainland. "And I don't know how long she'll be gone. They're getting such a late start as it is, she'll probably miss the last ferry back."

"Frank's going with her," Paolo said. "You can stay in his loft."

"I guess I should go pack some clothes," Maria said.

"And we're taking care of Brutus, too," Hattie said. "Pack his food, dishes, and leash."

But before Maria left the kitchen, a swirl of red lights filled the window.

"That's the EMTs." Hattie opened the kitchen door and waved to the driver of the ambulance. "Go around to the front!"

Maria joined her at the open door. She watched the ambulance pull around the drive to the front entrance. The EMTs left the lights on, but there was no siren. Maria started out, but Hattie put her hand on her arm.

"Now, they don't need us getting in the way," she said. "You wait here with me."

Maria went to the side garden instead. Brutus followed. At least they could see the front entrance and the waiting ambulance from there.

After a moment, Paolo and Hattie joined her. Hattie put her arm around Maria's shoulders and pulled her close. She kissed the top of Maria's head.

"I know you're worried," Hattie said. "But he's got your mom and Frank, and they'll take good care of him."

The EMTs appeared at the top of the grand front stairs with the gurney. Mr. Ironwall hardly made a lump under the sheet and straps. Celeste and Frank followed, carrying overnight bags.

As the EMTs loaded Mr. Ironwall into the back of the ambulance, Brutus barked. Maria held him back by his collar and pushed the big dog's rump down. Brutus sat hard. He scratched the air with his paw, whining.

The ambulance pulled away, followed closely by Frank's truck. Celeste turned and waved out the passenger window.

"We'll be okay!" Hattie called to her, waving back.

Maria watched the vehicles disappear down the long clamshell drive. She felt hollow, as if someone had scooped her insides out.

"Do you think he'll be all right?" she asked no one in particular.

"Of course," said Hattie. "He's just got a little water in him. The meds'll pull it out. You'll see. I bet your mom calls us tonight with good news." She wiped her hands on her apron. "Now you two run along. Paolo—help Maria pack. I'm going to give Frank's room a thorough cleaning while he's gone. That place hasn't been aired out in decades."

30

ENGAGING THE ENEMY

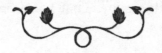

PAOLO SAID TAYLOR WOULD BE WORKING AT the yacht club that afternoon. As soon as they finished packing her stuff, Maria and Paolo headed into town on their bikes. Heat rose in waves off the black asphalt bike path, and sweat plastered their shirts to their backs. Maria would have enjoyed the ride if it were ending at a swimming hole, but she dreaded having to talk to Taylor alone.

"You'll be fine," Paolo called over his shoulder. "He won't do anything to you where he works."

"But what if he won't listen to me?" Maria said.

"He wants the Murdefer treasure as much as we do," Paolo said. "Every kid on the Island has dreamed about that treasure at one time or another."

They locked their bikes to the rack at the edge of Edgartown, and walked the rest of the way.

The yacht club was a cedar shake structure that loomed out over the bay. It had a dock on the starboard side crowded with catboats like the one Paolo had "borrowed" the day he took Maria sailing. On the port side, a landing with more docks jutted into the bay. Sailboats crowded these docks and more bobbed at their moorings. The whole place bustled with boats coming in and going out.

Just as they approached, a large explosion shook the air. Maria saw a puff of smoke rise into the sky.

"What was that?" Maria asked. "A bomb?"

Paolo shook his head. "Cocktail hour. They fire the cannon at five o'clock so everyone knows it's time to start drinking."

"Are you serious? A real cannon?"

"It doesn't fire a cannonball." Paolo shrugged. "But it *is* a real cannon. Rich people are weird. Come on."

When they got closer he pointed to a motorboat puttering out in the bay with a few passengers. "That's Taylor. He ferries the yachties from the club to their sailboats that are moored out there. When he comes back, tell him we need to speak with him somewhere private.

I'll be waiting in the park next to the bookstore." Paolo looked over his shoulder. "I have to get out of here. I'm not supposed to be on the grounds."

Maria watched him trot back up the hill toward the center of town. Then she sat on a dockside bench to wait.

Across the bay lay Chappaquiddick, which she'd heard was the even smaller, more exclusive island. A small three-car ferry shuttled back and forth from another nearby dock.

To her left was the fishing pier, and farther along was the lighthouse beach where they'd watched the fireworks. To the right, the yacht club, a fancy water-view restaurant, and expensive homes.

"Hey, Captain Dirt's girlfriend."

Maria turned and saw Taylor pull his boat neatly alongside the dock and cut the engine.

"He wants to talk to you," she said. "Privately."

"I'm working," Taylor said.

Maria looked behind him. "You don't have any customers right now. And I think you want to hear what he has to say. About . . . *you know*."

Taylor climbed out of the boat, came over to where she sat, and looked down at her. He wore a red polo shirt with the yacht club insignia, white shorts, and brown deck shoes. He stood too closely for her to get off the bench without touching him, so she stayed sitting.

"We've been considering your offer," she said to his tan forearms. Her mouth felt dry after the hot bike ride, and she wished she had a drink. "We'd like to negotiate."

"Fine. Take me to him." Taylor went back to his boat and took a wooden sign from under the seat, which he hung around the console: BACK IN 15 MINUTES.

As Maria led Taylor up the hill to the park, she noticed he did not walk beside her. He probably didn't want anyone to think they were together, but instead of feeling insulted, she smiled to herself. It struck her as funny and slightly pathetic.

Paolo was waiting by the old mill wheel. He'd had time to visit Vineyard Scoops, and he handed a sweating waxed cup to Maria.

"I hope you like vanilla. I didn't know what to get," he said.

"Thanks." It was the first time a boy had ever bought her a milk shake. Or anything, for that matter. It tasted cold and sweet and felt good going down.

"Hey, when you're done with your girlfriend," Taylor said. "I don't have a lot of time."

Paolo went over to the bench and sat on its back, his feet on the seat. "Taylor, we know you trashed the boat"—he held up two shushing fingers against the other boy's protest—"and we know why. You want the map. You thought you might find it, or maybe stop us from going for the treasure on our own."

"I don't know what you're talking about," Taylor said.

Paolo continued as if he hadn't spoken. "We're prepared to make you an offer. As long as you don't trash our boat again, we will include you on the treasure hunt."

Taylor didn't react. He stood in the center of the path, arms folded. A passing young couple had to unlock hands to fit around him and avoid the flower beds on either side.

"In fact," Paolo continued, "we'd like to use your boat. You get a one-third cut. But you don't include Josh. 'Cause I'm not dividing the treasure any more ways. Take it or leave it."

Taylor pretended to think about it, but Maria could tell he would go for it.

"Okay," Taylor finally said. "When do we go?"

"The night of July seventeenth," Paolo said.

Taylor squinted as if he was suspicious. "How's it gonna work?"

"We'll meet you at your dock at eleven o'clock sharp. It's up to you to find a way out of your house." Paolo took a final slurp of his shake and chucked the cup into a garbage can. Then he stood, brushed his hands on his shirt, and said, "Don't keep us waiting."

"Aye-aye, Captain Dirt," Taylor said with a smirk, heading back downhill toward the waterfront. His swagger indicated he thought he had put one over on them.

"What if he didn't go for it?" Maria asked. "Did you even have a plan B?"

"I thought maybe I'd have to punch him or something. I don't know."

Maria laughed and Paolo blushed as they headed back toward their bikes.

31

BATTEN DOWN THE HATCHES

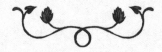

THE NEXT FEW DAYS PASSED BY IN A BLUR OF activity. With Mr. Ironwall in the hospital, Maria and Paolo could devote the entire day to preparations for the treasure hunt. After exercising Brutus, they set about fixing the damage Taylor Bradford had made. While Brutus slept in the cool cabin, they rigged under the hot deck tent. The canvas acted like greenhouse glass, trapping the sun and stale air beneath it. But they didn't dare unlace it from the rail for fear someone would see them, and then all their plans would be ruined again.

Of course, Taylor Bradford already knew what they were up to. But they counted on him to keep up his end of the bargain and not bother them anymore. One day he buzzed by on his jet ski and gave Paolo a mocking salute, but that was it. Since he thought they were partners, he had no reason to bother with them or *The Last Privateer.*

After a long day on the boat, they biked back to Paolo's family compound. Brutus, good dog that he was, trotted alongside. Upon their arrival, Grandma Newcomb insisted on a thorough tick check for them and the dog, then showers, then a half hour of "quiet time" while she and Hattie finished cooking dinner. Quiet time wasn't very quiet; extended family arrived from their various jobs with groceries, news, musical intruments, and all sorts of other distractions. Maria began to figure out who was who, and they all welcomed her to the family easily. This cousin taught her a few chords on his guitar, that in-law passed her a baby to bounce. Hattie gave her small jobs to do: stripping thyme leaves from the twigs, picking dandelion off the back lawn for a salad, or whipping cream and sugar for dessert. When Pops was up and about, he took Maria and Paolo to the garden to weed, pick cucumbers, tie up vines, and whatever other chores involved too much bending for his bad back.

After another gourmet dinner of strange foods, the extended family would disappear to their various homes and the main house would become still and peaceful. Maria thought this time of night felt like the tide going out; all the movement and noise drained away, leaving quiet ripples. She read or played a board game with Paolo and his grandmother while Hattie finished in the kitchen and Pops took a twilight stroll. Sometimes they simply sat on the patio, listening to the peeping frogs Vineyarders called pinkletinks and watching for fireflies and shooting stars. It would have been completely wonderful, except that she was so worried about Mr. Ironwall. Hattie and Grandma tried to reassure her that Mr. Ironwall would get better soon, and her mother would soon come home.

But Mr. Ironwall didn't get better, and her mother didn't come home.

"I *know* it's been three whole days, *chérie*," Celeste said on the phone. "But he needs someone here to deal with the doctors and nurses. And he's trying to get his affairs in order."

"What does that even mean?" Maria gripped the only phone in the Newcomb household—an old-fashioned rotary dial that actually had a curly cord connecting the handset to the base, so you couldn't walk around the house and find privacy. All their conversations had to happen right there in the kitchen with Hattie and whatever other Newcombs were home at the moment.

"Just that he has lots of paperwork to do. Legal things."

"Like his will?" Maria said. "Is he going to die?"

"It's nothing you need to worry about, *ma chère*," Celeste said. "I'll be home in a couple days."

"A couple days is what you said a couple days ago."

"Aren't you having a good time with the Newcombs? Hattie said you and Paolo were building a tree fort and biking all over the Island."

"It's fine, Ma. But I just want to be back in the cottage, with you." Maria allowed a little whining to creep into her voice.

"By Saturday, the latest," Celeste said. "I promise."

"Why can't Joanne just take over?" Maria asked.

"She is here when she can be. But she has taken another job."

"She took another job!" Maria said. "That's bad, right?"

"Maria—" Celeste began.

"I know. He's very old, and very sick. I don't want to hear it!" Maria slammed the phone down. Immediately it began ringing.

Hattie gave Maria a meaningful look.

"*You* talk to her!" Maria yelled, and ran out into the garden.

Paolo was helping Pops and Grandma wrap their fruit trees in burlap and twine.

"What are you doing?" Maria asked.

"Battening down the hatches. Nor'easter's coming," Pops told her. "Expected sometime late Saturday. People are scrambling to get off-island before the ferries stop running."

"What's a nor'easter?" Maria asked. "And why would the ferries stop running?" If the ferries stopped, her mother couldn't come home.

"High wind and flat-bottomed boats don't mix," Pops said.

Grandma turned to Maria. "And what did your mother have to say about Mr. Ironwall?"

"She says she'll be home soon."

"Well, that's good news, isn't it?" Grandma said absently. She'd gone back to untangling the twine.

"I guess." Maria stared intensely at Paolo, trying to send him a message with her eyes. He bugged his eyes back at her but didn't seem to understand.

"Paolo, I think we better get to the library today," Maria finally said. "You know that question we had about the constellations? I found some new information you need to learn. You know, now, in case they shut the library in the storm."

"Oh, yeah." Paolo finally caught on. He handed the burlap to his grandfather. "Yeah, we should go."

They grabbed their bikes from the shed and sped down the dirt road. As soon as they reached the bike path Maria pulled up alongside Paolo. "Mr. Ironwall's going to die."

Paolo slowed. "How do you know?"

"He's writing his will and his night nurse took another job." Maria panted. The wind off the ocean pushed against her, and she felt as if she were riding up a hill, though the path was flat. "Tonight might be our only chance. 'Cause I'll be going back to the Bronx any day now."

Paolo pulled ahead and stopped his bike in front of her. Maria was forced to stop also.

"Are you okay with this?" he asked. "I mean, with the old guy dying?"

"Of course I'm not okay!" Hot tears filled her eyes. "But I have to be realistic."

"But it's not even the right date," Paolo said.

"That doesn't matter. We don't know the right time anyhow, so we don't know the correct heading. We were always just gonna guess, right?" Maria swiped her eyes with her sleeve. "I mean, that's just movie nonsense—magic doors that open only on one particular day according to the position of the moon or whatever. This is a real-life rock, or hole, or something—we just have to go look for it. I'm going to get the boat ready." Maria hopped on her bike and took off. She didn't bother to see if Paolo was behind her.

32

THE QUEEN'S DOOR

THAT NIGHT MARIA WENT TO BED IN HER clothes. She clutched the headlamp Paolo had borrowed from his grandfather's camp equipment. Her mother's walkie-talkie lay next to her. Paolo had the other downstairs with him. He would click with his transmit button twice to signal the old folks were asleep, and twice more when he was under her window. Paolo could just slip out of his own ground-floor bedroom window. But since Maria was in Frank's loft, she would have to climb out the window just as she'd planned to climb out the window of the cottage—there was no way for her to sneak through all the shotgun bedrooms without waking Hattie, Pops, and Grandma.

Maria hoped they would have enough time.

If only they knew *which* island!

If only she could have cracked the mystery of Cassiopeia. But now it was too late. Now they just had to hope that something popped out, something obviously door-like, when they got there.

Outside, the wind blew in noisy gusts and rattled the trees against the roof. Though the storm wasn't supposed to arrive until Saturday, advancing clouds scudded across the sky. Even if she knew the right time for the constellation, it wouldn't matter. The stars hardly showed behind the clouds.

Maria shone her headlamp up at the rafters in the ceiling. They weren't that different from the rafters in her attic room back at the cottage, except those had dates and initials carved all over them. It seemed she would never figure out who *FH* of *1718* was, and *SI* of *1812*. And she'd never figure out the weird *1230* . . .

She clicked off her headlamp and stared at the glowing red numbers of the clock across the room. When would Hattie, Pops, and Grandma go to sleep? It was 10:29, and if they wanted to get to the island and back before morning they had to get started soon.

The clock clicked over to 10:30. She counted the hours to sunrise on her fingers. 10:30. 11:30. 12:30 . . .

12:30.

1230!

1230 wasn't a year. It was a time! And it had been carved on the rafter where she'd found the map!

Maria got out of bed and slipped quietly across the floor. She located the sheaf of printouts from the library and examined the different angles of the Cassiopeia constellation on July 16, arranged by hour. She pulled out the star map for midnight, and the one for 1:00 a.m. Cassiopeia's feet pointed to northeast in both. Slightly more north by 1:00 a.m.

Maria sat back and reasoned it through. She compared the star charts to the compass on Murdefer's treasure map. If she was right, even though they weren't sailing on the correct date and they couldn't see the stars, they could still follow the correct compass heading. As long as they sailed with the compass pointed around 33 degrees, they would be headed in the right direction!

Maria was so excited, she almost missed Paolo's signal. Two taps on the walkie-talkie. She peeked out and saw him waiting beneath the burlap-wrapped peach tree with both their bicycles.

The rope ladder worked as it was supposed to: she tied it to the bed and then used it to lower herself to the grass.

She grabbed Paolo and pulled his ear to her mouth. "I know where the treasure is!"

"How? We can't even see the stars."

"I'll explain on the way."

She looked back at the rope swinging from the open window. The wind blew it back and forth, but it was nearly invisible in the starless, moonless dark.

"You think it's okay to leave it like that?" she asked.

"You'll need it to get back in," he said. He climbed on his bike and pushed off.

"What if someone sees it?"

"My mom is in the back room, and she never gets up. Grandma took off her glasses and hearing aids, so she wouldn't notice anything, even if she did wake up. And Pops is whacked on painkillers for his back. Frank is off-island, and Harry's at his girlfriend's house." Paolo coasted beside her. "Tell me about the treasure island."

Maria explained her discovery about the star maps.

"That's amazing! You're amazing!" Paolo said. "I can't believe how smart you are."

"No. You could have figured it out yourself."

"No way. I just don't think like that," Paolo said.

Maria was glad he couldn't see her blush in the dark. She pedaled ahead and let the night air cool her hot face. The wind bent the tops of the pines and made a loud shushing that sounded like the ocean. No cars passed by them. It was late. Everyone was either off-island already or in bed.

* * *

They got to the Ironwall Estate quickly and hid the bicycles behind the Old West Shed. Then they ran through the field, past the Great House, and onto the empty beach. In less than half an hour they had the canvas off the boom and the sails raised. Though the waves were choppier than usual and the wind was stronger, they managed to maneuver the boat smoothly from the dock. Maria still could not believe they were finally, after so many weeks of preparation, sailing toward the outer islands, toward the treasure.

The first leg was not as easy as it had been on the shakedown sail, as the wind was against them, but the island largely protected them and they were able to slowly tack their way east. But as soon as they left the lee of the island and hit the open sea the temperature dropped, and *The Last Privateer* plunged headlong into a huge wave.

It felt like a cannonball had struck the hull.

After a lull of smaller waves, another large one hit, pounding their little boat. The red and green running lights swung in crazy circles. A great gust of wind pushed the sails over so the deck tilted and the shrouds dipped toward the water.

"I thought the storm wasn't coming till Saturday!" Maria said.

"It's not; I guess this is just the rough seas ahead of the storm," Paolo said. "No one is out in this weather. Except us." He stared at the black waves. "This is stupid."

Maria knew he was right, but ignored him. The wind drove splashes of water from breaking waves into her face. She swiped her fingers across her glasses and took a step forward.

Suddenly the boat shifted under her feet. She fell down through a hole and hit her left shoulder against something hard. She gasped with the sudden pain. A gush of water doused her from above. She looked up.

Paolo shone his headlamp down at her. He stood at the top of the companionway. Maria realized that she must have fallen into the cabin.

"Are you okay?" he shouted.

"I fell." Maria tried to raise her hand to block the blinding beam of his headlamp and pain shot through her shoulder. She immediately sat on the nearest bunk. Paolo disappeared.

"Paolo!" she yelled. The wind whipped her voice away and she heard no reply. "Paolo!"

She pulled her feet onto the mattress and hugged her injured arm. It felt better if she didn't move it.

Finally Paolo came back.

"Where were you?" she yelled up at him.

"I had to take in sail and tie the wheel," Paolo said. "I need you up here. This boat is too big for me to handle alone."

Maria stood. Then the boat rolled and she skittered sideways and grabbed for the companionway. An electric pang zinged up her left arm.

"I think we should turn back." Paolo sounded concerned.

"I don't want to turn back," Maria said. "We still have time to find the treasure if we hurry."

"Forget the treasure," Paolo said. "You're hurt and we have to get home before this weather gets worse."

"No!" Maria clung to the companionway with her right hand and breathed deeply, willing herself not to puke. "We have to try!" She groped for some way to convince him. "Anyhow, we're closer to the outer islands than home."

"You can't even use your left arm." Paolo looked at

her. "I bet your shoulder is dislocated. I dislocated mine skateboarding once; it hurts like crazy."

"Then if it was dislocated, I'd be passing out with pain. I'm fine. Just bruised a little." Maria climbed the ladder as quickly as she could one-handed to show him she was okay. "Don't tell me we stole a boat for nothing."

Maria took the wheel before Paolo could argue. She breathed slowly and evenly; in through the nose and out through the mouth, four counts in, eight counts out, willing her nausea away. Her shoulder did hurt like crazy. Paolo was probably right, it probably was dislocated and it probably was stupid for them to go on.

Then, suddenly, the clouds parted and Maria could see Cassiopeia.

"Look!" She pointed her chin to the sky. "It's a sign!"

Paolo looked at her for a long minute, his mouth set in a hard line. "Okay," he finally said. "But only because we're probably closer to the outer islands than home. Keep her steady on this course. I'll be right back."

Paolo went belowdecks. When he came back up he had a sheet he'd torn and folded in a triangle.

"At least let me tie it up for you," he said. He made a sling and gently positioned her arm against her stomach, tying it securely in place.

"I really am okay," she said.

"Sure you are," he said, as if he didn't believe her.

They pointed the prow as close to the correct heading as the wind would allow and sailed on, tacking back and forth. Maria steered; Paolo handled the sails. The boat still creaked and bucked against the waves, but the swell gradually lessened, broken by the small islands somewhere ahead in the dark. Now and then Cassiopeia winked at them from behind the clouds.

Then, ahead, Maria saw a dark mass, more like nothing than something.

She shone the high beam of her headlamp over the bowsprit. "I think I saw an island," she told Paolo.

Paolo shone his light with hers. "There's something out there," he agreed. "I don't see a door, though."

They peered together into the night. The stars had disappeared behind the clouds again. It was so dark it was nearly impossible to see the difference between land, sea, and sky. But then a cliff face came into view.

"Hold the light high and watch for rocks," Paolo said. "We need to find a safe place to anchor."

"But can't I keep our heading at 33 degrees?" Maria asked. "Just in case it *is* the right island?"

"Right now I just want to get off this boat," Paolo said. "I don't care where we are."

Maria kept her light trained on the approaching

island, and her compass heading as close as she could manage. Just as they were about to hit land, a wave tossed them and the cliff opened up. There was a cave! It had been hidden by a large rock that had created the illusion of a solid cliff.

"The door," Maria whispered. Small waves curled into the mouth of the cave. "We found it."

"What?" Paolo said.

"The door! It's there!" Maria pointed with her chin.

Paolo shone his light in the direction she pointed. There it was. A cave. A door.

"Let go the anchor!" Paolo shouted, as he let the anchor go.

33

TREASURE ISLAND

THE RED AND GREEN RUNNING LIGHTS ON THE *Privateer* grew smaller and dimmer the farther they rowed from her. To Maria, sitting one-armed and useless, the waves felt bigger and more dangerous now that they were in a small rowboat, but Paolo pulled them steadily and confidently toward the beach beside the cave.

When they came to the shore break, Paolo jumped out and Maria followed. She used her one good arm to hold the dinghy's painter while Paolo lashed it to a rock. The ocean wind had modulated to a cold, damp breeze. Their headlamps shone on the rocky beach and cliffs. It was so dark, and they were so far from any other humans. If something happened to them, no one would know where they were. No one would find them.

No one came to this island except park rangers and biologists—and then only rarely.

"It feels like we're the first people to ever land here," she said.

"Well, I hope we aren't. I hope pirates landed here." Paolo pointed his headlamp toward the cave. He took her good arm and helped her scramble over the slick rocks. Even so, each step jostled her bad arm, and her shoulder throbbed with her heartbeat. But they were here! This had to be the treasure island. She steadied her breathing and walked carefully on.

The cave was bigger and deeper than it had looked from the boat. A curved dome of rock, about six feet at its highest point, formed the ceiling, and on the floor a stream of outgoing water weaved around boulders of varying size. Water dripped from the ceiling, and the floor was slippery with greenish-black slime. The rock walls sheltered them from the outside wind and the relative silence was a relief. The warmer air smelled of mildew and moss.

"What if we followed this stream?" She pointed her light at the rivulet. "It seems to be coming from somewhere back there." Her light disappeared in the recesses of the cave.

"Okay. You first." Paolo let her lead.

She picked her way carefully to what seemed like a dead end. But as she got closer, she saw that it was really a large boulder that had created a false back wall to the cave, and that behind it lay a tunnel through the cliff.

"It's like a passageway," she said. She peeked into a long rock hallway. Her light disappeared into the murk. "I don't want to go first. There might be bats."

"There aren't any bats anymore," Paolo said. "They all died from some weird bat disease. Don't you read the news ever?"

"Oh, so we may be stepping on bat skeletons? That's too creepy."

Paolo didn't answer, but he took the lead. All along the cave walls natural shelves jutted out at various heights. Paolo and Maria shone their lights onto each one, but each one was empty. It got colder and damper the deeper into the cave they went, and the dark walls closed in around them. She took hold of the back of Paolo's shirt and he didn't complain; he just reached back and took her hand in his. They crept like that through the narrowing passage for a long time. And then, suddenly, Paolo stopped.

"Look!" he said.

Maria came up beside him. Their headlamps shone

into a large, round room. There were no exits but the passageway they'd come through.

"This is the end of the line," Maria said. "If it isn't here, it isn't anywhere on this island."

They shone their lights around the walls. Here, there were no weird rock shelves. Just smooth granite flecked with bright bits of mica. The floor, unlike the rest of the cave system, was oddly sandy.

"That's weird," Maria said.

"What?"

"There shouldn't be sand here." She got down on her knees and began sweeping away at the sand with her good arm. "All the rest of the cave is rocky. And we're really far from the beach. This sand is too perfect, like it was trucked in and dumped. To hide something. Help me look."

Just as she spoke, her hand brushed against something hard. "Come here and dig."

Paolo got the shovel from the bag, but it wasn't necessary. The chest was buried so shallowly they could find it with their hands. A brass corner poked from the sand. A little more digging revealed a leather handle.

Paolo whistled. "I never really thought . . ."

He grunted and pulled, but could not haul it up. Together, they dug away the sand to expose the top half of a wooden treasure chest. A large padlock secured the front.

"Oh, wow." Paolo sat back. His hands raked his hair. "Oh. Wow. Can you believe it?"

Maria lifted the padlock and let it drop. It was real enough. Some kind of heavy metal. But the skull and crossbones carved on the back seemed theatrically pirate-esque. It reminded her of something.

"We don't have a key. I guess we could carry it out." Paolo tried to lift the chest. "Jeez. This thing weighs a ton."

"Wait a second," Maria said. She fished through her backpack. There it was, down at the bottom. The key with the skull and crossbones. The key she'd found on the boat.

She slid the key into the lock. It fit perfectly. With an easy turn of her wrist, the tumblers clicked over and the lock sprang open. Maria sat back on her heels, surprised.

Paolo stared at her with a puzzled expression. "How'd you get that key to work?"

"Remember how this didn't fit in the engine starter?" Maria said. "Because it wasn't for the boat. It was for this treasure chest."

"But why would Mr. Ironwall have the key to this treasure chest in his sailboat?" Paolo asked.

"Why would he have had the treasure map in his cottage?" Maria answered. "Maybe all these artifacts were handed down to him from his ancestors, but he just didn't put two and two together."

"Well, let's open it!" Paolo cried. He sprang forward and lifted the lid.

They both peered in, shining the beams of their headlamps together. There, nestled on a bed of sea-smoothed rocks, sat a fork.

"That's weird," Paolo said.

Maria picked the fork up and inspected it. It was badly tarnished, but it felt heavy and expensive. She rubbed a bit of black off and silver shone through. She rubbed a bit more, and the letter *I* appeared in the handle. The shape looked oddly familiar. Like the silverware she'd found on *The Last Privateer* that first day she'd gotten aboard. The set that was missing one fork.

"Oh," Maria said. A horrible feeling washed through her. "I think I'm going to be sick."

"What?" said Paolo. He hovered near her shoulder. "That looks like real silver. Are there more in there?"

Maria's head swam and she thought she might pass out. She bent over and took a few deep breaths. It felt like cold black oil was filling her lungs and she couldn't get enough air.

"Well, it's worth taking back," Paolo was saying. He scrabbled around in the chest, moving rocks. "But it's not enough to make us rich."

"Don't bother," Maria said. "That's all there is."

"How do you know?" Paolo said. He kept lifting out rocks and chucking them on the sand. "I bet the treasure is under all this—these rocks are just a decoy."

"No. I know who the fork belongs to," Maria said. She straightened up and shook the fork at Paolo. "See? The initial says *I*."

"So?"

"*I* is for Ironwall. Mr. Ironwall," Maria said. "And this is his fork. There were only three in the boat. There should've been four."

"So what?" Paolo said. But he stopped chucking rocks.

Maria shone her light over the ground, carefully this time. A corner of paper stuck out from the bone-dry sand. She pulled it gently free and held it under her light.

It was a map, not unlike the map she had found in the attic, except this one was torn and brittle. She showed it to Paolo.

"So you're saying there were two maps?" Paolo said.

Maria dug about in the sand. "Mr. Ironwall got here before us."

"Is that why he's so rich?" Paolo asked. "He already found the pirate treasure?"

Maria continued to pull things from the sand. She found a cocktail napkin. A toothpick with faded green cellophane decorating one end. A lady's bobby pin. An oyster shell. Another beat-up copy of the same map.

Maria showed him the items in her hand.

"I don't understand," Paolo said.

"Do you remember the story Pops told about a party Mr. Ironwall threw?" Maria said.

"No." Paolo pulled his headlamp from his head and shone it on the cave floor. Now they could see many small bits of litter. Another napkin. Another oyster shell. A peach pit. A corner of a picture. Paolo picked it up and held it to the light.

It looked like part of an old movie poster. Maria could make out:

ast Privateer

ilm by Peter Iro

in

Technicolo

She showed it to Paolo. "Mr. Ironwall liked to throw elaborate parties. Your granddad told us about one where he put real pearls in the oysters to impress the guests. Where a lady cracked a tooth—don't you remember?"

Paolo stared blankly at her.

She sighed. "Okay, so you don't remember. But I do. I think this was a party like that. Maybe this *was* that party. To celebrate his new film, *The Last Privateer*." She held up the shred of movie poster. "I saw a poster just like this in a room in his house."

"Wait," Paolo said. "You're saying this was all for a party?"

"Yes." Maria waved the poster over the littered sand. "This was all for a party. The maps. The treasure chest."

"So there *never* was a pirate treasure?" Paolo said.

"There never was a pirate treasure," Maria said. "But there was a treasure hunt. The maps were the invitations. They said when and where the party was going to be."

Paolo stared at her. Then he kicked an oyster shell across the cave. It shattered on a rock.

"But our map looks so real!" Paolo cried. "It's so old!"

"It just looks old." Maria plucked other maps from the sand. "And this one looks old, and this one looks old, too. I guess it isn't so hard to make things look real when you have Hollywood professionals making your props."

"So that's why the key fit," Paolo said. "And why it was in the boat."

"Yes," Maria said.

Paolo squatted and put his head in his hands. "Now *I'm* gonna be sick."

They sat down on the sand and leaned their backs against the fake treasure chest. After a while Paolo said, "I can't believe we stole a boat for this. We're idiots."

"Yeah," Maria said. "Kids like us don't find real treasure maps."

"Or become millionaires," Paolo said.

"I guess I'm going back to the Bronx, now."

Paolo took Maria's good hand in his. "I'm really sorry."

"Yeah, me too." She squeezed his hand. "Well, it's been fun anyway."

"Seriously?" Paolo said.

"Yeah." Maria thought about the last few weeks, the last few days, and the last few hours. "It really was kind of fun," she finally said. "Even if it was all stupid and useless. I mean, I never even used to leave my neighborhood. But since I moved here we fixed up a sailboat. And stole it!"

"And we tricked Taylor," Paolo said.

"And we escaped in the middle of the night," Maria said.

"And you solved a pirate riddle," Paolo said.

"And we sailed to an unknown island on a dark and stormy night . . ." Maria said. "That's kind of a lot of adventures for someone like me."

"Yeah, I guess," Paolo said. "Still, I'm going to get teased so bad when Taylor hears about this. I'm going to be Captain Dirt forever."

"Maybe he won't hear about it," Maria said.

"Of course he will," Paolo said. "He thinks we're going for the treasure with him on the seventeenth. We'll have to explain why that's not gonna happen."

"Maybe not," Maria said. "Maybe we won't even make it back home."

"Of course we will," Paolo said. "Then we're gonna wish we didn't."

Maria stared at him. He was right. They'd stolen a boat in the middle of the night. Even with the wind at their backs, it was unlikely they'd get home by morning, and the adults were going to be seriously worried. And then who knew what kind of trouble they'd be in when they got home. The thought washed through her like ice water. She felt exhausted, and her shoulder hurt terribly.

"Paolo?" Maria said. "I think I really might have dislocated my shoulder."

"Come on." Paolo helped her to her feet. "Maybe we can still get home before anyone notices."

But they did not have a chance. As they stumbled from the mouth of the cave, they heard the violent chop of helicopter blades and the roar of an approaching motorboat. Bright white lights flashed on them and an amplified voice boomed from the boat: "This is the U.S. Coast Guard. Stay where you are. We're coming ashore."

34

WHAT KIND OF TROUBLE

HER MOTHER'S SOFA BED WAS SO WARM AND cozy. The quilts felt heavy and reassuring, the pillow felt so soft. Maria wanted to stay burrowed in it forever, but the late-afternoon sun streamed through the kitchen window, and the shadow of her mother fell across the bed. She couldn't pretend to be asleep anymore.

"Mr. Ironwall wants to see you as soon as you are dressed," Celeste said. She turned her back to Maria and started washing dishes.

"He's back?" Maria asked. She felt an odd mix of relief that Mr. Ironwall was alive and terror about having to face him.

"He came back this morning. Joanne had to take time off from her other job to bring him home. I was too busy dealing with your nonsense."

Maria hung her head so her hair formed a dark curtain. Her nonsense. Her mother had met her in the ER of the Martha's Vineyard Hospital, where her shoulder had to be reset by an overworked resident. Then came X-rays and an awkward immobilizing sling, and painkillers that had blissfully knocked her out until now.

"Of all the idiot ideas!" Celeste suddenly burst out. She turned with a coffee cup in hand and shook it at Maria. "And stealing from Mr. Ironwall! His boat! Not yours!"

"We were supposed to get back before anyone noticed."

"Do you realize that if Mr. Newcomb hadn't gotten up, you two could still be lost?" Celeste continued as if Maria hadn't spoken. "You hurt yourself, you could be dead from hypothermia . . . And do you think I'll even get another job after this fiasco?"

"I'm sorry, Mama," Maria said.

"Sorry doesn't even come close to making up for this." Celeste turned her back again to Maria. "You have no idea how bad this is."

Maria did have some idea. She realized now that she and Paolo had put themselves in great danger. She understood that they never would have made it home by morning, and if the storm had been worse, they might not have made it home at all. They had been saved by luck and Mr. Newcomb's love of peaches.

Pops Newcomb had never been a good sleeper—not since he broke his back and started taking the pills. Luckily, he slept even more poorly that night, out of worry for the wind. And that worry woke him up. He thought he heard a creaking; he'd peeked outside to see if his precious peach trees were losing limbs, and he saw the rope ladder swinging against the house. He hobbled as fast as his bowed legs could carry him to wake Hattie and Grandma. Of course, once they woke, they found the empty beds.

Then he called Uncle Harry, who got dressed and came over immediately.

Meanwhile, Hattie called the police. The detective on duty suggested Paolo could be with one of his friends. He seemed to think it was only a matter of childish mischief. "Teenagers are like that. Sneak off with their friends."

Grandma Newcomb looked at Hattie. "We both know Paolo doesn't have any friends but that fool girl who's clearly gone off with him."

Just in case, Hattie called Taylor Bradford. She had a bizarre conversation with his sleepy and confused mother. There'd been a sleepover planned for the sixteenth, at the Bradfords, Hattie said. Perhaps she'd gotten the date wrong? No, Mrs. Bradford explained, as far as she knew, there was no sleepover, and Paolo certainly wasn't in their house.

Mrs. Bradford put Taylor on the phone, and finally, after Mrs. Bradford threatened Taylor with the loss of every electronic and motorized gadget he owned, the story came out—how Taylor had bullied the two to include him in the hunt for Captain Murdefer's treasure. "They were fixing up that old sailboat," Taylor said.

Grandma called Celeste, who was dozing in the chair beside Mr. Ironwall's bed. The ringing cell phone woke them both up. He made Celeste tell him what had happened.

"I'm afraid I know where they may have gone," Mr. Ironwall said.

Meanwhile, Uncle Harry drove like a madman to the Ironwall Estate. The bicycles were discovered behind the Old West Shed, *The Last Privateer* was found to be missing, the Coast Guard was called, and the rescue was enacted.

Now Maria put her feet on the cold floor and hauled herself from the bed.

"If you're looking for clothes, they're there on the table," Celeste said.

Maria looked at the sad pile. She didn't like the blouse her mother had selected. "Can I wear something else?"

"Everything else is packed."

"What do you mean?" Maria asked.

Celeste gestured toward the door. The four large duffel bags that they'd brought from their apartment lay beside it.

"We're leaving?" Maria asked. "But I thought Mr. Ironwall was better."

"What do you think, Maria? How can Mr. Ironwall trust us anymore? As soon as Joanne gets a replacement for me, we're gone."

The oily feeling washed through her. She'd ruined everything. He was better; they could have stayed.

Frank pulled up in the golf cart. He glanced at Celeste as she climbed, wordless, into the front seat.

"I need something from my backpack." Maria ran back into the house and pulled out the leather-wrapped map. Even if Mr. Ironwall couldn't trust her anymore, at least she could explain why they'd done it. Then, maybe, at least he wouldn't hate her so much.

* * *

Paolo was already standing with Hattie outside the double doors of Mr. Ironwall's room. He gave Maria a grim smile and Hattie shot him a fierce look. None of the adults said anything to the children or each other, yet somehow Joanne must have sensed their presence in the hall, for the door opened and her big hand ushered them in.

"Just the children," Mr. Ironwall said. "You wait out in the hall, too, Joanne. I'm sure Maria can yell loudly enough if I need any assistance."

Brutus leaped out of the bed and hurried to Maria, licking and wagging and snuffling at her. He was probably confused—she had been in the hospital all morning and hadn't taken him on his beach walk, and she felt bad about that, too. She wanted to bury her face in his fur instead of facing Mr. Ironwall. She forced herself to look at the thin figure in the great white bed.

He looked better than he had when he'd left. The oxygen mask was gone, but a big silver tank, with gauges and nozzles and plastic tubing, stood by the bed should he need it again.

"I'm so sorry; we're so sorry—" She glanced at Paolo, who was pale-faced and nodding mutely.

Mr. Ironwall raised his hand. "You stole my boat."

"We were just borrowing it," Paolo said.

"As you have apparently been borrowing it for a very

long time," Mr. Ironwall said. "I hear you had a little clubhouse in the cabin, and spent a great deal of money at the marine supply store."

"We fixed it up first, really nicely," Paolo said.

Mr. Ironwall closed his eyes. Then he opened them and fixed his gaze on Paolo. "The fact that you went to such expense and trouble to repair my boat before you stole it scarcely mitigates your crime."

Paolo looked at Maria, confused.

"It is hardly an ameliorating factor," Mr. Ironwall said. Paolo still looked confused. "In other words, it barely makes things better."

"We're still in a lot of trouble," Maria whispered.

Paolo looked at the floor. Maria reached over and touched his hand with her pinky.

"I'm sorry, Mr. Ironwall," Paolo said. "We're sorry."

"Of course you are." Mr. Ironwall pinned both of them with a steely gaze. "But stealing my boat—that is not the real crime."

"We betrayed your trust!" Maria cried. "I know! My mom told me! But it's not her fault. It's mine. So you don't have to fire her . . . and you don't have to kick us out. I promise to be better, I'll never mess with your stuff again—"

"Enough, Maria," Mr. Ironwall said. "Control yourself!"

Maria stopped.

Mr. Ironwall's eyes softened and he patted the bed. "Come sit."

Maria sat. Paolo moved closer, but remained standing.

Mr. Ironwall took Maria's right hand. He held it for a long time—long enough for Maria to inspect all the painful knobs and blue veins in his hand.

"Maria, look at me," he finally said.

Maria couldn't bear to meet his eyes. There was a purple bruise on his wrist where an IV needle had been. She kept her focus there.

"You were badly hurt," Mr. Ironwall said gently. "You were quite in over your head. Something much worse could have happened. You do realize that, don't you? How could any of us have survived that? I couldn't have borne that. Nor could your mother have, or Hattie . . ."

Maria shook her head. She didn't trust her voice.

"It grieves me terribly that I put you up to this." Mr. Ironwall pressed her hand. "All my stories about pirate treasure and adventuring nonsense."

"You didn't put me up to it. I found a map!" Maria

fished the leather tube from her bag. She handed it, with the map rolled inside, to Mr. Ironwall.

"I know it's fake, now," Maria said. "But it looked so real."

Mr. Ironwall inspected the leather tube for a long time. Then he untied the straps and unrolled the scroll. He touched the parchment gently, turned it over, and gazed at the back. Then he placed it on the bedspread.

"We realized it was a fake when we found the treasure chest filled with rocks," Paolo said. "We found the invitations and the party stuff all around."

"But the treasure, fake or not, could have waited!" Mr. Ironwall said. "Why did you go out on *that* night, in such weather?" He turned toward Paolo. "Of the two of you, you should have known better."

Now Paolo looked down.

Maria found her voice. "It was my idea. I thought that you might not come back from the hospital. And that my mom and I would have to leave the Island. And the cottage. And I just couldn't stand it! I didn't want to go back to the Bronx—and we needed money to stay—we needed that treasure. I thought it was our only chance before . . ."

"Before?" Mr. Ironwall said.

"Before you left them high and dry," Paolo said.

"Left them high and dry?" Mr. Ironwall pushed himself up on the pillows. "Wherever did you get the idea that I would do that?"

"Something my mom always says," Paolo said. "When you die we'll all be left high and dry."

Mr. Ironwall chuckled. Maria looked up to see him shaking his head. "I would never leave Maria and her mother high and dry. Or your mother, or Frank. In fact, I took the opportunity, while I was on the mainland, to see my lawyer. He came to the hospital to help me get my affairs in order."

"Oh!" Maria gasped. "That's why I thought . . ."

Mr. Ironwall smiled at her. "Just because I see my lawyer doesn't mean I'm planning on dying tomorrow. It is just prudent at my age not to leave such things to the last minute."

"I'm sorry," Maria said.

"You will be happy to know that you will never have to quit the cottage, regardless of my status." His eyes twinkled as if he'd made a joke. "I'm leaving it, and the surrounding acre, to you."

"What?" Maria said. "I mean, excuse me?"

"You heard me perfectly well," Mr. Ironwall said.

"You are the inheritor of my cottage. And its surrounding acre."

"Really?" Maria asked. "You can do that?"

"Of course I can!" Mr. Ironwall looked indignant. "It's mine and I may give it to whomever I wish."

"But what about your family?" Maria said. "There must be someone else expecting . . ."

Mr. Ironwall wagged a scolding finger. "You know very well I have no one expecting anything. You're the closest thing to a granddaughter that I'll ever have. So there. It's done. The cottage is yours. Now stop making me repeat myself. It's tiresome."

"Oh, thank you, thank you, thank you!" Maria lunged forward and gave him a one-arm hug. He reached awkwardly around her and patted her back.

"I'm not used to such enthusiasm," he said. "Remember I'm rather fragile."

She pulled back and looked directly in his eyes. "But you have to promise me," she said in her most serious voice. "You are not allowed to die ever. Even if you do leave me the cottage."

"Well, I can promise to *try* not to," Mr. Ironwall said. "But I don't think I'll succeed. Now call the adults in."

There was a brief shuffle in the hall, and then Frank, Celeste, and Hattie entered as sheepishly as if they, themselves, were in trouble. Joanne clicked over Mr. Ironwall, fussing with his blankets and standing resolutely by his side, demonstrating with her superior expression that it was she, and only she, who hadn't caused him any heartache.

"Mr. Ironwall," Celeste began, but her voice was drowned out. Hattie said Paolo was headed off to reform school on the mainland, while Frank said kids will be kids and he and Hattie weren't much better at that age, and Joanne stated none of this was good for Mr. Ironwall's heart. When no one calmed down, she put her fingers to her mouth and whistled.

"Mr. I's had enough already and I need to get home," Joanne scolded. "So could you all shut up now and let the old man speak?"

They nodded and quieted.

"I want all of you to listen to me now," Mr. Ironwall said. "I'm very tired from all the excitement and I don't want to have to repeat myself."

He turned his gaze back to Maria and Paolo. "Show them the treasure map."

Paolo glanced at Maria. She took the map from the bedspread and handed it to her mother.

Celeste unwrapped the map and read it. "'Twice twice two, then twice that more. Take one from the first, the Queen treads upon the door.'"

"I used pirate maps such as these as an invitation to a party I threw years ago," Mr. Ironwall said. "For my film *The Last Privateer.* People sailed to the little island where the children were found and we had a picnic in the caves. It was, as Maria would say, a *fabulous* party."

Celeste shook the map at Maria. "Why didn't you just show me this in the first place? I could have told you it was utter nonsense."

"It's *not* utter nonsense." Mr. Ironwall scoffed as if he'd been offended. "The quote is historically accurate. In fact, my whole film was well researched. It was based on my ancestor Captain Murdefer. I used his old ship's log as source material."

Celeste passed the map to Frank. "But we could have told them it wasn't *real*. If only they had come to an adult instead of sneaking around . . ."

"Maybe that's why they didn't come to an adult," Mr. Ironwall said. "Because an adult would have told them it wasn't real. And they needed to believe it was."

"We compared the map to charts of the Island," Maria said. "And there were stories about real pirates that really hid real treasure around here."

"The *Whydah* was real," Paolo said. "Dad took me to the museum in Provincetown."

"And Captain Murdefer was a real privateer—he was Mr. Ironwall's ancestor." Maria gave up. It sounded so lame now.

Paolo turned to his mother. "It looked so old. And real."

"Please," Hattie said.

"But the children were correct!" Mr. Ironwall said. "Captain Murdefer did in fact bury treasure on *that very island*. In that very cave!"

"But there was no treasure," Frank said. "You just said the pirate map was a party invitation."

"The invitations were based on an actual map. One that the captain had copied into his log after the original map had been lost. The children followed their map to the *exact right spot*." Mr. Ironwall pounded the bedspread for emphasis. "And if there had still been a treasure to find, they would have been extremely rich."

"So there really once was a buried pirate treasure?" Maria couldn't help asking.

"Of course," Mr. Ironwall said. "Right where you found the fake one. Murdefer went back for it himself once he was cleared of racketeering charges. How do you think we Ironwalls came to own all this?" He spread his hands through the dusty air.

"Figures," Paolo said. "Everything is always already found, or used up, or whatever."

"But we were right!" Maria glanced at her mother. "Though I guess it was pretty stupid to think it would still be there for *us* to find."

"Well, I suppose that makes me pretty stupid also," Mr. Ironwall said. "Knowing my ancestor Murdefer had already dug up his treasure didn't stop *me* when I was your age. You see, I found his old log and followed it to that very island myself. I told Maria how my cousins and I hunted treasure also, in case Murdefer didn't get it all."

Mr. Ironwall took a deep breath and closed his eyes. When he opened them, he looked uncharacteristically uncertain. "I'm afraid I owe everyone here an apology. I led Maria to believe hunting pirate treasure should be something all children do. But, then again, we never *stole* our boat, and our parents always knew where we were." He gave Maria and Paolo a long, serious look. "And we never went out in the middle of the night."

Hattie took the map. "Anyone can see these stains are tea." She glared at Paolo. "How could you ever believe this map was real?"

"But the children *were* right," Mr. Ironwall insisted. "Their map *is* real."

The adults turned to Mr. Ironwall.

"But it's just an invitation to a party, you said so yourself," Maria said.

"The ones you found at the cave were just invitations. But this—" A smile glimmered on his thin lips. "*This* one is the original map of Captain Murdefer. It is of great value. Historians thought it was lost. *I* thought it was lost." He looked at Maria. "Wherever did you find it, my dear?"

"In the cottage," Maria said. "Behind an eave in the attic."

"Well, we'll have to get the Island Conservation Foundation in there," Mr. Ironwall said. "Maria's little cottage may be worth more than we all realized. I hope you don't mind if the old historians snoop around *your cottage*, Maria dear." He gave her an exaggerated wink.

"Why are you saying, Maria's cottage?" Celeste said.

He turned to Celeste. "Oh, did I neglect to tell you? Maria owns the cottage now."

"Maria owns the cottage?" Celeste said slowly, as if the words were in a language she barely understood.

"Now and forevermore. Nothing you can do about it," Mr. Ironwall said to Celeste. "No going back to the

Bronx for you. So just unpack your bags. I still need a nurse."

"We don't ever have to leave!" Maria said. She jumped up and wrapped her good arm around her mother.

"I don't know what to say." Celeste looked bewildered.

"How about congratulations?" Maria suggested. *"Mabrouk!"*

"Mabrouk," Celeste murmured. She reached for something to steady herself. Frank stepped over and gave her his arm. "It's a miracle."

"Of course it is," said Frank. "None of us wanted you to go."

"Especially not you." Hattie hit her brother in the shoulder with the back of her hand.

35

The Last Privateer

MARIA AND PAOLO WANDERED AROUND THE
Great House lawn, checking out the party. The tents
were packed beyond capacity and people spilled out
onto the grass. They'd planned to have the screening in
the Great House's movie theater, but when the tickets
sold out on the first day, Frank called Tilton Rentals
and booked the largest tents they had and a giant out-
door screen for the showing. Still more people wanted
to come, even if they couldn't fit under the tents. So
Mr. Ironwall let people bring lawn chairs and beach
blankets and settle down anywhere they could.

Food had come in from all corners: Hattie and
Grandma Newcomb had been cooking all week, a
smoker was brought in for a pig roast, and Pops directed the Newcomb men to dig huge pits on the beach

for the largest clambake ever seen in local memory. Cater-waiters carried enormous platters of steamers, lobster, and corn on the cob to the guests, while Grandma ladled her famous clam chowder and dished out slices of pie. Even Tante Farida had come up from the Bronx bearing *meze* and pastries: tubs of *hummus*, *baba ghanoush*, *tabbouleh*, and stuffed grape leaves, cartons of olives, rounds of cheese, trays of *baklawa*, and *knafeh*. Hattie grilled Tante for recipes, and the old woman happily obliged.

Under another tent strung with twinkling white lights, a jazz band played old cinema classics. A woman in red sequins crooned about dancing cheek to cheek, while Celeste and Frank spun around on the parquet tiles. Frank said something and Celeste tipped her head back and laughed. Maria noticed that her mother laughed a lot lately. And smiled and sang. Now Celeste smiled at Maria over Frank's shoulder, and Maria smiled back.

It seemed everyone was happy and smiling. Taylor Bradford had come with his mom, and nearby sat other kids Maria had just recently met, now that school had begun. School on Martha's Vineyard wasn't so scary after all. Hattie hadn't sent Paolo to reform school, so Maria saw him every day. And there were no more snarky comments. When the story came out that she had found Captain Murdefer's real map and followed it to the right place in a stolen antique schooner, no one cared that the treasure had been long gone. And more than a few kids were envious that Paolo and she had had such an adventure, and that their adventure had made it onto TV news. Now, when they called Paolo Captain Dirt in the hallway, they said it in a friendly way.

Surveying all, Mr. Ironwall, dashing in his tuxedo, sat at the head table, eating a bowl of chowder while Joanne hovered anxiously by. He had insisted she was not allowed to mash it into "pureed pablum" or spoon-feed him. He would eat it as Grandma Newcomb cooked it, using his own hand, and if he choked to death, then at least he would die happy. But he seemed to be in no danger as far as Maria could tell. Maybe he *was* getting better. He certainly seemed better, lately.

Something was happening in front of the screen, and the guests closest to it began clapping. Maria turned back to see Joanne wheeling Mr. Ironwall toward a podium. A man in an elegant suit and a bow tie stepped up to another round of applause.

"Thank you, thank you." The man adjusted his notes and his tie. "We are all here as guests of the esteemed and talented Peter Ironwall. I wonder how many of you remember his movies from your youth . . ."

As Mr. Ironwall sat regally in his wheelchair, the man talked of Mr. Ironwall's long movie career, his history on the island, and finally the wonderful gift he was making to its people.

"When Mr. Ironwall agreed to this showing of *The Last Privateer*," the man said, "he contacted the old studio to send any costumes, props, and photos they had. After the film, this valuable memorabilia will be auctioned off in the Great House Ballroom and the proceeds will go toward the Conservation Foundation."

"Let's go sit up front," Paolo said. He took Maria's hand and steered her to a blanket near the screen. The man finished his speech and passed the microphone down to Mr. Ironwall.

Mr. Ironwall waited patiently for the applause to end. Then he cleared his throat and said, "Well, now, you're all very welcome to my humble abode."

More applause, a few whistles and whoops. Mr. Ironwall smiled calmly like a man used to waiting for his audience.

"As a young friend of mine would say, this is a fabulous party." He caught Maria's eye and winked. "But it wouldn't be fabulous if it weren't for all of you!"

People cheered in agreement.

Mr. Ironwall went on. "The money from this and future fund-raisers will be donated to the Conservation Foundation to preserve Island history and arts. I will be using my own private funds to restore Ironwall Estate to its original magnificence. The Great House, the grounds, the outer buildings, the beach, the boat, and the dock—in fact, the entire property with the exception of the cottage and its surrounding acre—have been deeded to the Conservation Foundation, to be used by the Island as an Arts and Nature Center in perpetuity."

Applause flooded the crowd. Paolo put his lips near Maria's ear so she could hear him.

"What's 'in perpetuity'?"

"It means forever," she said into his ear. "Ironwall Estate will be here forever."

"And you will, too," Paolo said. "Isn't it weird how everything worked out?"

Maria nodded. The chain of events that made up the past few months were so strange. If the Bad Barbies had never attacked her, her mother would not have looked for a new job. They would never have come to Martha's Vineyard. She would never have met Paolo or Mr. Ironwall. She never would have found the map, or fixed up *The Last Privateer*, or sailed to find a pirate treasure. She certainly would never have gotten the cottage. Mr. Iron-wall would have had a different nurse. And that nurse probably would not have had a daughter to stir things up. Most likely, Mr. Ironwall would have stayed in his room until he died, but now, because Maria had made just the right amount of trouble, he sat proudly at the podium, cheered by people who loved him. And Maria sat in the audience, surrounded by people who had become her family.

"And now, *The Last Privateer!*"

The audience applauded, the lights under the tents dimmed, and music swelled. Paolo leaned his shoulder against Maria's shoulder. Maria leaned back.

On the movie screen, a white sun shone in a silver sky, and silver waves crashed in a silver sea. A black pinpoint began in the top left corner. As it moved across the screen, closer and closer to the camera, it resolved into a wind-lashed schooner. Their schooner. *The Last Privateer.*

The shot pulled in, swooping down to a lone figure on the deck. Captain Murdefer gazed out over the stormy waters. He looked troubled and the music was ominous. But Maria was not worried. She already knew how the story ended. He would find this island and he would bury his treasure. It didn't matter that the gold and jewels were long gone. All that he had built with his riches was preserved here on this island, on Ironwall Estate, as long as Ironwall Estate itself still stood. And as long as Maria lived in the cottage, she would see to it that Ironwall Estate would stand, until the land upon which it stood fell into the sea, and the waters washed it away.